THE TURNING OVER

by

William McCauley

Library of Cogress Cataloging-in-Publication Data

McCauley, William.
    The Turning Over / by William McCauley
    p.   cm.
    ISBN 1-57962-058-2
    PS3563.C33758T8   1998
    813'.54--dc21   97-30147
                                                        CIP

THE PERMANENT PRESS
4170 Noyac Road
Sag Harbor, NY 11963

In Memory of Oleta M. and William F. McCauley

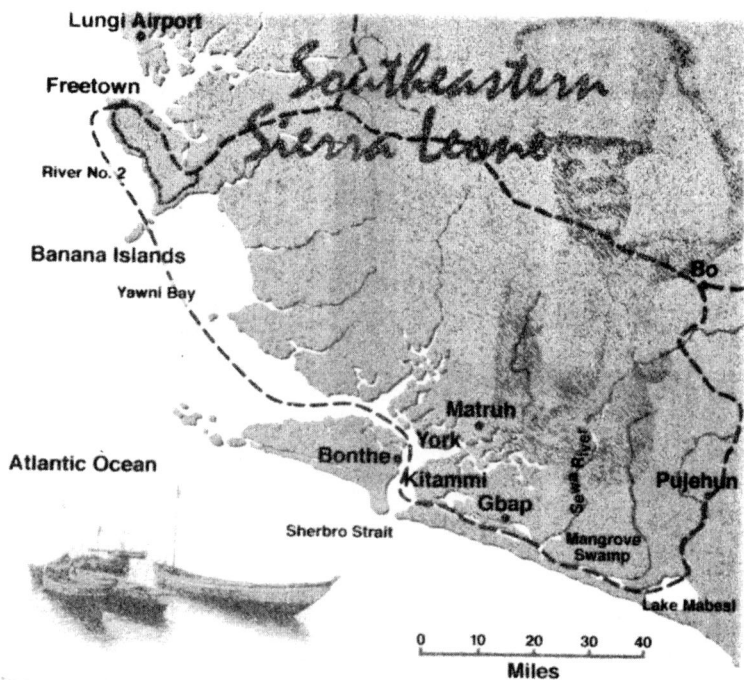

Lungi Airport

Freetown

River No. 2

Banana Islands

Yawni Bay

Atlantic Ocean

Southeastern Sierra Leone

Bo

Matruh
York
Bonthe
Kitammi
Gbap
Sewa River
Pujehun
Sherbro Strait
Mangrove Swamp
Lake Mabesi

| 0 | 10 | 20 | 30 | 40 |
Miles

Early one morning near the end of the rainy season Robert Kelley stood at the balcony wall brushing his sun-bleached hair. He faced the east where yellow light glowed in the space between the earth and the line of clouds over the mainland. A warm offshore breeze flowed over him. He put the brush aside and rubber-banded his hair into a pony tail and raised his cup and sipped the cardamom-scented coffee and watched the orange flare up out of the horizon and inch across the sky—broadening, edges brightening, the fire slowly cracking open and showing streaks of cool blue. The breeze, which was just vigorous enough to drive the mosquitoes to cover in the swamp, picked up, and the dense gray of the bay gave way to flashing silver, and the palms rattled cheerfully.

He saw Aminata walking on the path from the village and went back inside and down the hall to the stairwell. He pushed the door open and stood in the dusk, listening to her half-backs slapping up the stairs. She appeared on the landing.

"Mornin'-o," he murmured.

She came flap-flap-flap to the top of the stairs and kicked her half-backs off, then shouldered past him, ostentatiously ignoring his nakedness and his erection. He followed her to the kitchen where he leaned against the door jamb, watching her light the kerosene stove and fill a pan with water.

"I want you," he said.

She didn't even look at him. Her bare breasts, no bigger than tiny fists, jiggled stiffly and her dusty feet kicked up the frayed edge of her lapa as she moved about, banging things. Bony chest, plaited hair, hard little breasts, and petulant lower lip made her seem like the child she almost was. He began to feel ridiculous standing there with an ignored erection.

"Bring me coffee," he said crossly, and left the kitchen.

Grabbing the short handled broom, she leaned over and began furiously sweeping the floor.

Robert went to his bedroom and got into his shorts, then went to the balcony and sat, cocking his feet up on the railing. He picked up the book he had started the evening before, a coverless yellowed thing he had discovered during his last trip to Freetown in the heaps of tattered paperbacks and ancient textbooks on the table of a Garrison Street trader: *Black Mischief.* He opened the book to a dog-eared page and began reading, but the turn of his mood from serene to angry ruined his enjoyment of Waugh's satire; now it seemed supercilious, mincing, outdated. After reading a few sentences he closed the book and stared out over the bay, trying to recapture the euphoria that came after his run.

Aminata brought his coffee and leaned against the balcony wall in such a position that he could not avoid looking at her. He did not want the coffee—he had commanded her to make it to remind her that he still commanded her—but he took it anyway, so as not to give her a reason to restart the quarrel. These days she always arrived ready to quarrel. Anything could start it, but it always came around unerringly to what she called *you promise.* But there had been no promises, no hint that he would take her. Her assumption, like his so-called promise, had grown out of nothing.

At first he had scarcely noticed this girl, whom Pa Bia had brought to his house to cook his food, wash his clothes, clean his floors and windows. For weeks she had crept about like a frightened kitten, sneaking up the stairs in the morning when he was already at work and disappearing in the afternoon after hurrying through the preparation of his supper. Then, during a time when his longing for a woman was so sharp that not even masturbation assuaged it, he began to find reasons to come up to his living quarters when she was cooking or cleaning. He would lean against the door jamb and talk to her in his broken Krio, which amused her, and gaze at her narrow hips and thin waist, study the quiver of her tiny breasts and the flex of her flat hard belly as she moved about her chores. Robert forgot that he had regarded her as a child and she forgot that she had feared him. One afternoon after he had gotten her giggling, something strange happened. He watched his hand—as if it belonged to someone else—go out to one of her breasts, and heard his husky voice whisper, "I want you." She had lowered her eyes and padded off to the bedroom where she unwound her lapa and crawled up on his bed. Thereafter, whenever he wanted her he told her. Then one night he was too tired to walk her home—she feared the devils that lurked in the darkness—so he let her sleep in his bed. He encouraged her to stay for many nights thereafter and soon she was the mistress of his house.

It would never have gotten so out of hand had he known Marie when the young black girl came to work for him. But Aminata was already living with him by the time he met Marie, and since he always traveled to Freetown to see her it was easy to let things slide. To let no decision be a decision. To allow Aminata to stay a little while longer. Not that he actually planned his disloyalty to Marie. Indeed, he thought quite often of sending Aminata away, even practiced in his head the words he would use to tell her. But each time he got himself in a position to tell her he ended up with an erection, which focused his attention more on screwing than rejecting. He recognized his duplicity and thought it shitty; particularly as his long-distance relationship with Marie bloomed. More and more often he resolved that he would send Aminata away, but the right moment never came.

Looking up, he saw Aminata's eyes fixed balefully on him. She was about to resume the quarrel. He rose and went to the landing where he dipped the empty bucket into the water barrel and carried it to the bathroom where he filled the toilet reservoir, then dropped his shorts and sat on the toilet and thought that maybe it *was* time he left.

ϓ

He turned the magnifying ring to fifteen power. The dark smudge, flattened by distance and distorted by heat waves, became a silhouette of the sea car heading directly at him. Two figures wavered above the gunwale against the dark line of the mainland.

Below the balcony a young fisherman sat on a bench in the shade removing rusted hooks from coils of line. Alhadji and Pa Bia slouched glumly against the counter that blocked the store's big doorway, gazing seaward. In the shadowy interior behind the old men were shelves of netting bundles, packages of cord and hooks, tins of outboard engine oil. Against the far wall a locked wire cage surrounded two precious drums of petrol.

A breeze came and went, dropping down to touch the surface of the bay, combing it into rippled patches that drifted aimlessly. Kingfishers darted and dove and a couple of gray herons stood in the shallows and waited. The entrance to the bay was blocked by the shining black mud of a vast bar swelling out of the water, loading the air with a scent of rot that drifted back to the island and mingled with a similar richness rising out of the mangrove swamp behind the town. With the tide ebbing Hassan would have to steer the sea car around the flats and approach the landing through the channel along the north shore between the mangrove islands.

Robert went back into the living room, a large airy space bounded by high, whitewashed walls. The room retained the morning coolness in its tile floor. The Lebanese piassava trader who had built the house had possessed an eccentric taste in color, or more likely, an unsellable inventory of tiles, for the floor was a startling fruit salad of orange, green, yellow, purple, red, blue.

A table stood just inside the French doors. On it the work of the evening before was arranged as Robert had left it: kerosene lantern, ledger, spiral notebooks, paper, pencils. A corner table supported a short-wave radio, and along one wall the shelves of a book case sagged under rows of frayed paperback novels, technical manuals, and the only possessions he really treasured: the volumes of African history that he had collected in his five years in Sierra Leone. The

8

two bedrooms were whitewashed cells containing beds and mosquito nets that were spotted with the tiny droppings of bats that came and competed with the geckos for nighttime insects. Big, iron-barred windows admitted the glaring heat of late morning.

Robert connected the radio cable to the battery terminals, turned the radio on.

"Zimi Freetown, this is Bonthe, over."

He turned the squelch control until the static diminished. He called again and a distant voice responded.

"This is Zimi, over."

"Hello, Kevin—they're coming in the bay now."

"Good. How's it going with you?"

"It's coming together."

"Robert, something's come up. I wonder—can you be finished in five days?"

"We agreed on three weeks; it's going to take all of that."

"I'm afraid three weeks is out of the question now. Chief Kamara's invited Minister Kargbo down to Keilahun for Constitution Day. Wants to bring Kargbo out to the station and show it off—successful Sierra Leonean development project, that sort of thing. That'll be awkward if a white man's still around looking like *he's* running things."

"Every village has planned a ceremony, Kevin—it's important that we turn it over properly."

Kevin's voice came through the static. "This event is also important. There's increasing trouble between President Momoh's Freetown bunch and the First Vice-President's Pujehun crowd, and they both see this as an opportunity to show they can cooperate. A step toward cooling things down. We'll just be in the way. C'mon, now, Robert, it can't be that difficult to change things, can it? Can't you make do with a visit to York Island? It's the most important village, anyway, and you can do York in a day. Or two, at most."

"I can leave tomorrow if that's what you want."

"I'm not asking you to leave tomorrow. I'm asking that you hurry things up a bit, that's all. We do need to accommodate Kamara."

"Accommodate Kamara. Right. We both know what

Kamara wants. He wants to get at those new Yamaha twenty-fives, before Kargbo can get at them. And the inventory." The scratch of static for a several seconds, then Kevin's voice, still patient: "We don't own this frequency, Robert."

"The villagers at York and even the Kitammi have all but quit the cooperatives already. They know what to expect when the Ministry takes over." He heard a knock at the door to the stairwell and lifted his thumb off the talk button. "Come!" he shouted.

Alhadji entered, kicked his half-backs off, waited for permission to advance into the room.

Robert waved the old man inside.

"There's no chance they'll work with Alexander unless I take him around and hang heads with them. There needs to be talk and ceremony, and they need to look him over. If we don't do it right they'll simply quit the cooperatives."

"I'm sure you've got a point, Robert, but we do have this problem. I'll go along with whatever you can do in five days—but no more. I need you out of there by then. It's already arranged."

"If it's already arranged, what the fuck is this conversation about?"

"Professional courtesy, old boy."

"It's going to come apart, Kevin."

A long silence. Then, tiredly: "Robert, no one is indispensable, not even you. Believe me, it won't come apart because you leave."

"We made promises to these people. We owe them some warning, a chance to get their money out of the cooperatives before Alexander gets control."

The anger in Kevin's voice came through the static: "Goddamn it, Robert, negative on that." Silence for a moment, then, in a mollifying tone: "Impress on the villagers that we'll oversee things, that we'll continue to provide inventory. We'll be there as long as they need us."

"They know better than that. When we're out of sight we won't control a fucking fishhook." Robert waited for Kevin to respond, but the static went on uninterrupted. Finally, Robert shrugged and raised the microphone to his mouth. "I'll be out in five days."

Kevin curtly signed off and Robert disconnected the batteries. As he coiled the cable he looked at Alhadji. The old man had a worried look.

"How de go de go, Pa?" Robert said.

Alhadji's old, nearly blind eyes squinted. He wore shorts and a T-shirt. With the big toe of one bare foot he scratched the other foot. "No bad," he said.

"Come and sit down. You want coffee?"

The old man nodded and came across the room. He drew a chair away from the table and sat uneasily on the front edge.

Robert went to the kitchen. Aminata had heated the water for his coffee before going off to the market. He got the stove going again and spooned the Lebanese coffee into a cup, added several spoons of sugar, some powdered milk, and when the water started rumbling, lifted the kettle and filled the cup. He returned to the living room and put the cup before Alhadji and sat across the table from him.

The old man lifted the cup and noisily sipped. He squinted out through the French doors for a few seconds, then turned to Robert and asked him why he wanted to leave.

Robert smiled. They had been over this the day before. And the day before that. "My work done finish, Pa."

Alhadji considered Robert's words like it was the first time he'd heard them. "Make we get udder white man," he said, as if this idea was also new.

"I no able, Pa."

The old man persisted. "Beaucoup white man dey inside Freetown."

Robert went over it again, as patiently as the first time.

Alhadji frowned. "No fine for lef we. No fine a-tall. Black man de come now—'e go spoil de station."

"No, Alhadji."

"Yes, mastah. Black man go chop all dem t'ing." He pointed at his feet, through the floor, to the Project store with its pair of gleaming Yamaha engines, its stock of petrol and engine oil, its shelves of priceless British, Japanese, Norwegian, and American fishing gear.

The sun blazed hot on Robert's bare shoulders. Sweat tickled down the small of his back. He stood on the path that ran along the shore, watching Sori sink up to his calves in black muck as he waded out to the sea car. Hassan stepped out of the boat, slogged around to the bow and tied the painter to a float laying in the mud, then lifted a box out of the bow and settled it on his head.

Alexander stood in the boat, hands on hips, the sun flashing on his mirrored sunglasses. His khakis, where the orange life vest had encased his torso, were dark with sweat. His flabby bulk suggested well-being, his arrogance power—he had the bearing of a Big Man.

Hassan waded slowly through the mud to the shore and he lowered the box.

"Aftahnoon, Mistah Robaht," he said.

"Hello, Hassan—the engine run okay?"

"Yes sah. No trouble." Hassan took a plastic-wrapped packet of letters out of his back pocket and handed it to Robert.

Robert removed the wrap and glanced at the envelopes. Each was addressed to Maxwell Bush at the United States Embassy, and each had a little star at the bottom left corner, the code Robert's correspondents used for distinguishing Robert's mail from Max's. One letter was postmarked three weeks before in Seattle and addressed in his brother's hand. The others showed Marie's return address in Mali. He shuffled through the letters, arranging hers by the date stamps, putting his brother's on the bottom. Glancing up at the balcony, he saw Aminata leaning on the rail glaring down at him. She always knew when he received letters from Marie, and though she was illiterate she let him know she knew which ones were Marie's by leaving little juju bundles among the letters in his chest—magic to break his ties with Marie: once a feather wrapped in a piece of paper torn from a school workbook, another time a chicken's egg and an alligator pepper wrapped in a fragment of orange paper, another time a pinch of dirt tied in a patch of red cloth (the dirt from a grave, presumably).

Robert opened the oldest of Marie's letters, a single page of lined notebook paper filled with the neat script of her handwriting. He skimmed the first paragraph, in which she told him her trip back to Bamako had been okay, that as usual she began missing him as soon as the plane lifted off the runway at Lungi, that she missed him most at night and hoped he missed her as much. He paused guiltily at this, reassured himself that of course he did. He read on into the second paragraph.

> *I gave Fletcher a copy of your résumé. He said he liked what he saw, but he has budget problems and can't even think of adding staff. He did say that he heard the UN is expanding one of their projects. I went down to the offices but no one there knew anything. I'll keep looking. I'm not discouraged, something will turn up. There's a lot going on here now, and that always means change. And it doesn't really matter whether you find anything right away because you'll be living with me. But I'll keep looking and when I can I'll put your résumé out. And remember to keep working on your French! It needs to be better.*
>
> *I wish you were here right now. I think about you all the time. I try not to because it makes me miserable. The first day I get back is the worst because I'm used to being with you and the last days with you are so fresh in my mind. I am thinking right now about River Number Two, but I shouldn't, because I'm going to bed in a few minutes and it'll make me crazy. I'll probably be up half the night, reading. Hurry up and come to me! I miss you!*

He looked up when he heard Alexander say something crossly to Hassan. Alexander spoke again, this time sharply. Hassan hesitated, then turned and backed up against the boat. Alexander put his arms around Hassan's neck and set-

13

tled his weight on the young man's back. Hassan's legs slid deeper into the mud. He steadied himself, pulled up on his right leg; but as he did the left went deeper. He wavered, tried to lean back against the boat, but it was too late: he tilted forward helplessly and fell, twisting to avoid falling with Alexander's weight on him. Instead, he landed on Alexander with a great *splat* that sent black mud flying.

Sori dumped a box on the trail and hurried back toward the boat. He pulled Hassan off Alexander, then he and Hassan hauled the grunting, sputtering Alexander to his feet. The big man slapped Hassan, who fell. The effort made Alexander slip, and he went to his knees. He allowed Sori to help him to his feet, then pushed him away and waded laboriously through the muck to the beach. He came up to Robert, the ooze sliding in gobs down his back, dripping from his arms and face and hair. "I have sacked that boy," he hissed. Quivering with indignation, he looked down at the muddy khakis. "Ruined! The station must pay for this. Absolutely."

"We'll take care of it," Robert said. "But let's get you out of these and have Aminata wash them."

"It's impossible. Absolutely. The station must pay for this."

Robert turned and called: "Sori, make you carry de box go upside."

"I must get out of these things and bathe," Alexander said. "Look at my clothes, they're ruined. I want that boy out of my sight. It was deliberate."

"It was my fault," Robert said soothingly as he led Alexander across the bare earth of the yard toward the stairwell. "They're not used to tying up here—the planks of the dock were tiefed a few weeks ago when I was in Freetown, and I haven't gotten around to replacing them. It's a bitch coming in at low tide without a dock. I should have repaired the dock for your arrival."

Behind them Hassan detached the engine and heaved it to his shoulders. He slogged disconsolately back through the mud toward the store.

At the top of the stairwell Alexander shrugged out of his trousers and shirt, leaving them in a sticky black heap.

Robert dipped a bucket of water out of the barrel and led Alexander to the bathroom. While he bathed, Robert went downstairs and found Hassan in the store talking worriedly with Pa Bia and Alhadji. They fell silent when he approached. Robert motioned for Hassan to follow him outside. "Mister Alexander done sack you?"

Chewing his lip, Hassan nodded.

Robert told him not to worry, that it was a mistake; he would take care of the matter.

Hassan looked down and muttered that in a few days Alexander would be the master of the station.

♈

Spirals of smoke from mosquito coils rose around them in the still air. Candles at each end of the table gave off yellow light and added heat to the stifling evening. The shirts of both men were wet with sweat.

"The sea car has built-in floatation," Robert said reassuringly. He'd already heard Hassan's story of the crossing, knew about Alexander's fear of the sea. "Even if it fills with water it can't sink. It's quite safe."

Alexander sucked his teeth to dislodge a piece of rice. "I have seen hundreds of Sierra Leonean villages. Why should I go motoring about all those islands?"

"I was thinking you might want to meet the villagers, visit the cooperatives—" Robert began.

"It is a waste of time. I can meet them when they come to the store. I am a Sierra Leonean, I understand the situation perfectly." He spooned rice and fish into his mouth. With his tongue he separated the bones, spitting them onto the table beside his plate. "Probably even as much as you," he added. For a while he concentrated on his plate, ingesting one heaping spoon of rice after another. He belched and drank some water and glanced over his shoulder toward the kitchen where Aminata worked in the light of a lantern. "The girl?" He turned back to his plate and spooned more rice.

"She cooks and cleans," Robert answered, but in the silence that followed, his explanation seemed incomplete.

He added: "She's been my woman for two years."

"And now you are leaving," Alexander said. He belched once again and shoved his spoon into the heap of rice. "My family will stay in Freetown. I will keep the girl. To cook and clean."

That night Robert asked Aminata to stay with him. She tossed her head and said contemptuously that he could make love to his hand.

♈

"You give her too much money," Alexander said. "You are making this girl rich. It is not good to pay so much, it creates jealousies in the village."

Robert would not let Alexander change the subject. "About the village visits—there's a good deal of anxiety, we need to—"

"I have already said I do not want to visit the villages."

They were standing at the balcony railing. The sun was still low, the morning breeze soft, cool. A few minutes before, Pa Bia had come for the key to the store and there was already a murmur of voices from the porch below the balcony. Alexander drank the rest of his coffee and went back through the French doors. Robert heard him say something, then heard Aminata's laughter.

In a few minutes Alexander came back with a steaming cup of coffee. "Mister Kelley, we will forget this business about visiting the villages. I want to prepare for the visit of Minister Kargbo and Chief Kamara."

"I don't think you understand how much distrust there is down here of Fisheries Division. We need to convince the fishermen they'll be protected."

"Indeed? Protected from whom, Mister Kelley?"

"I am talking about perceptions." Robert was suddenly cautious about his words. He remembered the trouble that had come to him two years before when he'd accused Chief Kamara. He had saved his job only through the humiliation of a public apology.

"And these perceptions—" Alexander said amiably, letting the sentence trail off.

16

"There is a perception that Fisheries Division—that certain officials unfairly exploit fishermen."

"Ah. I see. So you wish to take me about and show me as your protégé—a black man well-enough schooled in white man's principled behavior to be his successor."

"Not at all, Mister Alexander," Robert said, mindful of the cleverness of old Kamara in turning an accusation of corruption into a racist attack. "I am not talking about Fisheries Division or blacks or whites or about you. I am arguing that the cooperatives are in danger of collapsing because the members fear Fisheries Division. That is all."

"I see. I thought you were suggesting we must protect the villagers from black oppression." He smiled condescendingly. "Mister Kelley, these are my people."

"Not exactly. They're illiterate back-country Sherbros. You're a Freetown Krio."

Alexander puffed up. "We are Sierra Leoneans. And *Africans.* We share the same goal, to build our country, and we will do it the African way, not the white way."

"These people don't care about your goal. Their goal is tomorrow's food. And one other thing. This isn't about race."

"Quite right," Alexander said, facing Robert. "It is about how things are to be done. I am head of station, and African. Things will be done in the African way."

Robert reddened. "It's not a matter of African way or white way, it's a matter of doing it the right way. And you're not head of station, I am."

Alexander sipped his coffee and smiled at the horizon. After a minute he went inside and said something in Sherbro to Aminata—rather loudly, Robert thought—which was followed by her giggles.

They closed the store before noon and began the stocktaking. Robert counted stock and called out the numbers to Alexander while Pa Bia and Alhadji, forced to surrender their territory, stood resentfully on the porch and watched. They could have finished in a half-hour had they gone to the file cabinet and extracted the inventory reconciliation. That document would have been accurate enough, but Alexander's arrogance had put Robert in a foul mood, and so Robert, knowing that a precise accounting would be taken as an insult, insisted on measuring and counting every loose hook, every fragment of netting, every nut and bolt and screw. They even measured odd scraps of plywood and corrugated roofing metal, old two-by-four end-cuts, the odds and ends of rope hanging on the wall, the plastic bags of nails.

Robert did not mind the heat. Stripped down to shorts and halfbacks, still invigorated by his morning run, he forgot his anger. Alexander—made to copy numbers like a clerk—sweated like a laborer. By mid-afternoon the store was an oven and Alexander no longer even pretended civility. Finally, he slammed the clipboard down on the counter and declared that he was finished. They quit at the hottest hour of the day and climbed the stairs side by side, Robert contemptuous, Alexander fuming.

They found Aminata singing in the kitchen. She lapsed into tight-lipped silence when Robert berated her for cooking in the hottest part of the day—which of course she did every day. When Alexander came up to her and said something in Sherbro she laughed. Robert went out to the balcony and plopped down in a chair with the Waugh.

After Alexander finished bathing, Robert dipped a bucket out of the barrel and carried it to the bathroom where he stepped out of his shorts and into the tub and poured cups of the cool water over his hot skin until the bucket was empty; then called Aminata to bring another, which she did, after making him wait long enough to make him understand he was being made to wait. But the cool water had soothed his spirit as well as his skin and he did not mind the wait. Moreover, his change of mood had got him to thinking he needed to be more generous with Alexander. He was letting Alexander's arrogance bother him, and he shouldn't, for if he provoked Alexander it would be the villagers who would pay for it. And, to be fair, he needed to see the world from Alexander's point of view. After all, he was a senior biologist, and a Big Man: a politician with connections and ambitions, and perhaps even the abilities that could one day make him a minister. Yet here he was, isolated from the center of power, and subservient, if only for a few days, to a junior white functionary in a remote posting that no one cared about, except the few hundred primitives the post served. He had every right to be irritable.

Robert came from his bath pleased that he had gotten past pride to the essence of the problem, and had the generosity of spirit to deal with it. He would win the African over, and would begin by sharing a beer with him and listening to what *he* wanted to do, and would offer help and advice only if asked.

The flat was filled with the oily, earthy odor of the potato leaf plasas that simmered on the kerosene stove. He got two bottles of beer from the cabinet and went to the balcony. It was deserted. He looked up the beach toward the trail leading into the mangroves, then the other way, where it disappeared in the elephant grass bounding the stream. Beyond the grass and the palms were the thatch roofs of the village, and beyond the village, the ruins of the town. Aminata had gone off to the house of her father and mother or to the market, perhaps, but what of Alexander? Probably a nap. He put one of the beers on the table and opened the other and took it out to the balcony. Moving the chair to its familiar position, he sat and picked up the Waugh. After reading for a few minutes, he decided he wanted to get high, put the book aside, went to his bedroom. He closed the door, rolled and lit a joint, drew on it a couple of times, pinched the fire out, and went back into the living room. He heard a strange sound—a faint creaking of metal against wood. He went to the window and looked down through the bars at the bare earth behind the house. Nothing moved, not even the air. He heard the sound again and went into the hall. From behind Alexander's door came murmurs, grunts, the whisper of cloth over cloth, the creaking of a bed, labored breathing, a liquid, slippery, slapping sound. After a time the rhythm picked up and the slapping grew louder and the hoarse breathing became an urgent keening that ended in a long moan.

Robert's high was no longer the good jamba high. His heart boomed like he had run five miles, filling his chest with tightness and his head with thumping echoes. And then the bed creaked explosively. Panic seized him: he saw Alexander approaching the door, his spent dick swinging

19

like a pendulum beneath his bulging gut; saw Aminata spread upon the bed behind him, her breasts and her belly and her still presented cunt wet with his sweat; saw the door swing open; saw Alexander's smile—

He fled across the living room and down the stairs and out the door into the withering heat. The panic eased before he went twenty paces down the trail. Feeling foolish, he slowed to a walk, stopped at the edge of the mangroves and looked back at the blocky, white-washed building, so out of place against the palms and the elephant grass. He thought about going back, but was too high and too confused about what he should be feeling. He thought he ought to be angry. On the other hand, relieved made more sense: Alexander had just removed his problem. Of course there was the insult, the damage Alexander had done him—though when he pressed himself to describe the damage he could find little to say except that Alexander had fucked Aminata. As if Aminata had nothing to say about it.

He told himself it really didn't matter. In a week he would be in Marie's bed, where he wanted to be, and Aminata would be another African story. And yet—goddamn it, it did matter. He gazed at the house, wondered if he ought to go back. But he shrugged, knowing he didn't care enough to confront either Aminata or Alexander; moreover, it was too confusing to sort out when he was stoned. He would walk off the high and think about it.

He followed the path into the humid mangrove darkness. The path tunneled through shoots and runners so densely tangled that he could see no more than a few feet into the darkness on either side. The trail was black and damp and lumpy with roots, and in the low places muddy.

He walked for twenty minutes before the tunnel grew brighter and the trail opened onto a sandy beach occupied by a dozen palms and a hut falling to ruin. Rain had washed much of the mud out of the hut's wattle framework, leaving a rain-gullied talus skirt around its exterior walls. The thatch was gray and heavy with rot and ready to fall through the bushpole rafters. The hut had once sheltered a man and his wife and six children and the man's mother, but the man and his wife and five of his children had drowned when the pampam on which they were passengers had gone aground. Robert walked around the hut and found an old woman squatting in the shade before a pile of cassava roots, a pipe clenched in her teeth. She was peeling a root with a knife. She squinted up at Robert, then broke into a grin.

She rattled off something in Sherbro and Robert squatted beside her.

"Kushay, Ma."

Grinning and nodding and murmuring Sherbro phrases—a few words of which he understood—she peeled a cassava root. Her paper-thin breasts fell away from her rib cage. She puffed noisily on her pipe as she worked. She looked up and pointed toward the bay. "Hassan," she said.

He nodded.

She seemed satisfied that she had discharged her social obligation, for she now ignored him. He remained beside her for a couple of minutes more, watching her peel one root, then another, then rose and walked across the sand to the water's edge. The sand was white, and still hot, though the sun was low over the mangroves and the palms. He looked out over the bay and his eyes caught a dark object on the boundary of sea and sky. As he watched, it took on the shape of a man in a canoe.

Robert removed his halfbacks and stepped out of his shorts. He looked down at his brown body, with its band of pallid skin, against which his pubic patch stood out in brunette contrast to the yellow hair of his head and chest. He liked nakedness, liked looking at his own body, which was slim and well-defined, though by African standards it was effeminately soft.

He strode into the warm water until he was waist-deep, pushed forward and swam a few strokes, then stopped and lazily treaded water as he looked seaward. The canoe was close enough now to distinguish the movement of arms and the flash of sun on the dipping paddle. Robert began backstroking toward the canoe, enjoying the lift of his body each time he flung his arm back and pulled. Rolling over, he swam toward the canoe, raising his head every few strokes to see that it was pointed directly at him. It was a little bigger each time he looked, until it was right on top of him, and then it was sliding by an arm length away, and he reached out and grabbed the stern as it slid by, felt its momentum change as it began pulling him along. He rested and watched the white sand of the beach approach as Hassan dipped the paddle on one side and then the other. When he felt the sand under him he released his hold on the canoe and found his feet and walked up out of the water and onto the beach. He drew his shorts up about his waist as Hassan dragged the canoe up and lifted a small skate and a sizable barracuda out of the dugout.

Robert walked with Hassan through the sand to the hut where Hassan dropped the fish beside the fire.

The old woman had put the pot on the fire. She pushed a couple of dry sticks between the stones. The fire flared. She dropped pieces of cassava into the brownish water.

"You de eat with we, sah?" Hassan asked.

Robert shook his head, saying he had no torch to light his way through the mangroves.

Knowing Robert would not drink the brackish water in the earthen jug, Hassan went to the hut and came out with his cutlass and a coconut. He balanced the green globe in his hand and struck it a glancing blow, slicing off a chunk of its fibrous cover. Then he turned it and struck again. When he had worked his way around the coconut, thinning the two-inch husk, he struck it several times around one end, then with the tip of the blade lifted the top and flipped it off to the side. All this he did with deft strokes, without spilling a drop of the coconut milk. He handed the open coconut to Robert, who drank from it and passed it back. They walked back to the beach and sat in the sand. Behind them the sun was down in the trees.

"Mistah Alexandah go sack me wey you de go."

Robert said nothing.

"Duya I beg—talk for me, Mistah Robaht."

Robert nodded. "I will."

After Robert drank the rest of the milk Hassan held the coconut in the palm of his hand and split it open with a blow of his cutlass. With the tip of the long blade he delicately lifted the gelatinous, immature coconut meat from one of the shell halves and offered the gleaming white slab to Robert.

♈

A lantern in the kitchen spilled light into the living room and mosquito coils gave off the scent of smoldering wood. Sensing rather than seeing Alexander and Aminata on the balcony, Robert went across the living room to the French doors.

A full moon was rising yellow and huge out of the eastern horizon, flooding the bay and the sea with a pale gold that lit the sky and illuminated the shoreline, the house, the balcony. Far to the east lightning played in the tops of thunderheads. Aminata sat on one chair, Alexander on the other. Both clutched bottles of Robert's beer. Aminata had never before taken his beer without asking him.

"You found the beer, I see," Robert said dryly.

"Yes," Alexander said. "I didn't think you would mind—there are so many of them."

"I don't mind."

"I have already eaten," Alexander said. "I didn't know when you would return."

"I went to Hassan. He's very worried that you will not keep him when I leave."

Alexander raised his bottle and drank.

"He asked me to speak for him and I told him I would."

"Mister Kelley, you have already spoken for him. I don't want to discuss what I will do after the turning over."

"Hassan's an expert boat operator. He's been with me for three years. He knows this coast better than any man. And he's steady. Absolutely dependable. He's been indispensable to me. It's in your interest to keep a man of his experience and loyalty."

"Loyal to you."

"To his duty."

"I don't want to talk about it."

Robert realized that he was not helping Hassan. He felt helpless and futile. He looked at Aminata for the first time. "Hungry de catch me," he said. "I want chop now."

She stirred, but did not rise.

"Now," he said roughly, feeling a little surge of satisfaction when she rose and slid past him.

He got a bucket of water and washed the sweat from his body and the mud from his feet and legs and when he finished went to his room and prepared himself against the mosquitoes by slipping into the unwelcome confinement of long pants, socks, shirt. Sitting on the bed in near darkness, he smoked the rest of the joint he had rolled earlier in the day and reflected gloomily that Alexander had been there not quite two days and the station was already coming apart: Hassan sacked; Alhadji, Pa Bia, Sori grumbling and fearful; the cooperatives wanting their money; Alexander impatient to get him out of the way and to get on with the looting. The irresistible impetus to dissolution: Alexander's African way. Even Aminata. Already fucking the new man. But he pulled back from his judgment of her, thinking why not, who else will provide rice for her family when I am gone? When I am gone only one human in her world can do that.

His body did not like the confinement of all those clothes, and showed its dissatisfaction by sweating. The wetness trickled down his face and down the small of his back. He rose and went to the window, hoping for a cooling puff of wind. The moon's brightness reflected off the silvery leaves of palms and elephant grass, lighting even the ruined walls of the long-defunct piassava warehouse back through the trees. The evening rain would come soon, leaving dry air and a cool night.

The jamba moved in him, and he was filled with that pure, uncomplicated longing that came to him from time to time, like the love he felt for Marie. He longed to remain part of this Africa of mosquito-infested, mangrove-strangled islands and stunted tribesmen whom even the slavers of two hundred years before had regarded as worthless, and who were as organically connected to the islands as the black mud and the miles of mangrove thickets and the warm sea, hanging on and dying while they struggled to live long enough to procreate. He had not imagined a life of such richness before he came to Africa.

He looked out through the bars into the darkness, wanting to permanently fix in his memory every incident, every moment that gave substance to his time in this place, so that he could take it away with him. It was there, where the hard-packed earth of the yard gave way to knee-high grass, that he had stepped on the black cobra. When he had felt the movement under his foot he had leaped back with his heart in his throat and seen the cobra's hooded head pointing up at him, its eyes as flat as the eyes of a dead thing: it was so utterly absorbed in the act of swallowing a toad wider than itself that it did not even see him. The lower half of the toad's body bulged out of the snake's distended jaws, which ever so slowly contracted and expanded, drawing the toad in, legs twitching and jerking. He had watched until only the tips of the toad's feet still poked out of the cobra's mouth before he'd called Sori, who came with a club and beat the snake to death.

And out there, across the miles of mangroves, on the seaward side of the island, was the uncharted rock on which the pampam had run aground, taking out part of its bottom; from which he had walked through a mile of sandy ocean shallows, sometimes knee-deep, sometimes neck deep, to reach the beach, while the crew got drunker and the fifty or so African passengers became immobilized by hysteria and drowned when the incoming tide floated the wreck off the rock and waves swamped it.

Robert got Marie's most recent letters from the chest, the three that Sori had brought with Alexander. He left his room and got a beer and ate his plasas and rice alone at the dining room table, then went to the balcony where he avoided talk with Alexander by re-reading the letters. Feeling Marie's presence and hearing her voice in the neat scrawl of words. And also Aminata's hostility, which felt good now because it seemed to finalize their break and to fix him more strongly to the idea of Marie. He was still high when he went to bed and listened to the snuffles and grunts and bed squeaks from the room across the hall. The noise made him want Marie and he thought of her last visit when he'd picked her up at the airport and they'd come back to Freetown on the ferry and bought a bag of apples and some bread and cheese from the Leb store on Siaka Stevens Street and driven right on through town on his motorcycle and out past Juba Hill and down the Peninsula Road to River

Number Two and made love in the beach baffa while the warm rain rattled on the palm frond roof and dripped on his back. She'd panicked and tried to push him off when the little boys appeared in the open front of the baffa, but he'd just kept going, and she'd let him finish, though he could tell from her tenseness that she wasn't going to finish, so he had come quickly, while the little boys giggled and begged, "Duya, mastah, gimme mon-ey."

At about the time Alexander gave off his long moan, Robert jerked and shuddered. He allowed his breathing to return to normal before sticking his arm out of the protection of the mosquito netting to find his T-shirt on the floor. In the minutes between cleaning himself and sleep he thought about Mopti and for the first time began to look forward to the turning over. He *could* be out in the five days that Kevin wanted. Hell, if it came to it he could be in Bamako in five days, and a day later in Mopti. They were finished with the stock-taking. He would finish the reconciliation tomorrow, pack, and then he'd take the sea car for a couple of days, alone, and visit the villages at York Island and down at Sherbro Strait, where the Kitammi comes out of the string of lakes that parallel the long straight beach. He might even motor up the Kitammi as far as Gbap and the River Sewa to where the great mangrove swamp began. He would make his good-byes properly.

They made the run across the glassy bay and the low oily swells of the strait with gray morning coolness rushing over them. A pale disk of sun materialized from time to time through wispy haze. Hassan crouched over the tiller, shivering in the breeze generated by their passage, while Robert sat on the middle thwart, grateful that the steady roar of the Yamaha made talk impossible, grateful that he was facing the bow and did not have to look at Hassan's face; full of sadness that this was his last trip across the strait; full of regret that in one way or another he had failed them all—Pa Bia, Sori, Aminata, the villagers, all of them. He had handled the turning over about as badly as you could.

How could he have misunderstood it? It seemed obvious, now that he was away from the station. He had put so much importance on preserving Hassan's job that Alexander saw it as an opportunity to show that his power surpassed Robert's power. Simply that, nothing more.

♈

Pa Bangura was waiting for them at the landing at Matruh village. Hassan nosed the boat into the bank, climbed out in the mud and pulled the bow up on the shore.

He passed Robert's bags to Pa Bangura, then walked to the Mercedes doublecab with Robert. They had spoken scarcely at all since leaving Bonthe and now, as Pa Bangura tossed the bags into the lorry, they stood facing one another, still wordless. Hassan offered his hand.

They bounced over the pot-holed road through the village, past children who came running to watch them pass, and then they were in the bush, following trails that were little more than paths, crossing narrow palm log bridges, traversing low swells of land separated by swampy bottoms that were green with rice. After hours of lurching over swampland trails they came into the upland hills, and the trail began to take on the double track look of a road. The road took them to Sumbuya Town and through its half-dozen dusty streets of mud houses, coming out on the road to Bumpe, which for the first time was a true road—complete with many potholes and rain gullies—and Pa Bangura pushed the lorry to a bone-rattling 35 kilometers per hour. Coming out of Bumpe the road improved still more, and soon they were through the crossroads town of Tikonko and passing the ruin of the Shell Station, the only petrol station between Bo and the coast. Pa Bangura bore down on the accelerator, and on the flat stretch past the Teacher's College and into the outskirts of Bo the doublecab danced and rattled over a wide washboard of road, scattering Africans and throwing up a roiling yellow cloud.

The air shimmered in the fierce heat. The town looked deserted: people, goats, dogs, all had found shelter in which to endure the afternoon. The doublecab was even hotter than the air outside it, and Robert had sweated his clothes sopping wet. He instructed Pa Bangura to drive on through the town and out along the Kenema road past the neat rice paddies the Chinese development group had created from a meandering stream. Pa Bangura turned off the dirt road and gunned the doublecab up the pot-holed track to the top of a rise where he turned into the gravel yard and nosed the vehicle between a pair of VW vans beneath the umbrella of a great breadfruit tree. Across the yard was a long, low house with barred windows.

Pa Bangura turned the engine off. "Mistah Robaht, we need petrol."

Robert had one foot on the ground. He stopped.

"You get petrol inside the rubbers, notoso?"

"Well—no sah, I done put am inside de lorry."

Robert pulled himself back into the cab and leaned over to Pa Bangura's side and turned the key on and watched the needle of the petrol gauge steady at less than a quarter of a tank. He turned the key off and got out of the truck.

"You been sell the petrol."

"Eh? Sell am? Oh, no sah, I no been sell am."

"Bullshit."

"Nar God, sah, I no been sell am."

Robert got out and pushed the door shut.

"Nar God, sah."

Robert walked across the gravel yard toward the house.

"Nar God, sah, I no been sell am," Pa Bangura called after him.

Robert opened the door and stepped into a large room with desks and typewriters and file cabinets. A black woman sat at a desk, typing very slowly with the forefinger of each hand. A black man sat at another, his feet up on a desk, reading a *Newsweek*. A murmur of German came from down the hall, blending with the hum of air-conditioners and the grumble of a generator. Robert's wet shirt was like ice against his body. He heard laughter, then a stubby fireplug of a woman with close-cropped, gray-flecked hair appeared in the hall. When she saw Robert her smile froze, then faded.

"Hello, Barbara."

"Good day," she said stiffly. She had disapproved of him from the first time she met him—his dress and habits and demeanor showed him to be just another undisciplined American. The disapproval had hardened to anger on a Saturday night two years before. She had been sitting with the Dutchman in Pa Jalloh's, and his whiskey had put her in a blearily generous mood. She'd shown that she forgave his Americanness by waving him over to the table she shared with the fat, chain-smoking gold miner and—after Robert drank a beer with them and got up to leave—by offering her extra bedroom; offhandedly: the way any expat in Africa routinely offers shelter to a transient colleague—because it might be the only decent place. It was late and he was tired and he'd already tried Gunter's house and found it closed, with Gunter in Freetown, and he had been out to the Teacher's College and found that Kathleen was off visiting a friend in Sefadu. He accepted her invitation. The room included amenities: a bottle of Canadian Club—which she planted on his bedside table with two glasses—and herself: chunky, hairy-lipped, hairy-armed, hairy-armpitted, ripely needing a bath. He had claimed a splitting headache.

"Robert!"

A slight, pale man with thinning hair appeared in the hall.

"Good to see you." He offered his hand. "You're out now."

"Hello, Gunter. Yes, I'm out."

"What shall I offer you? My congratulation or my consolation?"

"I'm not sure yet."

"It's the best thing. It would have gotten you eventually. Who's taking it?"

"Alexander."

"Really! He was on track to head Fisheries Division. Why would he take a posting like that?"

"Money. The inventory. Kargbo wanted his man there to protect it from the Paramount Chief, who's been maneuvering for months to get *his* man in charge."

Gunter smiled.

"Na Salone."

Gunter looked past Robert to Barbara, who sat at her desk frowning.

"Barbara, will you please ask Mohammed to bring us beer and lunch?" He glanced at Robert. "How does bread, cheese, and ham sound?" Without waiting for response he turned back to Barbara. "And ask him to prepare some rice for Robert's driver." He led Robert down the hall. "Any word from Marie?"

"She's fine. Looking for something for me to do."

When they finished their lunch they went to the warehouse, a long structure with corrugated metal walls and roof and big sliding doors at each end, which the clerk had pulled fully open to admit light and air. The walls of the building were lined with shelves of hardware behind wire fences. Only the middle of the floor between the two doors was accessible, and in it were stacks of boxed medical supplies and the components of two hospital beds, all of which Kevin had purchased from Gunter's project and arranged for Robert to bring back to Freetown. Gunter got a clipboard from one of the African clerks, looked it over, handed it to Robert.

"We had everything except the rehydration kits."

Robert glanced over the list. "Can I load in the morning?"

"Of course."

"There's one other thing. Pa Bangura seems to have lost track of forty liters of petrol on the way up here. Can you spare twenty liters? That'll get us to Freetown."

♈

Robert dropped Pa Bangura at a hut on a patch of mosquito-infested ground bordering the Chinese rice paddies— the home of Pa Bangura's daughter and son-in-law—then drove out to the compound of the Catholic hospital. He waited outside the surgery until Sister Hilary and Sister Janet finished with patients, went with them to their bungalow, visited for a while over coffee, then made his goodbyes and drove to the center of town, which was a street of two-story structures owned by Lebanese traders.

He parked before a building fronted with dusty iron-barred windows. On a faded sign above the door were the words *Jihad Darwish and Son*. Inside, ceiling-high shelves, most of which were empty, lined the walls. Tinned food and insect-infested packages of beans and pasta and bottles of ketchup and mustard huddled in dusty little clumps alongside spray cans of Shelltox, candles, bar soap, lanterns, mosquito coils, greasy boxes of tools: inventory that Toufic Darwish had bought in Freetown from his rich cousin Billy.

John, the fourteen-year-old son of the son of Jihad Darwish, dozed in a chair behind the counter. He woke, yawned, greeted Robert, then rose and led him through a

31

passageway to the high-walled dirt courtyard behind the building. A tiny hut leaned into a corner formed by the walls of the compound. From a fire pit a ribbon of blue smoke ascended. A black woman squatted beside the fire, peeling cassava roots. Nearby a pair of naked black children played with the head of a doll. At the base of the stairs John stopped and called for his father.

Toufic appeared at the top of the stairs. Seeing Robert, he smiled and waved him up. "Mother is asking about you. She is saying that you will not come to tell her good-bye, but I tell her you will come."

They went across the covered porch and into a high-ceilinged room containing a pink and black plastic sofa and wood chairs with plastic seats. The joints of the wood furniture already showed gaps from shrinking, though the dry season was only beginning. Religious prints hung on every wall: Jesus with upturned eyes and a forehead bleeding from a crown of thorns; Jesus on the cross; the gory martyrdom of one saint or another. Across the room French doors opened to the balcony where Toufic's wife and mother sat at a small table looking out over dusty streets and metal roofs that wavered in the heat.

Toufic's wife, younger and fatter than her husband, had a pleasant milky face and black, uncovered hair. The older woman was small, big-nosed, crinkly-haired, and as dark-skinned as her son. Her head covering was white, as was her gown, which ended at her ankles. On the table were glasses of orange juice, a bowl of ground nuts, coffee cups, an ashtray in which a cigar smoldered.

Robert sat with them at the table, sipped the thick Lebanese coffee, smoked one of the White Owl cigars, laughed at Toufic's jokes and stories. But mentally he had already made his good-byes. After a while he rose and said he had to go. Toufic looked surprised, then hurt, protesting that Robert must stay and eat. But Robert said no, he had much to do before he could leave in the morning. He hugged and kissed the women, made the customary promise that he would return someday, then walked with Toufic down the stairs, through the store, and out on the street to the doublecab.

He drove to the outskirts of town, to a quadrangle of four long structures with rusty roofs and peeling paint. Parking the doublecab in front of one of the buildings, he climbed a half-dozen unsteady stairs to a porch that stretched the length of the structure. Bushpoles supported the porch roof, which had rusted through in many places. A dozen laborers sat or dozed on a shaded bench along the wall. They lazily followed him with their eyes as he walked past them to an open door.

He found Daniel Sulaiman sleeping on the table that served as his desk. A file cabinet, from which two drawers were missing, stood against the wall behind him. Three shovels, one with a broken handle, leaned against the file cabinet; and a half-empty box of netting bundles rested in the corner (begged from Robert weeks before; ostensibly for harvesting his ponds, but which, Robert knew, Daniel had sold one at a time to buy rice for his family). Above the file cabinet a crudely lettered sign proclaimed *Koribundu-Gbundapi Inland Fisheries Development Project*. A paperback novel rested on the floor beneath the table. Robert read the title: *Things Fall Apart*. Below the title, the name, Chinua Acheba. He smiled: for all the years he had known him, Daniel had refused to read Acheba, or any other African writer, saying they were all too pessimistic.

Daniel stirred, opened his eyes, turned his head, studied Robert for a moment, then stretched his limbs and yawned loud and long. He asked the time and Robert told him it was nearly five o'clock.

Daniel pushed himself up, swung his legs off the table. "I'm glad you've come. It always makes me happy to see my brother Robert."

"I've come to say goodbye."

"Eh!" Daniel looked surprised, then groaned. "It is today? Oh, it can't be so soon!"

"Tomorrow morning."

"So soon, so soon!" Daniel groaned again, more loudly. "When you leave I will be unhappy forever—it will be like my brother dying. It is a great loss for Salone. We must drink a Star Beer. For the sake of our time together." He stood and put his arm around Robert's shoulder. "We will go to Pa Jalloh's and I will buy the beer."

"Sure," Robert said. As with all friendships, theirs depended on the equality of their relationship, and so this fiction was necessary. Robert did not mind buying; he did not forget that in his first year in Salone, Daniel and his brother Prince had been the rich ones and they had been generous. But that was before the inflation impoverished the tiny Freetown bureaucratic and professional classes, and Daniel's family, like most of the families that had run the government for decades, were reduced to the living standards of the most backward villagers.

♈

The warm air smelled of charcoal and roasted meat— which, charred and spiced up as it was, could have been beef or bushrat—and the kerosene lamps of street food sellers. Pa Jalloh's was full. A gaggle of young Peace Corps volunteers chattered over beers at one table, their unfaded shirts advertising their newness: PCVs fresh out of training. German and British development professionals talked at a table beside the big glassless window. An Irish aid worker and his Scots colleagues laughed at another table and a couple of Dutch gold miners discoursed over beers and a bottle of whisky at the table nearest the door. A few blacks were scattered among the whites.

Down the dusty street the generator behind the movie house coughed and sputtered, then settled into a steady grumble, signaling that the movie would soon start. A queue of Lebanese and blacks pressed forward into the tiny building. A bare-chested Rambo hugged a machine gun to his hip and glared out at the world from a poster at the door.

Lightning flickered in the tops of thunderheads far to the east, the thunder coming in subdued crumps and rumbles. Robert and Daniel sat on a bench on the porch watching the distant flicker of light. With his teeth Daniel pulled the last piece of roasted meat off a stick. He threw the stick into the street and wiped his hands on his handkerchief,

34

folded it, put it back in his pocket. Raising his beer, he drained it and belched.

"So you see the problem," he continued in a thick, uneven voice. "Minister Kargbo thinks he has convinced the English, but I know they want to do a frame survey before they will give more money." He smiled wanly. "Minister Kargbo agrees, but he does not understand. All he thinks about is the money—he does not understand that a frame survey will ruin everything."

Robert was tired and thinking about driving Daniel home and then going out to see if Kathleen would put him up for the night. He had started to leave two hours before, but Bill Cavanaugh had showed up, and then that burly Dutch gold miner whose unpronounceable name he could not remember had joined them on the porch with his bottle of whiskey, which they had passed around, and then they had gone off to his Land Rover and smoked some of Daniel's Kabala jamba and drank some more of the whiskey. After a while the Dutchman had become annoyed with Daniel's rambling self-pity and had gone back to Pa Jalloh's, where he joined his colleagues. A few minutes later Cavanaugh and Robert and Daniel had returned to the porch where they sat until Cavanaugh dragged himself to his feet and wandered away to find his motorcycle.

"How can I do it?" Daniel asked.

"Do what?"

"I am talking about these frame surveys. I told you."

Robert shrugged. "It's a sociology survey. You go out and talk to the villagers."

"I know how to do a frame survey. I have done frame surveys. That is not the problem. The problem is how to *avoid* the survey. I have begged Minister Kargbo, but he knows nothing about these things, nothing at all. He thinks only of getting more English pounds."

"I don't understand," Robert said. "What is it you want, anyway?"

Daniel drew himself up, frowning at the difficulty of conveying the delicacy of his situation. "When the English discover that the project is nothing but a few holes in the ground they will think that I have cheated them. Minister

Kargbo makes me report all those wonderful productions of fish and when he reads the reports he *believes* them and sends them to the English. They will think that I have cheated them, but I have not cheated them. Minister Kargbo—all I wanted—all I want—" He looked vaguely around, seeking the thought that he had been leading up to, but the thought had wandered away from him. Unable to find it, he grabbed an idea that sounded like a suitably fine sentiment: "I want to give the people—something for the sacrifice the people made for my education. I want to—" he paused to belch "—develop a few fish ponds that make meat. Make meat for the people. I want to show a few farmers how to make meat—" He stopped, looked with watery, blooded eyes down at his beer bottle, showing Robert with a helpless smile that it was empty. "Kargbo chops the money. Takes it all. Every farthing."

"Na Salone," Robert said, rising. "You want another beer?"

"Kargbo chops the money and I cannot even give my brother a job."

"Do you want another beer?"

"Kargbo will not even give Prince a job. Twenty pounds a year it will cost him from all the thousands he takes from the English. A white man spends twenty pounds in an evening of drinking. Minister Kargbo spends *more* than twenty pounds in an evening of drinking."

"Do you want another beer?"

"Robert, will you help my brother, who is your brother as I am your brother? Before you leave Salone? You knew him before you knew me, Robert. He does not hate you, Robert, he loves you. I know that he loves you, he told me that. Duya, I beg, Robert, ask Mister Beachley if he will give Prince a job. I do not know what will happen to him if he does not find a job. Duya, Robert, give my brother a job."

"Do you want another beer?"

Daniel nodded sadly.

Robert went inside and made his way through the tables to the back where Pa Jalloh sat on a stool behind a small table. The room, lit by candles and lanterns, was much hotter than the porch and the mosquitoes were active in spite of the smoke of the coils. Pa Jalloh's thin Fullah face glistened in the wavering yellow light. A white skull cap covered the bristles of his shaved scalp. Robert saw faded words— which he couldn't read—on the old man's T-shirt.

"Make I get one Star Beer, Pa," he said.

The old man opened the glass door of the beer cooler. The cooler cooled nothing; a decade before, when its motor still worked and when there was electricity to drive it, it had cooled beers; now it simply controlled access to the old man's inventory. Jalloh accepted a rubber-banded bundle of one-leone notes and expertly counted them. He dropped the bundle in among the others in the cash box and opened the cooler door and got a bottle and popped the top off and pushed it across the table. Robert carried the beer out to the porch and gave it to Daniel and resumed his seat on the bench. He watched dark figures in the street moving in and out of shadowy lantern light, glanced down at the almost empty bottle of Star Beer that he had nursed for the last hour: yellow star set in a blue oval. "Heavenly gold," that professor of geology at Fourah Bay College had murmured drunkenly as the crowded ferry drifted with the tide, marveling that a nation that could not make anything work— not a ferryboat, not a railroad, not buses, not water delivery, not telephones, not sewers, not street lights, not health care, not schools, not businesses, not politics—not a single one of that great suite of services that just about everyone agrees is the minimum support for a modern existence; that such a country could produce such a fine beer as this—this heavenly gold—and in such abundance; well, it was an amazing achievement, wasn't it? An achievement to be proud of. The white-headed black man had said this with great solemnity after drinking half of Robert's case of Star Beers while the ferry drifted and they waited for rescue; and in the last light of the day he'd looked up at a B-Cal Airbus rising out of Lungi into the sky over the bay, saying that he had a ticket, sent by his white colleagues in Reading University, for a seat on that plane.

Daniel stirred, like he was about to speak again, but he was too drunk now with jamba, whiskey, beer, and self-pity to make much sense, or to care if anyone listened. To escape him Robert rose and stepped to the edge of the porch and put his arm around a bush pole roof support. He looked down the street, feeling not drunk, just good. He had passed the whiskey bottle without drinking and he had had only a couple of beers, wanting not to spoil the jamba high.

He was high the first time he saw this street, though not from pot. From excitement. And optimism, of course, though it was hard to remember the optimism, hard to believe he was ever optimistic about Salone. Now that optimism seemed more like the white man's overweening confidence, which is really a sort of hubris. He smiled. Prince understood that before he did, understood it and threw it in his face every time they disagreed. Hubris and naiveté are related conditions of delusion, Prince had said, and he was right. Robert had brought both of those qualities with him from America, though at the time he certainly considered himself a man seasoned and tempered by experience. At one time he had regarded those twelve years in his father's business as significant experience. Now he seldom thought of them at all, and when he did, it seemed like a single indistinct event: 4,000 repetitions that now seemed like one monochromatic drone of sameness, so distant it was like an experience out of someone else's life.

Even his recollections of training had the feel of someone else's experience. The only day he remembered vividly was the steamy day of the swearing-in at the big court bari at Songo, after which the Ambassador—the one before Neggie—and his wife had chatted for a few minutes with the new PCVs, then made their excuses and hurried into the air-conditioned Cadillac with the tiny flags drooping at each front fender and lurched off down the pot-holed trail, and then Robert and four others gathered at Prince's Land Rover. They'd tied their bags on top and three had crammed themselves in the back and two in front and they had suffered through three sweaty hours of slamming up against the roof and bouncing down on the hard canvas seats before Prince dropped four of them at the Peace Corps office in Bo to hang around the dayroom while he took Michael Caldwell on to Mandu. Skinny little bug-eyed Michael, just out of college, just beginning to shave; and within the next few weeks, to drink and fuck—activities he pursued with the monomaniacal passion he had once shown for his devotions and his studies. Michael transfigured as much as Robert, but much more quickly, and in the end more violently—wrecking himself and his motorcycle while drunk—and going home strapped to a cot.

When Prince returned from taking Michael to his village, they'd loaded Robert's things and Prince drove him to his village, one of tens of other villages and towns called Njala, where he was to replace totally serious, totally committed, totally devout Nancy what-was-her-name, whom he heard praying in the morning when he got up and who was praying when he went to bed, and who went to Bo each weekend not to drink and party but to attend mass. And who was outraged beyond words when he acted upon his discovery that he really *could* fuck pretty much any of the unmarried village women he wanted to fuck.

He came to know the name of every man and woman in that village, every bobo and titi, every tree on the hillside, every house, every path for miles around, every rock and pothole and turn in the track between Njala and the Mono road. And now that he had no time for it he wanted to visit Njala once more—the village was only thirty miles north of Bo—to see it one last time, to see who had married whom, to find out which of the children had died.

By the time Prince had dropped him at Njala, he and Prince had talked about the role of development in the evolution of West African economies, and they had discussed the question of whether Marxist socialism or western capitalism was the ideal path. The discussion had been ninety percent Prince and ten percent Robert. Prince, promoted to manager of the Bo office only a few weeks before, closed the social distance that he was supposed to maintain between his position and that of the PCV by inviting Robert to his house the next time he was in Bo. Robert had been flattered by the invitation. Two weeks later, when Nancy backed him to Bo on her Honda so that he could pick up his own Honda, he had stopped at Prince's office and Prince had invited him in and they had talked for a while before

Prince reiterated his invitation. They went in the Land
Rover to the tiny house where he and his brother lived and
there he met Daniel. In those days Daniel and Prince had the
income of bright young bureaucrats on the make—the economy was stable then and their pay meant something—and
Robert had the stipend of a volunteer, which was just about
enough to buy what he needed: rice, beer, and a bag of
jamba once in a while. More often than not he drank their
beer and ate their food. At first Prince's endless appetite for
disputation had dominated the friendship; it was only after
Robert understood it was ideas and words that interested
Prince, not domination, that they became friends. Daniel
more or less tagged along, becoming Robert's friend
because he was there.

"Robert, I done chak," Daniel murmured.

Robert turned.

"Water rough too mos," Daniel was saying. "I t'ink say
I go make sick."

Robert studied Daniel sitting there with his eyes closed,
slowly rolling his head from side to side against the building, muttering, "All men get rotten belly, Robert. God
laugh."

♈

Kathleen welcomed him with a squeal of joy and
hugged him, saying she had been thinking about him, wondering if he would come to see her before he left. They
shared a joint in the light of a candle and drank a Star Beer
from the case he bought for her from Pa Jalloh. She was her
usual gregarious self, but there was something different
about her. She hovered at a level of excitement that he had
never seen before.

"I'm in love, Robert," she finally gushed, unable to
withhold the good news. "I wish you'd come earlier, you
just missed him."

"Who?"

"Babah Allswell."

"The math teacher?" Bug-eyed, apologetic, slope-shouldered, muttering Babah Allswell? He tried not to show his incredulity.

She nodded excitedly. "You know him?"

He nodded.

"He's so re*ser*ved! So *qui*et! I never imagined what he's really like! For a year we sat next to each other at faculty meetings, on committees, and he never looked at me, never said a word to me. Whenever I said something to him he just looked down. I didn't even think he liked me, and then he came one evening—"

He sat dully, not listening, the fatigue of a day that had started twenty hours before finally settling upon him, bearing him down. Her expression softened, her gaze became distant, she seemed to lose awareness of his presence as she recounted how they had been drawn irresistibly together. It was the most incredible experience of her life. A marathon of love making, she said—with no sense of indelicacy—on the bed, the floor, the table, yes this very table. Until they simply exhausted themselves. They'd wilt and fall apart and twenty minutes later he would be at her again. He was overwhelming, voracious, left her sore and bewildered and exhausted. She thought of nothing but screwing him, nothing else mattered, not another thought entered her head all the time he was gone from her presence, not another thought entered her head when he was *in* her presence; she had not a thought about her classes, her students; just screwing Babah Allswell—could Robert understand how incredible it was to be so fully and completely loved and in love? He did not answer. He was already asleep.

"Mornin' sah," Pa Bangura called cheerfully. "We de go?"

An old woman stood behind him, looking worried, her arms crossed over bare breasts. Three children stopped playing in the earthen yard and looked expectantly up at the white man. Pa Bangura's daughter, a young woman with plaited hair and a belly distended by pregnancy, came to the doorway of the thatch hut. Her swollen breasts bulged up over a frayed brassiere. A pair of goats pulled against tethers to reach the greenery of the embankment.

Robert understood immediately. His jaw went tight.

The pregnant woman hurried forward, squatted beside a basket and grasped its bottom as Pa Bangura squatted on the other side. They lifted together, the young woman slipping under the basket and settling it on her head. She moved toward the trail that went up the embankment, while behind her the old woman and Pa Bangura squatted beside a second basket.

"Wait," Robert said.

The old woman and Pa Bangura, still on their haunches, paused; they looked at Robert.

"We no able for carry am go," Robert said.

The old man stood. "Mastah, duya—"

"No possible."

Pa Bangura came to the base of the embankment, pleading earnestly that he was certain there was space enough in

42

the doublecab. At this point the old woman groaned so loudly that everyone looked at her, thinking she was suddenly stricken. His daughter, standing uneasily at the base of the embankment with the basket still on her head, rattled something in Mende, distracting Pa Bangura. He looked annoyed, waved her off, continued his speech. His wives had nothing to cook, he said, his children were hungry, he himself was losing weight (he lifted his shirt to prove his point), the breasts of his youngest wife were drying up, and she with a suckling child. It had always been the privilege of project drivers to bring food and firewood back to Freetown when they drove upline. In times like these they had to have that privilege or wives and children would go hungry.

Of course the old man was talking nonsense. Robert knew that Pa Bangura's fat wives were the sharpest traders in the Wellington market. This stuff was not food; it was goods to sell for profit.

Pa Bangura saw that Robert was no longer saying no. He solemnly repeated his promise to abandon any basket that he could not secure on top of the load. Even the goats he would abandon if he could not secure them. This he promised, "Nar God," and pointed skyward.

Twenty minutes later the old man unloaded the baskets and the goats in the gravel yard of the Pujehun Project warehouse and helped the warehouse clerk load the medical supplies while Gunter watched and Robert checked the list. When they finished with the paperwork Robert and Gunter went to the office for coffee. Through a window they watched Pa Bangura and the clerk load baskets one at a time until the cargo towered over the cab. They ran ropes back and forth over the load, then Pa Bangura climbed gingerly to the top and pulled the hog tied goats up. Gunter remarked dryly that there was still room for two or three dozen ties of fire wood.

They had only one mishap. A goat chewed through the line binding its feet and leaped off the mountainous load as the doublecab sailed along on a rare stretch of intact blacktop. They finally captured the bloody-headed animal a quarter mile off the road when it stopped to browse.

They arrived at Pa Bangura's mud block house in the

Wellington ghetto in the heat of the day. After unloading goats and baskets they continued their journey, through the abandoned industrial suburbs spread out on the plain below Mount Auriol, arriving at the usual jam-up of cars and lorries in Kissy Market. Pa Bangura nudged the doublecab through swarming customers, begging children, market women, and young men hawking old copies of *Newsweek* and *West Africa*. West of the Kissy Roundabout the crowds thinned enough for traffic to move at a walking pace through the Lebanese district, where two-story structures leaned shoulder to shoulder over the narrow cobbled street. Wiry porters glistened with sweat as they leaned like horses between the shafts of car-sized carts. Clothing hung from lines strung from balcony to balcony. Black women wove in and out of traffic, their headpans sailing above the crowd. A white-headed old Leb leaned against an iron balcony rail, staring down at the chaos.

They turned off on East Street and drove past queues snaking out of the bus station, past the new mosque, the abandoned Bata Shoe Store, the government book store with its empty shelves, to George Street, where they pulled over and stopped.

The Tropic of Capricorn was a relic of colonial time, a house converted to a hotel by its white owner in the 1940s to capitalize on the housing shortage that came with the wartime influx of administrators and soldiers. It had changed little in the intervening years, except that it sagged now with age, and electricity seldom lighted its rooms, and the water that sometimes flowed from its taps would likely as not give you cholera, and there had been no glass in its windows for decades. Despite these deficiencies, the tiny hotel still possessed the best part of what it had been. It was clean and it was known to have no bedbugs, unlike every other flophouse hotel in Freetown—even the once-grand City Hotel, which was directly across the street. But most important of all, it was secure; as secure as the Paramount Hotel or the Bintomani Hotel or even the YMCA rest house. Sturdy iron bars guarded the windows of every guest room and strong locks blocked the doors, and though the clapboard siding showed as much raw wood as paint, the walls were solid; there were no holes for thieves.

Mrs. Gooding operated the Tropic from a table on its shaded porch, from which she sold bean sandwiches, dried fish, cigarettes one-one, Star Beer, and Cokes. When she saw Robert she waddled off the porch and grabbed him into a hug. Calling for her daughter to come and tend the table, she escorted him up the narrow staircase to the best room, all the while puffing about how wonderful it was to see him, and asking if his white woman was coming from Mali. Behind them Pa Bangura dragged Robert's bags up the stairs.

Robert bought a Star Beer and a handful of cigarettes for Pa Bangura and sent him to the project office with a note for Kevin Beachley, then went back up to his room. On the table were a kerosene lantern and a tin can with edges bent down to form cigarette rests. A bare light bulb hung in the middle of the room. He opened the shutters and looked out on the street and the City Hotel where, according to local lore, Graham Greene had lived while he wrote *The Heart of the Matter*. To the left of the City Hotel was the Freetown City Hall, a disintegrating structure with broken windows and talus slopes of trash fanned out beneath every window.

He got soap and towel from his bag and went down to the shower baffa in the back yard. As he poured cups of cool water over his head and soaped his limbs he thought about the call he would make to Marie. He had already decided he would ask her to take some time off and meet him in Europe.

He went back upstairs, put on shorts and shirt, grabbed his knapsack, and walked the three blocks to the U.S. Embassy, a three-story white building facing the Cotton Tree roundabout. A young marine greeted him in the lobby. Robert asked to see Max Bush. The marine picked up the telephone, punched some numbers, said something into the phone, then told Robert that Max would be right down. He offered his hand, saying his name was Lenny, that they'd met at the Fourth of July party at the Marine compound. Max appeared at the base of the stairs, carrying a bundle of letters.

"Hello Robert," Max said, tossing the bundle.

Robert caught the bundle. "Hi Max." He glanced through the envelopes—a couple from Marie, one from his brother, a card from his father, one from a friend from his Peace Corps days. He looked up at Max. "Where's the Mali Embassy?

"There's no embassy—they have a consulate. Over on Goderich or Regent Street, in the back of a shoe repair shop, I think. Someone in the French Embassy can tell you where it is. C'mon upstairs."

"I want to get started on my visa."

"It's nearly five, everything's closed. C'mon upstairs."

"I need to buy some leones and I have to book a flight, and—"

"I got plenty of leones. I'll loan you some. C'mon upstairs, we'll have a drink." He took Robert's arm and Robert allowed himself to be guided through the metal detector and past the steel door, which a second marine opened from the inside, and up the curving stairs to the third floor where the stairwell opened into a circular antechamber with a secretary's desk, maroon carpet, white walls, and tables covered with stacks of *The Economist* and *West Africa*. They said hello to Ambassador Neggie, a fat black fellow with a fluffy ring of white hair about his head and a preoccupied look, who walked past them and down the stairs, followed by a woman carrying a pile of papers.

In Max's office Robert dropped his knapsack at the foot of the leather chair and sat, shivering when his damp skin contacted the cold leather.

"You won't believe what that asshole's done now," Max said. He closed the door and went behind his desk and pulled a bottle of scotch from the bottom drawer. He dropped into the leather chair and swung around and grabbed a couple of glasses and a pitcher of water from the credenza. "You remember that white paper I wrote on Momoh? The one Neggie wouldn't let me send. It was just after Pa Siaka announced Momoh would succeed him and the conventional wisdom had it—"

Robert remembered very well: it was when he met Marie. He was in Freetown for planning meetings. He and Kevin had driven down to the beach to talk privately, and he'd seen Marie emerge from the hotel and come down the stairs, lanky and brown in a blue bikini, and pass through a squadron of black youths chasing a soccer ball across the white sand. He'd stepped out of his halfbacks and run into the surf after her. "Wait," he'd called. And she had stopped and turned. The water was momentarily ankle-deep, and then hip-deep as a wave swirled up around them. "Will you join me and my friend for a beer?" he'd asked, and she had looked at him like he was crazy, then turned her back on him and stepped toward the next wave and he had said, "Okay, let's swim," and had surged past her and dove into the wave and came up and faced her with water streaming out of his hair and his shirt plastered to his chest. She'd studied him for a second, then glanced up the beach as if to ascertain the safety of her situation, and saw Kevin standing in the sun before the baffa—a rumpled man in sun glasses and flowing shirt and white shorts.

"I'm Robert Kelley," he said, offering his hand.

"Do you do this often?" she asked, ignoring his hand.

"What? Approach strange women or swim in my clothes?"

"Yes."

"Not very often. What's your name?"

A long pause; then, reluctantly: "Marie."

"You're American. Not Peace Corps, though."

Still cautious, she shook her head.

"Tourist?"

"I suppose. Traveling through, stopped in Freetown for the beaches."

"It's a long way to come to see the ocean."

Another wave, this one big enough to sway them.

"Mali's not so far."

"You work in Mali?"

Nodding. "USAID."

"Rural development?"

She nodded again.

"Then you've probably heard of Zimi Development Project. It's famous in West African development circles."

She shook her head.

"Well, that's who I work for. That's my boss up there by

47

the baffa. We're in planning meetings now, with managers from Zimi and Pujehun and Bonthe—that's me, I run the Bonthe Station. We get together in Freetown three or four times a year for these meetings. Kevin and I came down to the beach to get away from the others for a while, so we can talk about my fisheries program. Will you join us in the baffa for a beer?"

He had been surprised that she talked to him and even more surprised that she accepted the invitation. "Staying at the Cape?" he asked.

She nodded.

"Have you seen Freetown?"

"No. It was very dark when the bus came through. All I saw was candles and lanterns."

"You need to see Freetown, then you'll see this isn't the place to stay. It's a great beach, but one hotel's lousy—that's the one you're in—and the other's expensive. You should be at the Tropic of Capricorn, in Freetown. It's clean, secure, right in the middle of things, and it's only a buck a night."

"Bet that's where you're staying."

"Why yes, it is. How'd you know that?"

"Wild guess."

They were approaching Kevin, near the entrance to the baffa.

"Kevin, I want you to meet my friend Marie."

Kevin removed his sunglasses, offered his hand. "Pleasure."

"Marie works for USAID in Mali. Rural development."

"Women's programs," she said.

"Ah, USAID," Kevin said. "Know one of your chaps. Fletcher."

"Yes, I know him."

"Chaired the meetings two years ago in Accra. He gave a brilliant talk on the economics of upland rice cultivation. When you see him, tell him Kevin Beachley sends his greetings."

"I will."

"Women's programs, you say? Health or the business side?"

"Health, mainly."

"Lots of opportunity there. Women's programs are all the rage these days."

"And about time, too, don't you think?"

"Yes, certainly."

That afternoon Robert did not return to the meetings. Kevin went back alone and Robert spent the rest of the afternoon with Marie and took her to dinner that evening at Farah's, where they encountered Max and Julie. The next day Robert and Marie traveled with them down the Peninsula Road to Hamilton Beach in Max's official car. Marie had loved the air-conditioned luxury of the Cadillac with American flags snapping at the fenders, and she'd loved the opulence of the Embassy retreat at Hamilton Beach, with Sierra Leonean staff hovering about and looking for an opportunity to bring a cold beer or a sandwich, and she'd loved the party Max gave two days later, in honor of Third Assistant Minister Kargbo. There she met a junketing black U.S. Congressman and European and African ambassadors and Sierra Leonean leaders—each of whom noticed her and competed for her attention. On the fourth day of her visit she checked out of the hotel at the Cape and moved to the Tropic.

Robert remembered that period also as the time—it was a month or so after Marie's first visit—that Julie came on to him. She had come to the Tropic and had sat in the chair in his room chattering nervously, looking everywhere but at him, finally blurting that she wanted some pot and had no idea where she could get it. He said he had some and dug it out of his knapsack and split it into two parts and gave her one part folded in a piece of newspaper. From the little pile still on the table he rolled a joint. She smoked it like a cigarette; Robert warned her to be moderate, but she laughed and said she had years of abstinence to make up for. She became giddy and hyperactive, getting up and drifting to the window and looking out, then returning to the chair, jabbering all the while; until finally she spewed it out, the reasons she was at last (and for certain this time) leaving Max. The same transgression, tirelessly repeated: years of philandering; with whores, with colleagues, with her closest friends, with the wives of *his* closest friends (he had as a matter of

49

course tried Marie and Marie had informed Robert). The words came tumbling almost unintelligibly as she paced to the window and back to the chair, while Robert listened, not knowing what to do or say, until she stopped in front of him and pleadingly asked him—point-blankly, probably because she didn't know any other way to do it—if she was attractive: she thought she was, she tried to be, she wanted to be attractive, and he murmured of course she was attractive, yes, she was beautiful and very desirable, and she had said, okay then sleep with me. But she could not out-sleaze Max Bush, even stoned; she was too unpracticed; the appalling crudeness of those words, coming from *her* mouth, shocked her and she rushed out of the room and went banging and thudding down the stairs, leaving her purse and the jamba she had begged.

A couple of weeks later all the talk around Freetown was about the wife of the American Deputy Chief of Mission screwing the French economic attaché, and after him a chubby, balding, bewildered forty-eight-year-old Peace Corps volunteer. And then she exploded her family and left Freetown, dragging her shell-shocked kids onto the plane with her, and got herself home to Virginia just in time for her nervous breakdown.

"He lifted stuff from that paper and put it in one of his reports," Max was saying. "Whole pages of it. Without attribution, of course. Caroline showed me a copy. He didn't change a comma. But here's the good part: he doesn't know I sent my paper to a friend on the Salone desk, who passed it around—unofficially of course—to the other Africa desks. It got a lot of praise. Even from the Africa Secretary. When *he* sees Neggie's name on *my* paper—well, then he'll know what kind of sleaze ball he's got for Ambassador to Sierra Leone. The heart of the paper was that the Old Pa chose Momoh as his successor because of Momoh's political inexperience. It gave the Old Pa some security, but it's created a weak presidency, one that's ripe for a coup—you listening?"

Robert had been thinking about Marie. "Pardon?"

"You're not interested in this stuff any more, are you? Leaving Salone—Jesus, I wish it was me. Suppose you're still planning on going to Mali—"

50

"Of course."

"Hope you're not in a hurry."

"What's that mean?"

"Lungi's closed. IAA inspectors pulled a surprise inspection and found out the emergency vehicles don't work. Seems the firemen sold some unnecessary parts—pumps, hoses, tires, that sort of thing. Even sold the engine out of one of the firetrucks. Of course B-Cal, Air France, Nigeria Air all canceled their flights. All that's left is Aeroflot, and I think their nearest destination is Prague."

"You're shittin' me."

"That's what they said in Washington."

"Can't they get parts?"

"This is Salone, Robert. Suppliers don't just ship stuff to Salone. Suppliers demand money up front. So the government's mobilized every possible resource to resolve the crisis: they've sent ministers to every embassy in sight, begging. They talked to us first, and Neggie refused to even forward the request to Washington. And of course they went to the Cubans, who said no, and the Russians, and the Nigerians, and especially the Brits. The Brits finally caved to the pressure from the airlines, particularly B-Cal. The British government ended up guaranteeing payment. But it turns out the trucks are so old no one keeps parts anymore, so the supplier finally said forget it, the whole thing's a pain in the ass and they didn't want to do business with Sierra Leone, anyway. So now B-Cal's looking for the parts. Can you believe it? They're ransacking English villages and junkyards. And while all this is going on, air traffic at Lungi amounts to one landing a week by Aeroflot. B-Cal will probably end up buying new trucks just so they can get back in here."

"How the hell are people getting in and out?"

"Overland through Guinea. Local transport to Kambia, then poda-poda to Conakry. But there's still a lot of flooding up there, so it could take a while. The best bet is to book transport on a grain ship that's due in a couple of weeks. Get off in Dakar and fly to Paris, then down to Mali."

"Shit."

Max offered the bottle again. "You're the one always saying if you're in hurry you shouldn't be in Africa. They'll get those trucks running one of these days. In the meantime, where else can you live for next to nothing? That can't be bad for a cheapskate like you. I suppose you're staying at the Tropic again."

"Yeah."

"Amazing. Tell you what—I've got all those empty rooms, you can stay with me. I'll charge you a buck a day just like the Tropic, but I'll throw in breakfast. Real food, not rice and green slime."

"I like green slime and rice. Besides, Juba's too far out of town. On the other hand, I might do it if you'll throw in a car."

"I suppose you'll want a woman, too. I could give you Josephine to go with the car and driver."

"Who's Josephine?"

"Krio lady I met at a reception given by the mayor."

♈

Robert slept in the Krio lady's sister's bed that night. A sharp pain in his groin and a grinding headache woke him in the gray light of dawn. He pushed the net out of the way and rolled out of bed onto his knees, the effort setting his head to pounding so fiercely that he thought he had malaria again. And then he remembered the Algerian wine they had drunk after Farrah ran out of beer.

Slowly, so as not to get the blood pounding in his head again, he pushed himself to his feet. He looked down through the gray netting at the naked black woman curled on the mattress ticking. The sheet was a twisted knot of gray at her feet. Josephine's sister. What was her name?

He looked round, couldn't see his clothes, decided he couldn't wait. He followed a faint outhouse aroma through the bedroom door, the smell growing strong as soon as he came into the darkened hall. He found another door and pushed it open. The damp stench of old shit rolled out, stopping him in his tracks. But only momentarily, for the immediacy of his need urged him inside. In the dim light coming through the dusty window he looked down into a toilet full of shit and piss. The floor suddenly came alive with dozens of big-as-your-thumb cockroaches scurrying in panic about his bare feet. He retreated from the bathroom, went to the back door, which opened to a yard of hard-packed earth enclosed by a palm thatch fence. He went bare assed and barefooted across the bare ground in the gray of first light to the banana tree. The pain subsided as he urinated.

The house was a cinder block structure with a rusty roof and road dust caked so heavily all over that it looked like it was made of mud. The windows were opaque with it. A dugout canoe, gray and cracked and overgrown by weeds, rested upside down in the middle of the yard. A pawpaw tree had grown to shoulder height out of the weeds, its immature fruit nestling like testicles under drooping leaves.

His thirst and the ugly taste of dead cigars demanded water. He walked around the house looking for a water standpipe. Finding none, he entered the house and went through the empty dining room. As he moved across the dusty concrete floor a feeling came to him that he knew something about this emptiness; he could tell that it had come slowly, perhaps by the selling off of furniture piece by piece. Where did that certainty come from? He did not remember hearing it. Was it the look of the place? He went on into the living room, which was also empty. Dust everywhere, walls blackened all around at the height of children's hands. No furniture, no rugs, no brick-a-brack. Nothing but dust and gray light and silence.

Josephine's house: so different from this house; it had seemed as perfectly natural on her as brown skin and British accent. A wood house in a small neighborhood that could have been an old down-at-the-heels London suburb. A tiny bungalow in a pocket of colonial era bungalows with tiny, lush yards enclosed by seven-foot brick fences topped by shards of glass, guarded by wrought iron gates that opened off narrow lanes that one entered from the Main Motor Road, along which streams of Africans walked all day and into the night with headloads of wood or fish in pans or ties of greens. And inside her house a minuscule foyer and a tight stairwell spiraling up to a pair of small bedrooms; a house with faded and peeling wall paper and elaborate wainscoting and frayed upholstered chairs and scratched side tables and rugs worn down to tan backs, and old photographs of serious black gentlemen in absurd black coats and black ties and black bowler hats. Widowed thirty-five-ish Josephine sitting forward on her chair, young looking in her eagerness to please two white gentlemen, her legs turned demurely to one side, her hands clasped in her lap. And her son, a lanky fifteen-year-old in white shorts and shirt, wandering in with a tennis racket, looking them over with erratic eyes, muttering something and going out the door when they greeted him.

As Robert observed the ruin that was Josephine's sister's house it occurred to him that this desolation was as appropriate to that lady as Josephine's shabby gentility was to her. This house showed Josephine's sister's soul just as Josephine's house mirrored *her* soul. What the fuck was Josephine's sister's name? And what did she look like? He couldn't remember precisely, but he had a picture of hair conked straight and shiny black, the frizziness only at the ends, an accent that perfectly caricatured lazy-upper-lip upper-class English; and mannerisms so very British you might have thought her speech a parody, a part she had played in the *theatah* she had left. Yes—an actress, returned from failure to her dead father's dying house; to a precarious existence that had already narrowed and reduced her life to that of most black lives in this black land, which was mere subsistence. Rice and green slime. And a hole in which to shit. Sitting beside him at a table for white people under a string of colored lights that moved in the ocean breeze, seeking personal relevance in nervous chatter about the relevance of modern theater; as unAfrican as she could make herself; straining forlornly and absurdly to be not-Sierra-Leonean-and-not-African while he wondered why he was there with her. How had Max managed to drag him along? He had wanted to come to the beach for a run, not to sit in Farrah's and drink and listen to this poor wreck of a woman.

He went into another room: a kitchen, apparently, though it was hard to tell in the gray light, for someone had deracinated sink, faucet, and cabinets. It was now a dustbin full of unsellable junk. This room seemed as appropriate as the dirty walls and the water closet full of cockroaches and old shit. He returned to the bedroom and got down on his knees and looked under the bed and found his shorts and shirt in the dust. Then he realized he did not see his knapsack, and for a breathless second panic squeezed his chest: his passport was in that faded green knapsack, as were the yellowed shot records going back to his ROTC days, and his international driver's license, and the wad of documents proving he was a legal resident, that he'd paid his Salone taxes, that he could legally work for money in Sierra Leone. And legally leave. And most important of all, proving his United States citizenship: certifying, thereby, the priority of his existence.

He went around to her side of the bed and lifted the net and touched her shoulder. A frown tensed her face and she curled tighter. He studied her profile against the gray mattress ticking and saw a black face devoid of Negro roundness, a face that possessed the sharp nose and hard lips of whiteness, framed by jet tangles—an appealing black-skinned white-featured face. He shook her. "Where's my pack," he asked, his voice rough and gravelly from the cigars his mouth told him he'd smoked the night before, and thick with thirst.

"Umm."

He shook her again, more roughly.

"—bad man, Bo—lef me," she murmured, her eyes still closed. She slid her hand down her naked leg, feeling for the sheet. Not finding it, she curled tighter and shivered.

"Where's my pack?"

"Duya, Bo—lef me."

He dropped the net, went down to his knees and looked under the bed once again. He rose and kicked through a pile of clothes, uncovering several bundles of two-leone notes, which he kicked aside. Then he stepped into his shorts and without looking back, walked out of the house into full daylight, under a brilliant rainy season sky, a sky devoid of the Harmattan whiteness that had been coming and going; and having added worry about his knapsack to his burden of headache and thirst, he went barefoot around the front and out to the dusty road, now cheerfully yellowed by slanting sunlight.

♈

Robert limped up the stone stairs, leaving blots of blood on every other step. He opened the door and stepped into the air-conditioned lobby. President Reagan looked benignly down from the wall above the desk, behind which Lenny stood. The young Marine looked down at the blood seeping from between the toes of Robert's left foot.

"You're bleeding, man."

"Is Max here?" Robert said. He ran his hands through his hair, which hung in tangles about his head and shoulders.

Lenny picked up the intercom handset. "DCM's office, please." As he waited he leaned over the desk and looked down at Robert's foot. "There's a lot of blood there, man."

Robert looked down. The blood was puddling around his foot.

"This is Lenny, Mr. Bush. Robert Kelley wants to see you, sir. He's got a cut foot." A pause, then, "Yes sir." He put the handset in its cradle and came around the desk. "He's coming down. You want me to call Mike?"

"I guess you better." Robert put a hand on the desk to steady himself and lifted his left foot. The glass shard had entered straight on, slicing deeply from the ball of his foot back to the instep. It had happened as he walked along the rutted track that meandered down the hillside through the hundreds of squatter shacks. It had come from out of nowhere, like a spear, and he'd cried out and tumbled forward, and a half-dozen blacks came running from shacks near the trail. They'd knelt beside him and murmured solicitously while he sat in the dust with his left foot in his lap, steeling himself to pull the glass out, and when he managed it, they'd helped him to his feet, and one of them, a young laborer, offered Robert the loan of his halfbacks, and then had walked down the hill with him, strutting his pride in being selected to help the wounded white man. They'd

56

joined the stream of Africans moving along Congo Town Road, Robert reduced to silence by the pain, while the boy—who called himself Alimamy—chattered familiarly about coming from a village near Kenema to live in his cousin's shack while he looked for work. The wound had bled steadily for a while, then stopped, clogged by the dust of the road, but in the half-mile stretch from the Krootown market to the Cotton Tree and the American Embassy the bleeding had started again.

The metal door opened and Max came out carrying the green knapsack. He stopped when he saw Robert. "Jesus, what happened to you?"

Robert took the knapsack, relieved that Max had it, annoyed that Max had been the one who was alert enough, even when drunk, to rescue it from wherever the hell he had left it, annoyed even more that he looked so fresh, so undamaged by their night of whatever the hell they had done.

"How much money did you have?" Max asked.

Robert opened the knapsack and found his damp underwear and the half-backs and the soggy Evelyn Waugh, and most importantly, the leather Bo bag in which he carried his documents and checkbook. The rubber-banded bundles of two-leone notes were gone. "I don't know."

"Your money's gone."

"I can see that."

"The princess got in your skivvies."

"How do you know that?" Robert said crossly, feeling his annoyance at Max turning into an idiotic defense of Josephine's thieving sister. "Maybe I spent it."

"It was at the beach," Max said. "My driver saw her going through it."

Swimming: the missing part. Farrah had sent the waiters and cooks home at closing time and brought some bottles of that awful Algerian out to their table and sat and drank with them in the darkness until the stars disappeared and the wind came whipping and rattling the palms and the rain came and they dragged the tables inside and went upstairs for more wine, and there the camaraderie had dissolved in a screaming, arm-waving, hysterical hala-hala between Farrah and Max after Max had lit into Farrah about drugs, insisting that he was practically the fucking Ambassador, that there was a war on drugs and he wouldn't stand for drugs in his presence, while Farrah's acne-scarred face got blotchy red and he pointedly rolled a joint no one needed or even wanted and lit it and blew a cloud of smoke into Max's face. Then all that yelling and the thudding, banging, rattling, arm-waving descent of the stairs and they were out in the parking lot, as inexplicably laughing in the roaring warm downpour that followed the squall line as they had been angry moments before, and they woke Max's driver and fell into the car; and then Max was shouting past Robert's ear at the driver, who stopped the Cadillac, and they'd all tumbled out onto the rain-firm sand and stripped off their wet clothing and stumbled through the black moonless night toward the swish and swash of phosphorescent surf; and then there was only the soothing surprising warmth of salty blackness lifting and lowering him under the clearing sky that became a glittery smear of Milky Way, showing itself in rainy season clarity; mesmerizing him as he floated and stared straight up, while the Southern Cross hovered low in the southern sky.

Max eyed Robert's bloody foot. "What happened?"

"Stepped on some glass."

"Martino's upstairs."

Robert looked down. There was quite a bit of blood on the floor.

"C'mon," Max said.

"Okay. But first I need some leones."

"What d'you need leones for?"

"How much do you need?" Lenny asked.

"Ten."

Lenny went behind the desk, opened the bottom drawer, took out a wallet, removed some bills, gave them to Robert.

Robert limped toward the door.

"Where you going?" Max asked.

"I want to give some money to the kid who helped me."

"I'll take it to him," Lenny said.

"No, I want to," Robert said. He pushed the glass door open and went down the steps.

Alimamy waited for him, bloody halfbacks dangling

from his left hand. His scalp bristled with stubble and the tight skin of his muscle-rounded shoulders glistened. He had a flat-nosed Mende face. His only clothing was a pair of colorless baggy shorts. The inverted triangle of his body was short, muscular, hard-bellied. There was nothing extra about him, no reserve, everything about him seemed necessary. Robert offered the money.

"T'ank-ee, mastah, duya, I wan work. Duya, mastah, I beg, gi' me work."

"No possible, padi." Robert limped up the stairs, glanced back as he opened the door, saw the youth forlornly looking up at him.

In the four years he'd served as the Sierra Leone/Liberia Peace Corps Medical Officer Mike Martino had seen Robert for more medical problems than any of the hundreds of PCVs, missionaries, development workers, UN staffers, and diplomats he'd treated. Martino had come to his new post from a family practice in Washington D.C., just in time to take Robert into his basement clinic and nurse him through a case of malaria so severe that he'd tried to medivac him (Robert refused his permission). On another occasion he'd sewn Robert's scalp back in place after he ran his motorcycle into a storm gutter half a block from the embassy. That accident should have killed him. And Robert was the only person he'd ever treated for sleeping sickness (tropical medicine references insisted the disease was not indigenous to Sierra Leone). And a few months after the sleeping sickness Robert had appeared holding his swollen hands in front of him, saying he had boils on the palms, boils so severe that he'd traveled all the way from Bonthe just to get them treated—and a good thing, too, for they threatened bone infection. And he had treated Robert for worms. And for clap. And for a burn on the inside of his thigh which came from falling under a motorcycle. And of course for conjunctivitis, which the locals called Apollo, in honor of the Apollo astronauts, who happened to be flying around the moon when a particularly virulent epidemic swept through the country. So, when Martino came down into the lobby and saw Robert's bloody foot he was not surprised.

He motioned irritably for Robert to follow him up the stone stairway and down the hall to the second-floor bathroom, where he made him prop his foot up on the sink edge, manipulated the toes as he examined the wound, shook his head in disbelief, or perhaps disgust, and left him with his wounded foot dripping blood into the sink while he went back to his office. He returned with a brush and disinfectant soap and a box of sponges, rolled his sleeves up, studied the foot distastefully. Then he turned on the hot water and began none too gently scrubbing the foot. Robert clamped his jaws against the pain, stared at the bald spot on the top of Martino's head, and refused to give the doctor the satisfaction of hearing him acknowledge the pain. When Martino finished he wrapped the foot in a towel and motioned for Robert to follow him back to his office. After he gave Robert a tetanus shot and a percodan tablet he pulled a chair up before Robert and sat and lifted the wounded foot to his lap and unwrapped it. He manipulated the cut for a moment, then uttered the first words he's spoken to Robert that morning. "How the fuck did you manage *this*?"

"Glass."

"I figured it might be something sharp. Lost your shoes, did you?"

"Yes."

Martino raised his eyes from the wound, looked at Robert's dirty shirt and his tangled hair. "If I had more time, and if I was interested, I'd ask you how. I'll bet it's a great story. Did you get it all out or do I have to poke around in there?"

"I got it all."

"You got it all, huh? Well, I'm gonna look anyway."

Martino probed the wound—taking his time, Robert thought—then splashed the foot with disinfectant that burned like fire, and closed it with stitches. He wrapped the foot and told Robert to keep it clean and dry and to stay off it for a ·week, then come back. He left the office and returned with a vial of percodan tablets and a pair of crutches. "Stay off that foot," he said again, handing Robert the crutches. He called Max, and Max came and walked Robert down the back stairs to the Cadillac. Max told Robert he'd come to check on him, then instructed the driver to deliver Robert to the Tropic of Capricorn.

Twenty minutes later Robert came out of the shower baffa, limped up the stairs with a towel around his waist and stripped the plastic sack off his bandaged foot. He sat in the chair and raised the wounded foot up to the bed. The sack had leaked; the bandage was soaked. He considered removing it but decided it would dry while he slept. He picked a roach out of the ashtray, lit it, and took a couple of hits. Immediately the pot started lifting him out of the percodan low. He got the soggy Waugh out of his knapsack and stretched out on the bed.

$$\Upsilon$$

He wanted Marie's attention, all of it; but she wouldn't give it. Why? She had come to Salone to be with *him*, not with these giggling fish mammies and market women, to whom she spoke so earnestly about contraceptives and hygiene as he waited impatiently for her attention. He was aware that it was a dream while he dreamed it, but he wanted so much for the Marie part to be real that he willed it to continue, even as his consciousness returned him to his bed in the Tropic. He opened his eyes on the metal underside of the roof and the exposed rafters and the bare light bulb, his enjoyment of the dream diluted by disappointment.

Sunlight streamed in low and yellow. The mosquito netting was up and the air was hot and still and he had sweated himself slick with wet. He yawned and thought about his dream, retaining for as long as he could the feeling of being with Marie. The dream place had been indistinct, but it had felt rural, even remote. It didn't feel like River Number Two, where they often went when she visited. Nor did it feel like Bonthe. It felt more upland, rather like the hills south of Bo.

It was not a real dream; it was more like a continuation of the daydream that he had carried with him into the drowsiness. The feel of it reminded him of Bo; of the time they had traveled there on his motorcycle and made Gunter's house their headquarters for a week of adventuring about the countryside. They'd spent the days bumping and bouncing over rural trails from one village to another, and the evenings with Toufic Darwish's family, or drinking beer at Pa Jalloh's with Gunter. There Marie had met Cavanaugh, a Scottish radical whose only topic of conversation was revolution and the destruction of capitalism, and the Dutch gold miner who had an endless supply of good whiskey and talked very little, and of course the usual clutch of PCVs, of whom Kathleen was by far the senior member, having been in-country by then for over three years—and who, in an excess of emotion, had given Marie a new view of Robert by telling her how Robert had saved her sanity by being her friend as she figured out a way to teach in an environment of severe privation—of no books and no supplies; of sickly, tired students who ate nothing but rice and greens and bananas and mangos.

One day they went with Gunter to inspect a rural clinic. As they drove into the hills east and south of Sumbuya Town she and Gunter had become immersed in what was to become a day-long discussion of the technical and social issues associated with setting up and running a clinic in the bush. Robert became a tagalong behind Gunter and Marie and the village headman—as bored, as vaguely jealous, as irritable as he had been at Max's party when Marie's attention had been diverted by all that Big Man attention. By late afternoon, as they drove back through the bush, Robert's irritability had become so pronounced that it dampened even the professional discussion between Gunter and Marie.

When they got back to Gunter's house and were alone in their bedroom, Marie had let him have it.

"I need for us to talk," she'd said, as she closed the bedroom door.

Talking was not what Robert had in mind. He had managed to put his irritability behind him and had forgiven her, and his anticipation of sharing a shower and then a little lovemaking had put him in a good mood. He was already unbuttoning his shirt. The coldness in her voice stopped him.

"A talk? About what?"

"About this afternoon. It's happened before. Is that the way I can expect you to behave when a man comes around me?"

"What do you mean by *that*?"

"I mean that men are always coming on to me. I deal with that all the time. But I can't deal with how you react to it."

He opened his mouth to protest, but snapped it shut. She had him. He had no defense. Except anger, of course—the defense of last resort. He used anger.

"What the hell are you talking about?" he blustered.

"What am I supposed to learn from your behavior? That I am a piece of your territory?"

"No, but you do attract—" he began, then stopped when he saw her expression.

"It was *your* idea to come to Bo and stay at Gunter's. It was *your* idea to have Gunter take us out to Mabang to see the clinic."

Ten minutes later they had said what they needed to say, or perhaps more than they needed to say, and after taking separate showers they dressed in tight-lipped silence and joined Gunter in his living room, where they tried, with a forced affability, not to embarrass their now nervous host by making him a part of their dispute. The tension left by this, their only real quarrel, did not endure long. They slept in one another's arms that night. But one effect did remain with Robert—the effect she intended, presumably. He forced himself to stop noticing the way other men noticed her. Nearly a year later it was still difficult.

He was fully awake now, and still thinking about her, thinking about trying to get a call through to her that evening. He decided finally that he needed to figure out how he was going to get out of Salone first. His wounded foot had complicated things: there was no way he could get out by public transport to Conakry or Monrovia.

He rolled drowsily onto his side to cool his back. A stab of pain startled him out of his day dream. Holding himself still to quiet the pain, he gazed out the window at low puffs of cloud against blue sky and listened to street sounds—an occasional car, a child screaming, others laughing, Fullah traders haggling with customers; human sounds mostly, mingled and muffled by distance. He swung his feet out over the floor, lowered the undamaged foot, hopped to the chair where he sat and leaned forward and picked up the shorts he had left in the middle of the floor and found the plastic vial of percodan tablets in a pocket. He swallowed a tablet and lifted his wounded foot to the bed and considered what he would do next. Food, of course: he had to get something to eat. He hadn't eaten since yesterday. He'd go to Mrs. Wilson's—he could navigate that far—and get some rice and groundnut soup. And then he remembered he had no leones. He had to buy some leones before he could do anything. It was four o'clock—Billy Darwish's would be closing in an hour. He got into clean shorts and T-shirt, slipped his knapsack on and slid his good foot into the plastic sandal, got the crutches, made his way down the stairs.

He got used to the crutches quickly and was soon negotiating the labyrinth of trader's stalls that crowded the sidewalks down the five blocks of Lightfoot-Boston Street. He opened the door of Darwish Hardware and hopped inside and made his way through the piles of boxes and reels of wire and stacks of corrugated roofing metal to the long counter at the back of the room. A black clerk told him Billy Darwish was not in, but his brother Farid was in the back— would he like to see Farid? Robert said yes. The young man slipped off his stool and told Robert to come. Robert followed him through a large room filled with construction hardware and electronics and boxes of tinned and dried food and building material. At the back of the room was a hall, where the clerk gestured at a door. Robert opened the door and stepped into a tiny, air-conditioned office. A KayPro computer occupied one corner of the desk, which also supported an adding machine, a neat pile of papers, sharpened pencils poking up out of a water glass. Lace curtains covered a pair of iron-barred windows. From somewhere on the other side of the windows a generator grumbled. A swarthy young man looked up. "What can I do for you?"

"I'm Robert Kelley—a friend of Billy's. I'd like to buy some leones."

Farid's face remained perfectly expressionless. "We do not sell currency. It is illegal."

"When will Billy be in?"

"Tomorrow."

Robert started to turn.

Farid's eyes went to the crutches. "You've injured yourself?"

"A cut."

"Not serious, I hope."

"No."

"I'm sorry I cannot help you."

"By the way, Toufic sends his greetings."

Farid's expression changed. "You know Toufic? How is he? And his family? I have not seen him in a year."

"They're well. I saw him a couple of days ago."

"You are Toufic's friend?"

Robert nodded, adding: "And I think I met you at the casino—two years ago. I was with the American Deputy Chief of Mission and his wife. You were on one side of the roulette table and I was on the other and we were both losing. Billy came along and introduced us. You were studying in England."

"Yes, yes, I remember it—I was home for Christmas."

"Are you visiting now?"

"No. I've finished."

"Home to stay?"

"I don't know. Maybe I will go back to London, maybe I will stay. Freetown is home, but so is England. I miss London when I'm here and I miss Freetown when I'm there." He pointed to a chair. "Please sit down."

"I'd better go, I still have to get some leones."

"I'll take care of you. How much do you want?"

"What's the rate?"

66

"Forty-eight to the dollar."

"In pounds?"

"Seventy-five."

"Give me ten thousand."

Farid rose and left the room. He returned with an arm load of bundled notes. "All I have is two-leone notes."

Robert unzipped his knapsack and Farid counted the bundles into the opening.

"Will you have coffee?" Farid asked.

"Sure."

Farid turned to the window and opened it. "Yusef!" he shouted. "Make we get coffee!" He turned back to his desk and punched some numbers on the calculator, told Robert the cost of the leones, watched him write the check. "So you're Toufic's friend," he said as he took the check. "Tell me about Toufic. How is he doing? We worry about him and his family. He is drifting away, disappearing into the bush. It is not the time for that, it is a time to be among your own. He hasn't been in Freetown in over a year. And his sons never come. One has even married a black. An illiterate village girl who doesn't even speak Krio. And the younger— well, the younger is worse. It is what happens when you cut yourself off from family."

"Toufic says he is like his grandfather."

Farid shook his head. "No, no, no. Never. My grandfather lived in the bush to trade for oil palm kernels. Even though he saw no other whites for months at a time, he never broke with his family, never went native. Even when his first wife and all of his children died he did not go native, he always knew who he was. Toufic is isolating himself, he should bring his family to Freetown. We have a place for him."

There was a knock at the door.

"Come," Farid said.

The door swung open and an old black man in baggy shorts and a woolen ski cap entered with a tray. He put the tray on the desk and backed out of the room.

Farid poured the coffee. "You paid in pounds, Mr. Kelley—I take it you work for the British." He handed Robert a tiny cup filled with thick black coffee.

"The Zimi Project—I run the Bonthe station."

"One hears rumors that the English are giving up on Salone, that they are ending development support, like the Americans."

"Only the Kambia project. The Brits will renew Zimi. It's one of the few successful projects in West Africa."

"The troubles in Pujehun do not disturb your operations?"

"There's always noise in Pujehun."

"What do you think will happen?"

"In Pujehun?"

"In Salone."

"You live in Freetown—you know more than me."

"Sometimes you can be too close to the politics. The more I see and hear the more I think it will end badly. And yet it goes on and on, getting worse, not ending, just getting worse. After a while you do not trust your judgment. Your expectations—" He ended his thought with a flutter of his hand.

"What *are* your expectations?" Robert asked.

"Well, it seems clear—Salone is going back to the bush. But on the way there will be violence, because violence always accompanies collapse. Each time I return it is noticeably worse. And yet business continues, politics continues."

♈

Robert crutched his way through the crowds on Siaka Stevens Street, past beggars, lepers, polio-cripples, past young men who stood among the beggars hawking magazines stolen by postal clerks, past Fullah traders perched on stools at box-top displays of used spectacles, used books, envelopes, pencils. He stopped and bought a handful of roasted groundnuts from a girl, which he ate while he rested.

The project office occupied a remodeled two-story residence a half-block off Siaka Stevens Street, across a narrow lane from the high brick walls that contained the grounds of St. Joseph's Convent. When Robert pushed the glass door open Mrs. Kruma lifted her head off her arms, which were crossed over the typewriter, greeting him with a sleepy smile. But the smile faded to a look of alarm when she saw his crutches and the red toe of his sock. She jumped up and dragged a chair forward and commanded him to sit. He sat on the chair in the middle of the almost barren room while she hovered about him, clicking her tongue in sympathy; then she stepped to the stairwell and called up to Kevin, before hurrying off to the back room and reappearing with a plastic bottle of water and a glass, as Kevin came down the stairs. His eyes widened as he saw Robert's foot.

"Good God, man, what happened?"

"Stepped on some glass."

"Looks like you stepped on a bloody land mine. We'd better get you to Martino."

"He already stitched it up."

"You're bleeding. Why in hell are you walking around on it? Where did you cut it, anyway?"

"Across the bottom."

Kevin shook his head. "Bleeding like that—we'd better look at it, don't you think? I'll get the first aid kit." He went into the back room and returned with a red box.

"It's okay," Robert said.

"Bleeding like that? I don't think so." Kevin went to his knees in front of Robert's chair and peeled the bloody sock off. With scissors he cut the tape and unwrapped the blood-sodden bandage, then lifted the foot so that he could look at the wound.

Robert looked down at the bulky figure kneeling in sweat-darkened khaki shirt and shorts. A fringe of thin gray hair drooped wetly against wrinkles of neck fat. He winced and pulled his foot out of Kevin's grasp. "Hey, that hurts."

"Of course it hurts. You've pulled the stitches." Kevin grabbed the foot, lifted it, and looked at the wound again. "Look here, old man, I've never sewn anyone up before, but I have the tools here and I've always wanted to try. What d'you say, shall we have a go at it?"

"Yeah, right."

"I s'pose that means no in American. Well, okay. We'll deliver you to Martino, then."

The embassy was closed by the time they got there so they drove out to Signal Hill to Martino's compound. The watchman opened the gate and came out saying, "Mastah no dey."

Kevin asked when he would return.

"Well, I no saby. Maybe seven o'clock."

Kevin looked at Robert. "Let's go over to my house. We can come back in an hour or so—we need to talk, anyway. You can chop with us."

Kevin drove down the hill past the President's Palace, which was a hump of white showing through the foliage of mango and breadfruit trees a hundred yards back from perimeter walls. Off to the left, at the base of the steep shack-crowded hillside, was Babadori Creek, beside which the rusty roofs of laborer's huts showed as patches of orange against the green of trees. Beyond the valley a gray shoulder loomed through a haze that had been building all afternoon: the steep flank of Juba Hill, which was not a hill, really, but the western extremity of the western-most spur of the western-most mountains in Africa. Along the crest of Juba Hill one could just see the outline of Pa Siaka's retirement estate, a sprawling fortress guarded by wire fences, high walls, and serious-faced young men with machine guns. Scattered over the hillside below the fortress were the walled estates of Lebs and government ministers and diplomats and white expats and the tiny huts and gardens of squatters. They followed the road as it descended Signal Hill, and soon they were driving into the sun, which the Harmattan haze had softened to a bright silver disk that would soon yellow, turn to red, and then to a dusty shade of rose that would illuminate the air like neon.

"Pa Bangura's angry with you," Kevin said.

"I'm not surprised."

"He pouted all day, complained every time I saw him that a man shouldn't talk to another man the way you talk to him."

"He's setting you up. Wants you in a sympathetic mood before I tell you he sold the petrol in the rubbers—to get money to buy a truckload of cassava and goats."

"He did? Where'd you find petrol to get back?"

"Begged twenty liters from Gunter."

"Ought to sack him, I s'pose."

"It's your rule."

"The problem is, he's so much smarter than the others. Quite dependable, if you can control his damned thievery. Though I must say he does use good judgment even there. Never steals anything important to *me*."

Kevin steered the Land Rover through the Lumley Roundabout, across the bridge spanning Babadori Creek, then turned up the hill on Pipeline Road. After a steep quarter-mile he turned off onto a potholed track that came round the shoulder into the open and looked out over the fishing village at Goderich Point, with its omnipresent pall of banda smoke, and the sun and the flat sea shining silver through the haze. The vehicle slowed as it approached the high walls surrounding a three-story house. The house and the walls were immaculately white, the roof glistened with new metal, and the iron gate and the iron bars were black and free of rust. The gate swung open and a blue-uniformed guard stepped into view. Kevin turned the Land Rover into the compound. The front and side yards were covered with clean-swept blacktop, and a row of parked vehicles: a Mazda lorry, the Mercedes doublecab, a tanker trailer, a white Honda sedan, all carrying the Zimi Development Project logo.

Rachel Beachley was on the balcony reading *West Africa* and smoking a cigarette. A glass of scotch and ice sat in a ring of condensation on the glass-topped table beside her chair. She looked up from the magazine when she heard the front door open, then heard her husband's voice. She watched two male forms come through the dusk of the unlit living room.

"Evening, darling," Kevin called. "I've found a walking wounded and brought him home for nursing."

Kevin and Robert came out of the living room and into the last light of the day.

"Robert! Goodness. What's happened to you?"

"A cut. Nothing serious."

They sat in cushioned wicker chairs on the verandah and drank the scotch that Tommy brought, nibbled roasted groundnuts, and looked out over the darkening valley, observing the flash of a late-season thunderstorm along the mountains that faced the sea south of Goderich Point.

Their talk turned—as it eventually did in any group of expats—to Africa and Africans. Rachel said she'd just read in *West Africa* that the Momoh government would soon move against supporters of the First Vice-President, who were stirring up trouble in Pujehun. She said this worried her, for Zimi was only thirty miles to the east of Pujehun. Robert said Bo was quiet and so was Pujehun, as far as he knew, except for the tribal dust-ups—the usual accusations of corruption and favoritism, quarrels over village boundaries, and occasionally, dark rumors of ritual cannibalism. These disturbances came and went, Robert said, but the price of rice in Freetown would always be the most important barometer of discontent.

Kevin and Robert usually got right down to disagreement when they drank together; sometimes amiably, often with a fair amount of heat. But on this night—Robert's last as Kevin's employee—Kevin seemed to be trying especially hard not to provoke Robert; and Robert accordingly restrained himself. When they discussed the details of the turning over Robert told Kevin one last time—though quite civilly—that Alexander would strip the station within six months; for which opinion Kevin neutrally thanked him. Then Robert opened his knapsack and handed over his last situation report, with the final inventory and the final accounting. As Kevin glanced through the report he reflected with a smile that he had read a great many of these reports. He and Robert had been together for—what was it? Four years? No, three, Robert said. They had met four years before. Yes, yes, Kevin said, and then he recounted—ostensibly for his wife, who of course knew the story, but actually because drink always loosened his tongue and gave him permission to indulge in nostalgia—how he'd found Robert on a cooperative oil palm plantation, a project he'd also been thinking about for the Zimi project. He was impressed by the work of the young PCV, and he offered Robert a job then and there. Robert had declined: he was a volunteer, not a professional, he told Kevin. But Kevin did not give up. He came back and offered to support Robert's program if he

72

would undertake a similar program for a few villages in the Zimi area. But Robert declined this offer also, preferring not to taint himself by associating in any way with Kevin Beachley's Zimi Project, which everyone knew treated its black employees like serfs and its client farmers just as badly.

As the months dissolved and Robert's close of service neared, he got serious about finding a way to stay in Salone to work as an expat. He remembered Beachley's offer, forgot his objections and went to see him. But he found that Kevin had hired two Sierra Leoneans, young men just returned from studies abroad, to set up a palm kernel cooperative, modeled on Robert's. However, Kevin was looking for a white man to run a new fisheries station. He planned to extend ZDP influence south to the coast by supporting the fishermen at Bonthe, training them to semi-industrial levels of fish production. The goal was to provide a stable supply of protein, in the form of smoked fish, for upland farmers. Would Robert be interested in discussions about that? A week later Robert signed a contract, and six weeks after that loaded a boat borrowed from the German Tombo Project, and motored across the seventy-five miles of Yawri Bay to Bonthe, so eager to get started that he didn't even return home on the leave he'd negotiated with Kevin.

The air turned to rose and they fell silent for the few moments it lingered. Then it was gone and the darkness came and Tommy appeared with candles shielded by glass sleeves. In the background the grumble of the generator went to a higher pitch as Tommy turned lights on inside the house.

When Tommy came to the balcony with the dishes and began setting the table Kevin suggested they visit Martino, so he and Robert drove back down the hill in the medieval darkness of Freetown night, a darkness that overwhelmed the puny glimmers of yellow coming from the candles and kerosene lamps of trader's tables and the weak squares of light from the houses of those rich enough to have generators and the petrol to run them. They went across the bridge and up the flank of Signal Hill to Martino's house. They had a drink with him while he re-stitched and dressed Robert's wounded foot.

When they got back to Kevin's house they found dinner waiting. While Kevin poured the wine Tommy came with the soup and bread. A cooling breeze from off the sea made its way up the hill, fluttering the candles and driving the mosquitoes.

Kevin ate like he worked—with enthusiasm. He finished quickly, mopped the bottom of his bowl with a heel of bread which he popped into his mouth and washed down with red wine. Then he sat back and crossed his arms over his chest and watched Robert. "A nice red, don't you think? Portuguese. I s'pose you've heard about the flap out at Lungi."

Robert nodded.

"Looks like you're stranded."

Robert took another piece of bread, buttered it, took a bite.

"What're your plans?"

"I'm going to Mali."

"You've not signed a contract?"

"No. Why are you asking?"

"Oh—something's come up, and since you're not committed to another position, maybe you'd like to hear about it."

"What d'you mean?"

"Staying on with Zimi—but in a new capacity."

Robert's eyes widened.

"I've been asked to take over an aquaculture project that the British government's been funding, and which the ministry's fucked up—pardon the French, m'dear—so badly that the home office decided to close it or bring it under ZDP control. Haven't told Kargbo yet—he's going to have a stroke. Believe you know the fellow that's running it now—Daniel Sulaiman."

Robert looked at him incredulously. "You just closed Bonthe because Zimi shouldn't be in fisheries."

"I didn't close Bonthe, I turned it over to the ministry."

"How is that different from closing it?"

"Aquaculture is an entirely different kettle of fish, old boy," Kevin said, grinning.

Robert ignored the pun. "You dropped Bonthe because you

74

wanted to concentrate on agriculture—that's what you said."

"Quite so. And that is why I have decided that Zimi *can* take on Sulaiman's project—aquaculture's a logical extension of the rice program, whereas marine fisheries was not. Bonthe was a mistake, but aquaculture fits; it's really just an extension of farming. Moreover, it promises to actually supply fish to the farmers of the project area—which, as you'll recall, was the goal for Bonthe, and which it never managed to achieve."

"They're both fisheries," Robert said.

"Come, Robert—they're as different as night and day. ZDP is an ideal situation for aquaculture; we should be doing it. Bonthe was different. We did everything for them—too much, in fact—provided an equipment store, organized fish processing and transport to Zimi markets. We tried everything to induce them to produce at commercial levels. And we failed, because most of 'em are subsistence fishermen. We cannot put our resources into subsistence programs. That is for others, not us. Bonthe was a failure—though not your failure," he added hastily. "In fact, you've done a marvelous job, I don't know anyone who could have done better. It is my failure, for giving you an impossible mission. Had we conducted a proper frame survey before we went in there we would have seen that your fishermen would not change their way of life, which is what we were asking them to do."

Rachel touched her husband's arm. "Darling—give us a light, please."

Kevin reached across the table and got the lighter.

"Perhaps we could talk shop later, what d'you think?" she asked, after blowing smoke into the air over the table.

"Of course, dear. We're boring you, aren't we."

Tommy brought the next course, the pot roast, on which Robert was glad to concentrate. It was followed by a salad, a dessert sauterne, then ice cream and coffee, during which the conversation moved to the inflation, which continued to worsen, and the burgeoning black market, which undercut the economy, and the persistent rumors of coup plots by Lebanese businessmen, disgruntled army officers, out-of-power political factions, all of whom claimed with increasing noisiness that Momoh's government was illegitimate and that the Old Pa had no right to simply hand power to a successor.

Rachel lit her second cigarette of the meal and watched Kevin pour cream into his coffee. He called to Tommy to bring the cigars. She smiled at her husband. "Now we can talk shop."

Kevin laughed, his face shining with the scotch and wine. "Poor darling. She lives in an intellectual wasteland—reads all those novels and poems and all about current affairs and shop talk is all she gets out of me. A person might think I never read anything but development stuff. And it's true. Monomaniacal is what it is. And yet she never complains."

Robert stirred cream into his coffee.

"Speaking of failure," Kevin continued. "I do want to make a point with you about that, because it relates to our disagreement. It is important that you understand that I accept the responsibility for Bonthe. If there was any failure there it is mine."

"It isn't a matter of failure, it's a matter of our responsibility to the villagers."

"It is matter of both. Projects fail when the managers quit managing. That is our responsibility: to manage. But white managers usually blame Africans for the failures— they're thieves, they're lazy, they're inferior, they've got no morals, they're this, they're that. But of course there's really only one reason for failure—when managers don't manage. When you're offered the management of a project somewhere—and you will once you stop being so sentimental— and so eccentric—remember that the source of failure is easy to find. Look for it in the management." Kevin refilled his glass with the sauterne and lifted it. He sipped, beaming, held the glass out before him. "A treasure! Darling, how many bottles of this do we still have?"

Robert was never sure whether Kevin's drinking showed in his preaching, or his preaching showed in his drinking. They went together, the drinking and the father-to-son preachiness. Robert managed to tolerate it.

"I am as accountable to my responsibilities as you are," Kevin went on. "That is why I closed—pardon me—turned over the Bonthe Station. It was a responsible decision, a decision made to strengthen the entire project. I call it *managing*."

"It was wrong," Robert said. "We failed; we promised things and did not deliver."

"Yes, we did deliver. But a promise is not forever—promises are made in a context and contexts change. As to wrong or right, you must always keep in mind the larger truth, which sometimes encompasses the lesser one—which, by the way, is a good test of the verity of the lesser truth—that the biggest moral failure is to endanger the goal by acting irresponsibly."

"I don't care about your arguments. The reality is we promised those villagers we'd support them. We made them trust us, then we screwed them."

"It *was* an unhappy ending; and a hard decision, saying it was all a mistake. But the thing is done now. Let us agree to disagree and move on to the future. I've got this so-called model aquaculture program and I want to make something of it, and I want you to do it for me."

"I can't. I've made plans, Marie expects me. If you'd told me a few weeks ago—"

"I did not know until a few days ago."

"Daniel is a good man. If you get an experienced expat to work with him, he'll—"

"All he wants is to get his fingers on the money," Kevin said. "They always do. But he's going to be as disappointed as Kargbo. Tell me what you know about this so-called aquaculture project."

"It's a boondoggle."

"Be specific."

"It's a few holes full of muck and weeds and maybe a few fish, though I doubt that. There's never been a harvest. The ministry chops all the resources. None of the money gets down to Daniel. He begs shovels and hoes from the Germans up in Bo, and sometimes gets a little help from the Chinese rice project, and some free transport from CARE and Catholic Relief. He tries, but he can't do much. Most of the time he sits in his office writing begging letters and making up phony progress reports and sleeping."

"That's about what I thought. But it doesn't matter. All that matters is the fit; if the idea fits we'll do it. I am open on how to organize it, though I have made up my mind that it must have a white manager—a person who knows Salone and is impervious to ministerial meddling. Someone who has worked with farmers. That's where you come in, of course. They'll trust you, they always do." Kevin had been toying with a fat cigar that he'd picked out of the box Tommy placed before him. He snipped the end, lit it, blew a cloud of smoke into the air above his head.

"I've made plans. Marie expects me."

"This is a rare opportunity, Robert. Bonthe was good for you—you may not realize how much you have changed from the young man whom I sent into the wilderness, but I do. You made the best of your experience, but you still lack the credentials of project management. This position will show on your resume as project management. It will give your experience the validation it needs to open doors, Robert. You want to stay and work in Africa. You have told me that and I believe it. With this opportunity you can secure the means to stay."

"Why don't you get one of your Brits for it."

"The thing is you're *here*, and you know the lay of the land. But mostly I want you because I can depend on you. We have our disagreements, but you know how to get things done. In Africa it is the most important thing about a man, that you can depend on him. And I can depend on you—in spite of your obstreperousness."

Robert reached across the table and picked a cigar out of the box. "I am not obstreperous."

"Of course you are. You are obstreperous right now."

Robert smiled. "It is not obstreperous to say what you think."

"It is obstreperous when you continue to argue beyond reason. By now you must know that I am right—as usual— and yet you still argue—as usual. Come, you must not desert Zimi, say you will do it."

"Do what? I haven't heard an offer."

"Manage the aquaculture project, of course."

"That's not an offer. On what basis will I manage? A British contract or a local contract? And for how much? You got me too cheap the first time around."

Kevin's cigar glowed red. He blew a stream of smoke into the air over the table. "In the three years you lived at Bonthe I have deposited—how much has it been? Twenty-thousand pounds? On your behalf in a London bank. I'll wager ten pounds against one that you've never withdrawn a quid from that account."

"And I've lived like a Sierra Leonean for three years."

Kevin smiled. "So you have—and of course you'll have more money. That goes without saying. But let us not talk about details now. Suffice it to say that I will be fair with you—nay, generous—as always. How shall we do it? I think we must go at it in stages, don't you? You must do a frame survey, of course. We must not repeat the Bonthe mistake of going in before we know what these people want. We'll need that data if we're to understand the scope of the task. And we need to know what we can expect from this Sulaiman fellow. Shall we keep him? Remember: if we take him we're stuck with him."

"We need him. We need a biologist. He's Krio, so there won't be any problems that come from putting a Temne in charge of a bunch of Mendes. Freetown family; intelligent; has a solid education."

"Is he honest?"

"Of course not."

"Can his dishonesty be controlled?"

"Yes. It will depend on my position."

"He's fairly senior. Been around a few years—I cannot put you over him. He has to be your counterpart."

"He invented the program and he's been managing it. He should be my counterpart."

"Can you control him if he's your counterpart?"

"He won't defy a Big Man who comes for some of the action, if that's what you mean. It will be up to me to do that."

His eyes were drawn off into the darkness. For the first time that evening power had come on across the valley, showing as a veil of yellow dots that swept over the contour of the land from the valley floor all the way up and over the shoulder of Signal Hill, the brightest lights a string of white splashes along the top: the white walls of the President's compound.

"Guess we'll have to see what he's made of, won't we," Kevin said. He drew on the cigar, blew the smoke up over the table. He spoke again, but with some hesitancy, and none of his usual bluffness. "Robert, there's one other thing—you must forgive me for mentioning it, but I think I must, for your sake and for the sake of the project." He paused. "I wish you to know that there is talk about your eccentricity—though of course I never believed it got in the way of your work. But this new position is a good deal more visible than Bonthe was, particularly to the people at the ministry, and it could make you vulnerable. I think I must let you know that—ah—"

Rachel leaned forward and addressed Robert: "He is trying to ask you to be more circumspect about your jamba."

Robert laughed.

"Look, old man, I really don't care—smoked a fair amount of the stuff myself when I first came out to Africa. Got to using it quite a bit, didn't we, love?" Kevin reached across the table and put his hand on Rachel's. "We have been uncouth company tonight, haven't we, darling. All this shop talk. Know it bores the hell out of you."

"It's all right." She drew on her cigarette.

"We'll be good now. No more business tonight, I promise. We will talk about uplifting things, intellectual things—like literature. We will talk about the last book we have read." He turned to Robert. "You are the guest, so you go first."

"I've discovered Evelyn Waugh," Robert said.

Rachel brightened. "Oh. That's *most* interesting. He is my favorite writer. A wonderful writer, and much neglected these days. Let me guess which book. Is it *Brideshead Revisited*?"

Robert shook his head. "An earlier book."

"Umm—a hint?"

"African setting."

"Ah. *Scoop.*"

"*Black Mischief.*"

"Good God!" Kevin exclaimed. "Who'd have believed it!"

♈

Robert declined an invitation to stay the night, so Kevin drove him back into Freetown. As they coasted down the side of Juba Hill into the valley, the hillside across the valley went dark, except for the bright string of lights at the President's Mansion. They drove up Signal Hill, past the President's compound, along the ridge named Hill Station by British administrators a hundred years before and which still echoed the presence of those first expats in the big colonial-era houses built on stilts and cooled by the altitude and the shade of mango and breadfruit and cotton trees and occupied now by latter-day colonials. They turned at the fork and spiraled down Hill Cut Road and into the narrow, utterly dark streets of the city. People clustered at traders' tables or walked in the streets, moving to the side for the Land Rover. Kevin steered the vehicle between rows of rundown two-story clapboard houses built three lifetimes ago by repatriated Nova Scotian slaves called Macaulay or Garrison-Smith or some ridiculous Scots-African concatenation such as Akibo-Murray, who'd carried the clapboard design back home to Africa in their heads. Those repatriates and their sons had built the small, squat buildings close upon one another and right out to the narrow, deeply-guttered lanes in a tight grid of street and house that lay like a blanket over irregular rocky terrain, and who never anticipated lorries and cars and motorcycles or the hordes of country folk who came into the city now to find work, and who crowded the streets in the day and jammed themselves into the tiny disintegrating houses at night, five or ten to a room.

The Land Rover sailed past the high brick wall of the prison, which came right down to the road edge, and turned onto Pademba Road, its halogen head lamps brilliantly

81

lighting the narrow, crowded street for a quarter-mile. Robert did not fear the desolation the head lamps revealed, nor the darkness at the end of that desolation. He'd lived 2,000 dark nights among dark-skinned people who survived far worse privation than that discovered by the head lamp cones, and he'd never felt threatened. Locking things up, that had become second nature—the incessant thievery a vexing detail of life that he now accepted, like skin rash in the rainy season—but he'd never worried about his safety.

In five years Robert had slowly accrued repute in the expat community as one of those eccentric whites who had almost but not quite gone native. But he knew how far wrong that was, how far he was from going native. His life was nothing like the lives of the blacks among whom he lived; indeed, his life was not so different from the lives of most expats. And though he lived his life with few luxuries—without walled compounds, or generator-powered lights, or air-conditioning, or freezers full of steaks and Tater Tots, or Land Rovers, or swapped-around VCR movies—he nonetheless possessed the essential element of a good life in Africa: the certainty that his white homeland would send an airplane to lift him out of pestilence if the pestilence made him sick. And he had enough food; he always had enough food. Today's food was always there and tomorrow's food would always be there, and there would be food for the day after that. The certainty of safe conditions of life separated him from his black friends and reminded them—as if they needed reminding—that their lives were not safe, that they had nothing except the cast-off rags they wore and perhaps today's food. Food: the heart of the matter. When you worried about food, as the blacks did, incessantly, obsessively—well, that was the essential distinction between them and us, wasn't it? Robert never worried about food, never worried about getting sick, because the safety net was there for him. Robert knew on which side of the line he wanted to be; and was: he was one of us, not them.

Familiar thoughts, called forth by the spectacle of this city of—city of what?—of the future?—of the past? Certainly the past. It was everyman's past. But it was also a city of the future—but whose?—his future?—Africa's future?—the white man's future? It was a ghastly, brutish, medieval accretion of misery: a thing throbbing with freedom and beauty and life and stinking of slavery and ugliness and death; the past and the present and the future, all in one place and time. Its reach was huge and he loved it.

That last night at Bonthe he'd forced himself to wander through the village handing out the money gifts, his face aching from all the smiling that went with the good-byes. He had gone to bed overwhelmed with loneliness, and in the morning that followed he would have made the bargain of Faust to stay in Bonthe. Now, a scant hundred hours later, he did not know what he wanted—did he really want to stay in Africa? And what about Marie? He wanted Marie very much. At that moment his hunger for her astonished him; and made him more than a little uneasy, for if at that moment he could have reached her by touch or telephone— what irrational thing would he do? He licked his lips and watched the Cotton Tree take brilliant shape against the blackness. He sighed, at once contemptuous of himself and grateful for the safety of his isolation.

"Kevin, could you turn left at the Cotton Tree, and drop me on Congo Town Road?"

Kevin looked surprised. "At this time of night?"

"Visit a friend," Robert murmured.

"You can't walk—how will you get to the hotel?"

"I'll hitch a ride in the morning."

Kevin shrugged and did as he was asked.

♈

The overturned canoe revealed itself in the starlight as a long slab of gray looming faintly in the black of weeds; the tree against which he had pissed was there beyond the canoe, and beyond the tree, the palm thatch fence circumscribed the visible world. "What the fuck am I doing here?" he asked aloud. The house did not answer, nor did the canoe. Could he make it back to the Tropic? He'd have to, or he'd have to sleep on the ground and be eaten by mosquitoes. For a second he considered making his way out the

Murraytown Road to Lumley Beach and Farrah's, but realized immediately that it was even further; and besides, after
last night Farrah would doubtless tell him to fuck off. He'd
try for the Tropic. A mosquito sang in his ear. He mentally
inventoried his knapsack, remembered no insect repellent,
sighed at still another foolishness, crutched himself around
the house and out onto the road, disgusted with himself,
glad that she was not home.

He made his way slowly down the hillside along the
track he had traveled less than 24 hours before, through
quiet squatter shacks, to the Main Motor Road. From time
to time a gentle voice came out the darkness, offering
"Evenin'-o" or "Kushay-o, how de body, sah?" as if it was
the most natural thing in the world for a white man to be
limping through scores of shacks crammed full of the poor-
est blacks in Salone—or in the world, for that matter—in
the middle of the night. He responded: "No bad, padi, way
you-sef?" as if he knew the faces behind the strange voices,
wondering if Alimamy owned one of the voices, thinking
once or twice that maybe he ought to call out to the young
man, give him the job once again of walking the white master to town. Twice he saw a shadow slip across the road in
front of him, a man or a woman going to piss or shit in a
rocky defile carved by rainy season downpours, a brushy
draw that paralleled the road thirty or forty yards to the
right, and whence an almost sweet outhouse smell drifted
on still night air. He rested for a while at the juncture of the
dusty track and the Main Motor Road, feeling the soreness
in the palms of his hands and under his arms, soreness that
he knew would soon be blisters. Then he got himself going
again.

His underarms and hands were sore as boils by the time
he got back to the Tropic. He wakened the watchman, who
let him in and followed him up the stairs, holding a lantern
high to light the way. Robert gave the man a two-leone note,
lit a candle, locked the door, dropped into the chair, and
allowed himself a minute of rest before opening the water
bottle and drinking half its contents. He rummaged in his
knapsack for the percodan vial, found it, swallowed one of
the tablets and drank again before climbing into bed. A

breeze drifted in the window, a dry Harmattan breeze that cooled and tightened his skin. Staring into the blackness, he thought about Marie, wished she was there beside him. He realized then that he had made his decision; and he wondered how he would tell her, and how she would take it. And he wondered if he had made a mistake.

Robert watched her jiggle across the sand. She was big, though not unattractively. There was no disproportionality in her bigness. She had big eyes, a big mouth and nose, big breasts, a bushy head of brunette hair. The only small thing about her was an overwrought bikini stretched to the breaking point. He returned to his reading as she entered the baffa.

She paused long enough to remove her sunglasses and look him over, then angled through a cluster of chairs and dropped her bag on a table near his. Dragging a towel out of the bag, she dusted the table, looked for a chair that might not be falling apart, glanced at Robert to see if her fussing had his attention and seeing that it hadn't, got it by selecting a chair at the other end of the baffa and screeching it across the concrete floor. She slapped at the chair with her towel, arranged the towel on the wire seat, and sat—gingerly, as if expecting the rusty thing to collapse. She removed a book from her bag, dropped it with a clatter on the metal table.

Robert looked up again a minute later when she hissed. The black man's eyes popped open. She hissed again and signaled with her crooked finger. The black man rose and ambled to her table.

"What do you want?" he asked sleepily. His once-white jacket was frayed at the cuffs and discolored by decades of food stains. A single homemade wooden button held it closed over his T-shirt.

"Coffee."

He gave a huge yawn. "Well—I no able—"

"Lebanese," she added.

"I no get—"

"Lebanese," she said again, this time quite firmly.

"But—look am—coffee no dey." He waved at the bamboo-veneered bar, a scabrous dusty thing fronted by a pair of stools so unraveled that no one but a drunk ever dared to climb them. He said hopefully, "I get Coke an' Seven-Up an'—"

She spoke with exaggerated patience. "Go to the hotel, tell the man in the dining room that the Italian lady desires Lebanese coffee."

"But—I no able for lef—"

"Go," she said.

He contemplated the wreckage of the bar, which it was his duty to attend, decided apparently that he could risk leaving it unguarded for a few minutes. He sighed, went out of the baffa into the sun and across the sand toward the hotel.

She took up her book and resumed reading.

Robert, who had watched this exchange, went back to his Waugh. He read a couple of paragraphs, then heard her speak once again.

"Do you stay in the hotel?"

He glanced up, shook his head, resumed reading.

She lit a cigarette and observed him: noted his long blond pony-tail, his almost hairless chest and legs, his nondescript and baggy shorts, the plump sock that covered his left foot, the faded green knapsack, the crutches; and around him the fitting chaos of a scatter of tables and chairs, randomly oriented, as if slung into the baffa over the low thatch walls, then righted where they landed.

"So few white people—"

He looked up. "Pardon?"

"There are no white people."

"This is a black country."

She smiled. "I meant tourists, of course."

"This is not the season."

"But the travel clerk said it is the season."

"It's not."

"She said it is a discovery. She showed me a book with pictures of beaches and grass huts and fishing canoes, but all I see are empty dirty tourist hotels that smell bad."

"You have to get away from here. Down the coast, or inland. Or even into Freetown."

"You're here."

"I come here to run. It's a beautiful three-mile stretch."

She looked at his crutches.

"Though I can't run yet."

"Yes—the beach is very fine."

They heard a distant yell and looked off down the beach. Africans—little boys, teens, young men—chased a soccer ball near the water where the ebbing tide had left the sand damp and firm. Their play was bringing them closer to the baffa and their yelps came more strongly on the breeze, which retained the morning coolness the sea had brought. The beach stretched southward through surf haze to the trees that marked the mouth of Babadori Creek. Beyond the creek the rocky flank of Juba Hill rose out of the haze, and beyond Juba a long train of white clouds and the coastal mountains converged on the horizon far to the south. The clouds had been pushing up against the dark slopes all morning, rising into coalescing clots that obscured the mountain tops. By evening they would be very high and black and growling with thunder, and in the night would come flashing off the mountains with the last rains of the season.

"But there are no tourists—it is not natural." She looked around for an ashtray, and seeing none, tossed the cigarette butt over the baffa wall. "The only good thing is the swimming. It is like a bath." She rose. "Will you watch my bag? These people are always stealing things."

He nodded, watched her walk past him and out the door and over the blinding whiteness of the beach. The soccer game had drifted off. She entered the water and waded out until the low surf broke round her hips, dove and swam straight out from the beach.

A movement drew Robert's eye to the hotel. A skinny old man came down the stairs through palm trees and rocks from the breakfast verandah, a book and a towel clutched to his bare chest. A young African in a white jacket followed with an umbrella and a beach chair. Then a middle-aged man and woman appeared, following the old man and the young African.

The old man came to the baffa, looked inside, then motioned for the young African to arrange the chair and umbrella in the sand a few yards away. The middle-aged couple came into the baffa, nodded at Robert, took a table. The woman said something in German.

Robert resumed reading. A few minutes later the waiter appeared with a cup of coffee. He looked around. Robert pointed out to the ocean. The woman was out beyond the surf, but was swimming back. The waiter shrugged, put the coffee on her table and went to the German couple, who also wanted coffee. Robert went back to his book. When he looked up again the Italian woman was wading out of the surf. He noticed then that a young woman had joined the old man beneath the stand of palms. She had stretched herself out in the sun, face down on a towel.

Robert watched the Italian woman approach. The disappearance of her bush of hair, which was plastered wet and dark about her neck and skull, threw her all out of proportion. Now she seemed thick and chunky. She stopped before the old man and spoke to him in Italian. His face clouded and he swung around and glared at Robert, then turned back to her with a sudden arm-waving volley of Italian. She withstood it, her arms crossed. When he ran out of words she reached down to him and said something—tenderly, it seemed to Robert. The old man pulled away from her.

The young woman pushed herself to a sitting position, looking disgusted. Robert watched her rise and come into the baffa. Her brown hair was long and straight and shining, her body slender and tanned. Seeing her mother's bag on a table, she pulled a chair out and sat and looked at Robert.

The old man was yelling again. The German couple had fallen silent and were watching—like Robert, like the waiter standing beside them with his tray. Then Robert looked once more at the young woman, who studied him as she lifted the cup of coffee and sipped. His gaze moved back to the Italian woman. Her face was red now as she shouted down at the old man, her hands on her hips.

"They are discussing you," the young woman said.

Robert looked back at the girl. He was confused—why was he part of this? What had he missed? It was like he had fallen asleep in the first act and awakened at the beginning of the third.

"My father says you are ridiculous." She raised the cup to her lips again, her eyes holding his. She sipped, lowered the cup. "He is a good judge of character."

The German couple glanced at the girl when she spoke, looked at Robert, then looked back at the big Italian woman and the old man, who were now shouting into one another's shouts. The waiter stood beside their table, his tray balanced at his shoulder, his mouth hanging open, his eyes bright with interest: he would bring a good story home to his shack on Juba.

"Shall I tell you what my father says?"

"I could care less," Robert said. He picked up his knapsack and opened it and slipped his book inside.

"My father is telling my mother that he is humiliated because she has chosen you. Choosing you demeans him. He wants to know where she has left her dignity—and when it was that her appetite consumed her pride." She smiled lazily. "And I wonder what has consumed *your* pride."

Robert leaned over and inspected the bandage. The pink spot that had appeared on it was no longer pink. The bottom of the sock was sodden with his blood. He worked the bandaged foot into the plastic sandal—the blood squishing out on his hands, which he wiped on his shorts—and picked up the knapsack and crutched his way to the entry, where he came face to face with the Italian woman.

"Oh." Her hands dropped off her hips. "You are leaving—" She did not move out of his way.

He moved past her and up the sandy slope to the road shoulder. When he came to the motorcycle he secured the crutches with rubber straps.

She came up behind him, took position beside the handle bars as he pulled his gloves on. Beyond her the young woman came out of the baffa and looked up at him, her shining brown hair falling down over her breasts.

"Do you do this sort of thing all the time?" he asked.

"What sort of thing?"

"Me. People like me."

"He is old—he has little appetite. It is our arrangement."

"What did he say about me?"

"Nothing—a comment."

"What was it?"

"He said you are disreputable, that I should find a more suitable companion to take me about. He says that you are young and you will hurt me."

"That's all?"

"Yes."

"What was all the yelling about?"

"He is angry because I brought him here. He tells me he hates this place, and he wants to go back to Milan."

Robert looked beyond her at the daughter.

"Come back for me in one hour. I want to see you again. I want you to take me to Freetown on your motorcycle."

He said nothing.

"I will be in front of the hotel."

She stepped back when he kicked the engine to life.

"I am Francesca Giuliani," she said, loud enough to be heard over the growl of the motorcycle. "What is your name?"

"Robert Kelley. " He said it past Francesca, at the young woman, who stood in the sunlight, showing herself to him. Like Marie, with the same kind of expression.

"One hour. I will be waiting."

He put the bike in gear and drove around the traffic circle, then took the dirt road along Man-O-War Bay and turned into the parking lot at Farrah's Place. Except for a rusting Volkswagen bug behind the kitchen, the lot was empty. He parked beside the VW. An old black man sat on the bench along the back wall.

The old man grinned, showing the void where his front teeth had been. "How de time, sah?"

Robert removed his crutches. "I de manage small-small, Sylvester."

"Yessah."

Robert entered the passage, which smelled of urine, beer, fishy cooking oil. He came out into the sand that surrounded the bar. The shelves behind the bar were empty and the door to the kitchen was locked. Stools rested upside down on the bar, and the folding chairs that in the evening would surround each of the square concrete tables were locked away. The sand between the bay and the thatch-roofed bar—all of it under leafy princess palms and strings of colored lights—was raked smooth. An invisible boundary separated Farrah's Place from The Cockerill Bay Cafe, the restaurant of another Lebanese—a distant cousin with whom Farrah had feuded for so long neither remembered the cause, their distaste for one another kept alive by habit and competition for the same few customers, though in fact their competition contributed little to the distribution of customers: some kind of natural filter diverted the English and Americans and the few Africans who could afford European prices to Farrah's Place, and the Germans and Lebanese and French to The Cockerill Bay. The restaurants occupied adjacent sections of beach: you could sit at a table in Farrah's Place and converse with an acquaintance sitting at a table at The Cockerill Bay. On evenings with high tides and a strong onshore wind, the water flowed over the sand and around the bar, and patrons would stand about ankle deep in warm sea water drinking Star Beer under the colored lights, their pantlegs rolled up, their sandals and shoes on the bar.

Robert went back into the passage, banged on a door, waited, banged again, then heard a voice.

"It's me," he bellowed at the door panel, "Robert!"

Another minute, then the hollow thump of feet descending the stairs, the click of the first lock, followed by the click of the second, and then the iron bar scraping back. The door opened enough to reveal Farrah's face and a patch of animal-hairy chest and the white of boxer shorts. "You.

What do you want?" Cigarette smoke curled up over his face. The cigarette dangled straight out from his lips, a mannerism adopted from some movie character, affected so long ago it had become a true part of him.

"I need to fix my foot. I have to meet Kevin and I don't have time to go back to my hotel."

Farrah coughed unexpectedly, the cigarette exploding from his lips and bouncing off Robert's chest. Still coughing, he kicked the cigarette over the threshold, past Robert's feet.

"Invite me in, Farrah, I need to fix my foot."

Farrah glanced at the bloody sock. "Now I am a fucking hospital." He stepped back. Robert went past him and limped up the stairs. Farrah locked the door and slid the bar across it and followed him up to the living room, where Robert tossed his knapsack to the sofa, which rested under the open windows.

A woman's voice came from the bedroom. "Bonjour, Robert."

He looked into the dark bedroom.

"Ça va, René?" he called.

"Pas mal." The lump of covers moved and René's face appeared against the shadows as she pushed herself up on one elbow. The sheet fell away from her upper body, which was covered by one of the *I just ate at Farrah's Place* T-shirts that in better times Farrah gave to favorite customers. She yawned. "Quelle heure est-il?"

"Onze heures et demie."

She pushed the sheet off and swung her legs out of bed, pulling the oversized T-shirt down about her hips as she lumbered to the bathroom and closed the door. A second later she opened the door a crack and said, "Farrah, il n'y a pas d'electricité."

"No shit," Farrah muttered.

A young African rose from behind a desk littered with yellow pieces of paper. He reached under the counter and got a slip of the same yellow paper and pushed it across the counter.

"Two," Robert said.

The young man got another slip of paper. He watched Robert print his name and a city and telephone number on each.

"How many minutes?" the young man asked.

"Ten minutes each."

The young man looked at a rate chart, scribbled some numbers on each paper. "Give me 760 leones."

Robert removed bundles of two-leone notes from his knapsack. The young black scooped the bundles into his arms and muttered, "Wait," and went through a door into the back room.

Robert turned. Lebanese, East Indians, Europeans, Americans, Africans lined the benches all around the room. Cigarette butts littered the cement floor and a haze of blue smoke hung in a permanent smog. Robert found an empty place between a white-robed African and a florid man in khaki shorts and shirt who introduced himself as an Irish priest from a mission in Kambia. Robert and the priest carried on a desultory conversation until the clerk called the priest's name and a booth number, whereupon the priest went into one of two halls that angled off the waiting room. Robert got his Waugh out and read. Every few minutes someone came out of the hall and went out the front door

94

and one of those waiting on the benches rose in response to the call of a name. An exhaust fan came on, hummed for a minute, then rattled and died. When the clerk called Robert's name and a booth number he rose and went down one of the halls, which was lined by booths on one side and dusty windows on the other. Some of the booths had doors that hung crookedly, some showed broken places on the jambs where doors had been ripped off.

Robert dropped his knapsack on the floor of the booth and sat on the bench built into the corner. From the doorways of other booths along the hall came murmurs and laughs. Cigarette smoke curled up into the hot air. While he waited he sweated and browsed the graffiti penned and carved on the walls above the telephone. Finally, the phone rang. He picked up the handset and heard a voice say, "Wait." Another two minutes, a distant click and a rush of static, then a voice speaking from such a distance that he could scarcely make out the words.

"Bonjour."

"Je veux parler avec Marie, s'il vous plait," he shouted.

"Robert, it's me!"

"I can barely hear you, sweetheart, speak louder."

"I've been waiting by the phone for days for you to call, I even tried to book a flight, but they said Lungi's closed. I have wonderful news, Robert, you won't believe it, it's the most fantastic luck. I met the manager of a new aquaculture program. It's a UN job—I told him all about you and what you've been doing in Bonthe and he wants to talk to you. He knows all about the Zimi project, and I think he was very impressed that you were associated with it. When can you come?"

He closed his eyes. "Oh shit."

"Did you hear me?" she shouted.

"Yes."

"What?"

"I said I heard you."

"When can you come? He wants to talk to you right away. They want to decide."

"That's what I called you about—I can't come right now."

"I can't hear you, you'll have to speak up!"

"I said I can't come right now," he shouted.

"Well, when *can* you come? They want to make a decision."

"Sweetheart—I don't know—maybe I can get free in a couple of weeks," he shouted. "About the job—I *have* a job now."

No response for several seconds, just the rushing sound.

"Marie, are you there?"

"Did you say you *have* a job? I don't understand—are you coming or not?"

"Not right now."

"Will you please tell me what you mean? Are you coming or aren't you?"

"No, not now. I got a job offer. I was ready to leave when Kevin offered me another job. Marie, I had to take it—it was a very good offer, too good to pass up. It means a British contract. I had to take it. Do you understand?"

The rushing sound went on for a long time; then: "Why can't you just come and look—this could be better—"

"I've already started, I can't come now."

"They won't—" And then a wave of static overwhelmed her words.

"Marie! Marie, are you there? I'll come up for a couple of weeks, as soon as I can get free. I can look at the job then. I love you, sweetheart, and I miss you—" And then he realized the line was dead. "Hello! Hello!" He looked at his watch. "Sonofabitch!" he yelled. He slammed the handset into its cradle and lunged out of the booth, limping out of the hall and across the waiting room. "I'm in fourteen," he said to the young man across the counter. "You cut me off after only two minutes. I want you to place the call again."

The young black looked at him with a blank expression, got a piece of paper from under the counter and pushed it across at Robert.

Robert flung the paper back at him. "Place the fucking call!"

The waiting room was full. Silence fell and every eye came to him.

The young black turned expressionlessly and went out of the room. He came back a couple of minutes later. "De pohson you colled broke de connection," he said lazily.

Robert wanted to say, you lying sonofabitch, but didn't. He returned to booth fourteen, got his knapsack, and came back to the waiting room, where he filled out another slip of yellow paper, then found an empty space on a bench and sat.

The clerk called Robert's name a half hour later. He looked up hopefully, then realized it had to be the second call he had placed.

"Robert! Where are you?" his brother asked.

"Freetown."

"When're you leaving?"

"I'm not. Kevin offered me another job and I took it."

"You're staying?"

"Yes."

"You're not coming home? At all?"

"That shouldn't be a surprise, Dave. How's everybody?" The connection was clear. Robert could hear his brother breathing, and behind the breathing the babble of a morning television program. Why did *this* connection have to be so goddamned clear?

"Dad's gonna be very disappointed. This is really—well, it's just plain unexpected. You coming home—it's all he's talked about for weeks."

"C'mon, David. He doesn't even write."

Silence for several seconds, then: "You're not even coming for a visit?"

Robert's eyes moved over the graffiti. "This should not be a surprise," he said again.

"Is it because of that girl Marie?"

"I got a job offer."

"You haven't been home in two years."

Robert did not reply.

"Dad's planned a backpacking trip with you. Wants to take you up to the high lakes for some fly fishing. He hasn't been up there since the last time you came home. There's still time before the snow."

"Are you getting my letters?"

"Yes."

"Then I don't understand what this conversation is about. I've been telling you and Dad for two years that I'm

97

staying in Africa. Africa is my home. It's where I live and work."

"This is your home."

Robert's eyes, roaming over the graffiti, came to a place high on the wall over the telephone where someone had carved *god laff*.

"No, it isn't."

"Are you gonna call him or do *I* have to tell him?"

Robert thought about Dave's letters. The last one little different from the one before it: resentment and complaint: sighs and whines: about sixty-hour weeks; about meetings of Merchants Associations; about hauling kids to Sunday school, baseball practice, soccer games, movies, skating lessons, swimming meets, sleep-overs, birthday parties; about helping Janice be a mother (she had a job, too— which brought in as much money as his, so he could hardly refuse half her motherly burden). David's good life: exchanging pieces of himself for a house full of useless stuff that he protected by giving away other pieces of himself. David hating the load, but perversely proud of accepting it, because there was courage in accepting it, and even the nobility of self-sacrifice.

"Seems like you could come home and we could at least talk about things."

"We're talking right now."

"We need to talk about the business."

"I don't know anything about the business anymore."

"Dad wants to retire, and I can't handle the business alone. We have to talk about how we're going to—"

Robert interrupted. "I've already told you I don't want anything to do with it."

"Same old Robert—Dave's worries, Dave's problems, Dave's responsibilities."

"Dave's choice. Sell the business if it's such a burden."

"Right."

"You love what you do."

"Yeah, sure, everyone loves twenty-hour days."

"If you didn't love it, why would you do it?"

"Someone has to be responsible—it would be nice if *you'd* face—"

"Dave—you're not hoisting it in. I—am—not—going—back. Period."

"Why do you have to be so ugly about it? Besides, I can't do anything. I don't own the business, Dad does."

"Sell the business, Dave. Get a life, for Christ's sake. You're better off working for someone else."

Another one of those sighs, followed by silence. Robert was supposed to say something conciliatory. But his anger wouldn't let him, so he sat and listened to Dave's breathing against a background of TV laughter and applause.

Whining now, sounding like one of his letters: "There's too much pressure on me, Robert, I really need help."

Robert looked across the hall at the dirty window and rusty iron bars, at the air outside that was turning pink. Dave was too weak to change, and he pitied him; but not enough to share his load.

"I'm not coming back," he said, but added after a pause: "But I will call Dad."

He waited another two hours for the second call to Marie, but the operators could not make the connection. He finally left at midnight, when they closed the telephone exchange, and went back to the Tropic and sat at the tiny candle-lit table in his room, sweating over a long letter explaining what he had so miserably failed to explain on the telephone, and promising that he would come for two weeks as soon as he could get away.

♈

They gathered in the shade of the long metal-roofed baffa, to help spread the food over the two long tables. Or to get out of the sun. Or simply to be close to the bar, behind which a pair of Marines popped the tops off bottles of Becks and Star Beer. The athletic among the guests were not in the baffa: they were in the pool or throwing horseshoes or chasing frisbees and footballs on the grassy hillside. And some escaped the afternoon heat by lazing about the air-conditioned day room inside the big house where they played pool or table tennis and listened to music.

Sergeant Sancho finished his welcoming comments and waved Neggie forward, clapping to encourage the crowd, who looked at one another and murmured; they had not come to hear Neggie make a speech. Sancho raised his hands over his head and applauded more vigorously. A couple of Sierra Leonean guests and the German Ambassador added a few limp, noiseless claps—enough to save Sergeant Sancho, whom they admired, the embarrassment of an unsuccessful introduction. Neggie appeared not to notice the anemic welcome, which he did not care about, anyway, because these people—except of course for Kargbo and the German Ambassador and the managers of CARE and CRS and a couple of development projects—were insignificant. He gained nothing by attending to their interests, though of course he knew that the most important part of his job was doing exactly that, or at least of convincing *them* that he did.

Robert had come up the hill to the baffa a few minutes before, to change the dressing on his foot, which he had gotten wet at poolside. While Sancho made his remarks Robert wound gauze over the dry dressing and then pulled a clean sock over it. He was leaning on his crutches watching Sancho introduce Neggie when Max came up behind him.

Two teen-aged girls entered the shade of the baffa, slipped past Robert and Max, and sat at one of the two long tables. Robert heard one of them say something about the Marines. The other giggled. The Marines of course were the center of attention and on their best behavior, ordered by Sergeant Sancho—on pain of Article 15 punishment—to drink nothing alcoholic until after seven o'clock, when the eating was finished and the food put away and the families gone and Thanksgiving could degenerate into the kind of party that most of the guests wanted.

"Neggie had him in his office yesterday, rehearsing," Max whispered to Robert. "Wrote Sancho's speech, then made him memorize it. Sancho was pissed."

Neggie cleared his throat and paused, as if searching for words. He glanced at Sancho. "Sergeant, you have caught me completely unprepared." He turned back to the crowd. "Sergeant Sancho is much too kind if he thinks that I am quick-witted enough to come up here unprepared and make a speech." He paused, looked thoughtful, then added: "But you know, as I look about me I see that I do have a word to say. Your presence here and the occasion we are here to celebrate suggests it. It is simply this, that I am humbled by the Americans I have come to know in my few months in Sierra Leone. You are America's best. You are the real American ambassadors."

Robert glanced at the girl, who was whispering to her younger companion. Her blond hair fell over one shoulder in damp strands, her skin was bare and golden and impeccable, the nakedness of her back—her bikini top was little more than a string and a pair of cloth patches almost too flimsy to adequately cup her immature breasts—conjuring Marie. She had Marie's long legs and lank sun-browned torso and Marie's triangular back, which tapered from wide shoulders to a small waist before flaring out to athletic hips. He'd never said a word to this girl, nor had she spoken to him, yet he felt a bond with her; in part because of her resemblance to Marie, but also because he sensed he stood out as pleasurably in her environment as she stood out in his. There was vanity in this observation, but also truth. For whatever reason, he *was* interesting to this girl. He *knew* it. The message of her interest was carried in glance and gesture and pause, as palpably as a message written on a piece of paper. She'd been there at the pool when he'd parked his Honda under the tree and made his way up the hillside: there, bouncing on the diving board: another Marie. He'd stopped at the end of the pool and stood leaning into his crutches, watching her from the privacy of his mirrored sunglasses, as she dove, climbed out of the pool in front of him, paused to wring the water from her hair and toss her head and give him a good long look at her, then go back and do it again. Showing a lot of herself, not just to him, but to a dozen Marines and PCVs who hovered, wisecracked, and drooled like fools. Moving about innocently, athletically, while her father—the taciturn Scot, Jimmy Cannon—watched with stony face and folded arms from a table at the end of the pool. All of it a game, of course. Except to the stiff dicks: it was no game to the stiff dicks.

Neggie gazed thoughtfully over the crowd. "In the faces before me I see America in microcosm. Black-skinned Americans, yellow-skinned Americans, white-skinned

Americans. All different. Yet all of the same community. All come to this God-forsaken, poverty-stricken, disease-afflicted land to help its backward people pull themselves up out of the morass of their ignorance—without a thought of reward, I might add. I am proud to be counted among those Americans, thankful to God that I am one of you, and that—like you—I am chosen to represent America."

"It's his nature to be devious, that's why," Max whispered to Robert, who'd asked why the Ambassador was bothering with such an elaborate subterfuge—why didn't he just say he wanted to say a few words? "Also, there's the tradition. It's the Marines' party. Neggie can't stand it that it's such a successful event and that these kids get credit for it. It's the only event in Salone that brings Americans to Freetown from all over the country. The Americans love that part of it—that it belongs to these kids, that they organize it and get it going. He can't stand that, because he can't take credit for it."

From the corner of Robert's eye he saw Jimmy Cannon's daughter roll her eyes up at him. He looked at her and she held his gaze for several seconds before smiling and looking away. He felt his blood rise, and he thought about Marie again.

"He hasn't mentioned our rutile," Max whispered.

"What?"

"The rutile. The reason we're here—to protect our rutile."

"Why the hell would he want to mention rutile?"

"The rutile mines—never mind, I'm being ironic," Max said.

"Ah. I get it."

"You're not paying attention and I know why, you're thinking about that girl's pussy. You ought to be ashamed—she's a baby."

"No, she isn't. She's been sending out mating signals all afternoon. I can feel the heat, she's glowing with it."

"Not for you, she's got the hots for Lenny. Haven't you seen how she rubs up against him? She wants a big-dicked Marine who can fight all day and fuck all night. You don't qualify on either score."

102

"I'd have a go at the fucking part if I had my foot on a pillow and she'd get on top."

"Thanksgiving is a uniquely American event," Neggie was saying, "a day we set aside to thank God for His benef- icence. No other holiday celebrates America like Thanksgiving. What does this tell us about ourselves? That we are a God-fearing nation? That is evident in the way we live. That we are a people chosen by God to lead humanity? That is also evident in the success of our arms. But if God has ordained that we are to lead humanity, how shall we lead? Well, I say there is only one way to lead: by getting out in front and going forward. That is the American way. To tell the world to get out of the way, we're coming through! Follow us!" His head went up, his chin went out, his gaze roamed the crowd. The fringe of white hair flared out like a halo and his generous lips were compressed into a line of determination. His pause drew a solitary, droll, British-accented "Hear, hear!" The Brits rolled their eyes at one another while the Sierra Leoneans kept their expres- sions diplomatically blank.

Third Assistant Minister Kargbo, at the far edge of the crowd in a gold-embroidered white gown and white skull cap, watched Robert. He broke into a smile when Robert's eyes wandered his way. Robert nodded solemnly. He'd met Kargbo three years before when he was preparing to go down to Bonthe, and had seen him perhaps four times in the next three years, at social events such as this one. In these contacts Kargbo had never really noticed him. Indeed, the only time they'd had more than incidental contact was the time that Robert had accused the paramount chief of cor- ruption, and Kargbo had lined up with the chief against him, seeing in the conflict a chance to remove Robert and get someone more manageable—one of his Sierra Leoneans— to run the Bonthe Station.

Kargbo had seen Robert at the pool as he and his wife had walked up the hillside from the parking lot, and he'd waved at Robert with such enthusiasm that one might have guessed he was greeting an old friend, and he'd led his wife up the stairs to the poolside table. There he'd said how glad he was to see Robert and then pulled a chair up and sat and looked around for a servant, realized that there were none, that he'd have to get his own beer, and had sent his wife on up the hill past the house to the baffa. He congratulated Robert on his appointment as program manager, saying Kevin had informed him that very morning. Kargbo added that he had been telling people for a long time to watch Robert Kelley—a rising star, a young man on the move. And he was very happy indeed to see his insight confirmed. Now, he suggested, they ought to discuss the ways they could work together as colleagues. He wondered if Robert would like to come to lunch. Robert said that in other circumstances he'd love to come, but unfortunately he was occupied with his duties upline. However, as soon as he came down to Freetown again he'd look in on the Third Assistant Minister. It was at that point that Max came down the hill from the baffa, escorting Kargbo's young wife and carrying a tray of cold beers.

After Kargbo and his wife left the table to pay their respects to the Ambassador, Max had asked, "What's he want?"

"Money," Robert had replied. "Trying to figure out how he can get at the money through me."

"And so, my friends," Neggie was saying, "we Americans are good neighbors and good Samaritans not only because it is the right thing to do, but also because we believe it is our God-given mission to deliver the American experience to the world. We are the world's model for civil cooperation and economic development. Our two-hundred-year democracy is the envy of the world. Our love of justice is unmatched. And our support for the backward poor of the world in their struggle to throw off the twin shackles of poverty and tyranny is unwavering. Our support of freedom is particularly important in Africa, where tyrants still hold sway—"

Max stiffened. He raised a hand to silence Robert, who had begun to say something.

"—only when the tyrants are gone and democracy is established will the nations of Africa—to which, as my own ancestral home, I feel both kinship and the deepest personal affection—only when the African people themselves push aside their tyrants, only then can the African people wipe out the poverty of their lives and make democracy a reality. And only when democracy is a healthy well-rooted plant will the people benefit from the development of their rich lands. In this regard, our own experience as a nation is the most successful model in the world. So, my fellow Americans—and my African cousins—" At this point Neggie paused and nodded in the direction of Third Assistant Minister Kargbo, who now watched Neggie intently.

"Dumb shit," Max muttered.

"As Americans threw off their chains to make democracy flourish, so must others break off the chains before—"

"Doesn't have the vaguest idea what he's saying," Max murmured.

♈

The word got round quickly after Kevin and Rachel arrived. Soon people were coming to Robert and congratulating him on his new contract. It was not the fact that Kevin had renewed Robert's contract that these expats acknowledged with their good wishes, but that Robert had obtained a *British* contract. This conveyed a status that Robert had not possessed while he worked under a local contract. A national contract conveyed virtual diplomatic protection and civil service rights. But more than anything else, it conferred professional standing. It implied career, not job.

Recognition was immediate. Harry Grimes, the Peace Corps Director, had once said of Robert: "Don't know him well—he was before my time. I'm told he was good, though he seems to have gone native. Decent sort, but irresponsible—drugs, that sort of thing." That same Harry Grimes now came to Robert at the poolside table and offered his hand, saying, "Hear we're gonna have you around for a while. That's terrific news, Robert. Kevin's been saying great things about the job you did down at Bonthe. Makes the Peace Corps look good. We're proud of you; you're a good model for what our young people can do here. I was thinking about grabbing you up myself, as Assistant

105

Director for Agriculture. If Zimi doesn't work out, come see me."

Even Chesty Koroma came down the hill to the poolside table and offered his congratulations. Robert had not seen him in months, though Chesty, as Kevin's counterpart and, putatively, Assistant Project Manager, was technically Robert's superior. He had always regarded Robert as just another white man between him and the resources of Zimi Development Project.

"Please sit down, Mister Koroma." Robert said with a smile after Chesty sat down.

"Thank you, Mister Kelley. Mister Beachley has told me that you are to lead the Koribundu-Gbundapi Aquaculture Project. I have come to offer my sincerest congratulations."

"Thank you, Mister Koroma."

"Not at all, Mister Kelley."

Robert glanced past Koroma's mirrored sunglasses to watch the Cannon girl climb out of the pool.

"Minister Kargbo has told me he is very happy that Koribundu-Gbundapi will have you as its new leader. He is confident that you will bring the project under control, perhaps even make it the flagship of His Excellency Doctor President Momoh's Green Revolution. As you know, His Excellency Doctor President Momoh believes that the future of Sierra Leone is in the hands of its farmers."

Robert nodded.

"I think that you already know that the project was almost ruined by our colleague, Mister Sulaiman. He was very clever. He concealed his many misbehaviors for a long time by building up a house of cards. But Minister Kargbo was more clever by half. He was hot on the trail of the thief and was actually on the very eve of ordering a grand inquiry into all of Mister Sulaiman's unbelievable misbehaviors when Mister Beachley came forward and announced that Her Majesty's Government would take over project administration. Minister Kargbo has showed me Mister Sulaiman's reports, by which Mister Sulaiman cleverly concealed his many indisciplines—but why mince words—I will say what it was, because we are colleagues and honesty among colleagues is important—his *theft* of project resources. Yes, theft. Minister Kargbo has generously forwarded copies of those clever reports to Mister Beachley. I think you will be amazed."

"Interesting," Robert murmured. The Cannon girl was standing only ten feet away, looking at him soberly as she toweled her hair. His heart thumped faster. He watched her turn away and become Marie as she walked slowly up the grassy slope toward the long metal-roofed baffa. The wet cloth of her bikini clung as sheer as paint to the globes of her buttocks. He groaned inwardly, sighed outwardly; he wanted his Marie.

Chesty Koroma drank from his bottle of Star Beer, belched sadly. "For Minister Kargbo it is a very painful thing—as it is for me, I might add, for I have known Mister Sulaiman for many years. Exposing his indiscipline—no, I will say the ugly word, though I confess that sometimes we Africans are reluctant to say it, because in this case it is so obviously the right word: corruption—such an ugly word, horrible"—he sighed again—"reflecting so unfavorably on every Sierra Leonean. But Minister Kargbo is a brave man, a man who squarely faces the truth, unlike some Sierra Leoneans, who, we must honestly admit, are sometimes— yes, I will say it—undisciplined."

Robert nodded gravely, while his eyes followed the girl up the hill. His heart skipped a beat when she paused and looked over her shoulder at him.

"I think Minister Kargbo will have Mister Sulaiman arrested. For his indisciplines."

Robert looked at Chesty. "That would be—that would be very unfortunate. Mister Beachley and I require his skills."

Chesty smiled. "There are other Sierra Leonean biologists. Minister Kargbo has one in mind, one of proven honesty. A brilliant man. One of Minister Kargbo's closest colleagues at the ministry."

Robert shook his head. "I am certain that Mister Beachley will be very disappointed. I believe that he will cancel the program if Mister Sulaiman's knowledge of the area is not available to us. Certainly that is what I will recommend. Mister Beachley and I believe that Mister Sulaiman's contribution is essential."

The half smile that Chesty Koroma had worn all the time he talked to Robert did not change. He nodded slowly, raised his bottle of beer and drained it. He belched and put the bottle on the table among the dozen empties left by Robert's well-wishers. His smile became rueful. "I think you are running a risk by keeping Mister Sulaiman. But you and Mister Beachley are very wise men. You have much experience in Salone—maybe you know more than Minister Kargbo. I will tell him of your wishes. And now I think I will go and find one more bottle of Star Beer. Again, let me offer my heartfelt and sincerest congratulations on your promotion. We Sierra Leoneans are very fortunate to have white men such as you guiding us."

A late-season squall came in the afternoon, darkening the day and driving everyone except a handful of swimmers into the house or under the metal roof of the baffa, and urging more than a few to their cars. Lightning flashed across the hillside above them, the thunder huge and violent, rattling the metal roof and shaking the tables, stopping conversations of even the veterans among the crowd. Robert wandered away from the bar and the tables where guests had coalesced into a dozen clusters. Leaning into his crutches, he watched the gray curtain sweep down the green valley, led by a skirmish line of tossing palms and waving banana trees. Robert welcomed the storm.

Under the metal roof a dozen women collected the bowls and platters on which they'd brought food. A pair of houseboys moved down one table, dragging a plastic-lined garbage can, into which they tossed abandoned paper plates of jello, mashed potato, chocolate cake. The meat from the plates they scraped off into plastic sacks to put aside with the leftovers the white women had given them, which they would carry home to their families and neighbors when their work was finished.

The sound of the Creedence Clearwater Revival came from the house. The dancing had already started. Robert looked down the hill. Car headlamps came on in the parking lot as guests with families scrambled into Land Rovers and Land Cruisers and Broncos before the rain hit. Below the parking lot, beyond the iron gates of the ten-foot wall, the potholed street was empty. Even the traders' huts at the corner, where the street entered Pademba Road, were shuttered. The hillside above the compound had also changed, the social babble quieted, the drumming, which had echoed across the valley for hours, silenced. When the rain stopped it would start again: the music of drums, the talk, the people drifting about the streets until the middle of the night.

They heard the waterfall roar of the rain before it advanced over the compound wall and across the grass and gardens. The wind hit them first, staggered them, sprinkled them with errant pellets of rain, chilled them with the surprising coolness of mountain air. Most of the two dozen who'd gathered at the edge to watch the squall approach disappeared into the house, leaving only the house boys and the white women and Robert. And at the other end of the baffa, near the bar, Neggie and Max were immersed in conversation.

Robert stepped back from the edge of the baffa as the rain roared down on the metal roof, the noise of it stopping all talk. The bushpole roof supports quivered and swirling wind filled the baffa with mist. Robert got the crutches under his arms and made his way down the length of the baffa and past the bar and down the three steps to the back door of the house. He glanced at Max as he passed, but Max was preoccupied.

"Racist nonsense," Neggie sputtered.

"Mister Ambassador," Max said patiently, "it has nothing to do with race. It has to do with the way words are interpreted."

"Why would they think any such thing? It was a speech celebrating American success and America's place in the world. It is part of the goddamned holiday, not a call to arms."

"Sir, words from the Ambassador of the United States carry a special significance. Those words will be interpreted to mean that the United States encourages a change of government. In Africa that is seldom accomplished by elections. Kargbo is close to the President. I think we must make it clear to Kargbo that your speech—"

Neggie snorted. "I will not explain my speech to anyone, Mister Bush, certainly not to a person like Kargbo. And you are presumptuous to think I will let you do it. You know, I really do believe you are a racist. Don't you, darling?" This last he said to his wife, a tan-skinned, sleepy-eyed, rather pudgy young woman.

She drew on her cigarette and blew the smoke off to the side.

"People who know me do not call me a racist, sir."

"Well, I think you are a racist, and I am damned tired of it. It is time you looked very closely at yourself, at your behavior, at your—at your—at your—your assumptions about Africans. Yes—that's it exactly. Those assumptions. That is the racism, those assumptions that Africans will do this or that. I won't have you assuming things in my Embassy."

Max reddened. "Mister Ambassador, it is my job to report on local conditions. It is what I am paid to do. And I do it pretty well—my views are quite respectfully received at State, as well as in the government of Sierra Leone. And that—"

"Don't you dare lecture me, Mister Bush. That's another aspect of your racism that I am tired of."

Max's voice quivered. "Sir, it is clear that we have reached a point where communication between us is impossible. My effectiveness depends on the freedom to—"

"*You* have the communication problem, Mister Bush. I will not release you, if that's what you're leading up to. If you go, you will resign and go without my approval. By the way, who is that young man with the long hair and the crutches that just went by here? I've seen him with you a number of times. Is that the American that Beachley talked about?"

"Yes."

"What's his name again?"

"Robert Kelley."

"Glad it's the British that've got him, not us. Can't imagine what they see in him. Disreputable fellow. You'd do yourself a favor if you did not associate yourself with him. He certainly can't do your career any good."

"Robert! You're *here*! But why? What's happened? Come in, come in."

Robert entered the tiny room, a case of Star Beer under one arm. The air was thick with kerosene fumes and the smoke of mosquito coils.

"What's happened?" Daniel asked. "You're not leaving Salone?"

"I brought some beer," Robert said. "Hello, Prince."

Prince, who had been asleep on his mat in a darkened corner, sat up. He did not return the greeting.

Daniel took the beer. "I don't understand—tell me what has happened, Robert. You're staying? Zimi is keeping Bonthe after all?"

"Kevin asked me to stay."

"But—that's wonderful, Robert! What wonderful news! It's what you wanted all along, staying at Bonthe—"

Robert had hoped Prince would not be present: he would make it difficult. "Fisheries stuff," Robert said evasively.

"At Bonthe, then," Daniel said, and called past Robert. "Eileen! Robert is back. He has brought us a gift of Star Beer. Bring something to open the bottles."

"Taking a black man's job," Prince said. "Like every other white man in Africa."

Daniel turned to his brother. "Do not begin that with our friend."

"Whose friend? He is a white man."

"Do not start that," Daniel said.

111

Eileen came into the room with a naked baby on her hip. She went to Robert and offered her cheek. "I'll get some rice," she said.

"I've already eaten."

"So you are staying?" Eileen asked.

"Yes."

"To protect the white man's rutile and gold and diamonds and their coffee and their palm oil and their iron ore—from the black savages who want to steal it."

"He has been reading the *Green Book*," Eileen said, speaking of Prince as if he was not in the room.

Robert shrugged. "It's okay."

"O-kay! The white man permits me to speak. You see, Daniel?" Prince slipped his feet into his halfbacks and jerked a T-shirt down over his shoulders and chest. He rose. "But I do not want to speak now. I want to leave this room because it smells of death." He brushed past Robert and Daniel and went out the door.

"I'm sorry," Daniel said.

"It's okay."

"He has changed so much," Daniel said. "He is obsessed with that *Green Book* and those foolish magazines—all he does is lay about and read and complain and when I cannot stand it anymore and send him away he goes off and talks to soldiers about revolution. They arrested him two weeks ago, and threatened to beat him, but even that has not—" Daniel stopped. "Robert, he needs a job, that is all he needs, that would change everything. Robert, can't you talk to the Peace Corps Director again—"

"Daniel, we've been down that road. I have no influence with the PCD. Prince has had two chances, there's no way they'll hire him again."

Daniel dragged a chair away from the table. "Still— there has to be—but this is not the time for that. Sit, Robert, and tell me how it happened."

Robert told him about his meeting with Kevin. When the gist of it became clear to Daniel, he interrupted incredulously. "You mean it's *my* project? Zimi is taking *my* project?"

Robert nodded.

Daniel leaped to his feet. "My God, Robert, you cannot imagine—you cannot know—oh, what wonderful news! Eileen! Come here! Robert and I are to work together! We will work together, won't we, Robert? Eileen, Zimi is taking control of my project! Oh, Robert, I could not have dreamed anything better than this." He went to the bedroom door. "Eileen, didn't you hear?"

She appeared in the doorway, the baby on her hip. "Yes, I heard. And yes, it is wonderful."

He began pacing. "First we must do a proper frame survey. I tried it once, you know, but it was impossible. No transport, no tools—but it doesn't matter now, Zimi will give us lorries, we will have money—and after the survey we will select villages for a true pilot program—like the one I told you about—I think we must have two villages—" He stopped and looked at Robert. "Do you think Mister Beachley will commit resources for three?" He continued pacing. "Three would be much better—if we could do three, for one year, it would be perfect—but of course we must conduct a proper frame survey to be sure. I have in mind several farmers who will be very good—one is a village headman who—"

He paced and talked. Eileen came back with opened bottles of beer. Robert drank and listened. After a while Daniel stopped pacing. "Robert, I thought the project was dead. A wife, two children, Prince—we would have starved."

Robert had been waiting for Daniel to run down so he could say the rest of it, the part that Daniel had not let him say. This seemed as good a time as any to get it out in the open. "Kevin's offering you a job as my counterpart," he said quietly.

Daniel's laugh became a smile. "Ah—so we will share authority."

"Well—not in the strictest sense. I will be responsible for the program and you—"

"You? But you are not a biologist. You have no experience in aquaculture, your work has been with marine fisheries. That has no relevance to growing fish in *ponds*." He added plaintively: "It is *my* project, I created it."

"We want you to be my counterpart. We will do things together."

Daniel studied the floor. "We will talk to Mister Beachley about this matter. It is clear that he does not understand. I think we must arrange for joint authority." He raised his eyes and tried to smile. "But that is for tomorrow. Today we will celebrate. My brother Robert is staying in Salone and we will work together."

He talked about his plans for the project, about the villages he wanted to bring into the program, the farmers he would work with, how many laborers he would hire. And again about how wonderful it was that he would be free of ministry control—Robert could not imagine, he said, how humiliating it was to plead like a beggar for a salary that was not even enough to buy a fifty-kilogram bag of rice. And to live with the knowledge that the thousands of English pounds his project brought into Salone ended in the pockets of ministers and vice-presidents, probably even the president himself. Now, for the first time since his university years he would have the resources to perform his duties, sheltered from that corruption. Of course his own productivity would be of singular importance, he told Robert as they sat in the smoky darkness slapping at mosquitoes and drinking beer, so naturally he would expect a lorry and driver, a suitable office with decent furniture, a typewriter, a secretary, materials for simple biological research—microscopes, metal trays, dissecting instruments, generator, lights, books, a computer like the ones in Zimi and at the Pujehun project—and money to cover his expenses. He must control supplies and equipment and the rice allocation of his African employees. That certainly. He knew only too well that the one who commanded the rice commanded loyalty. And as to loyalty—well, it was clear that he would have to control the hiring as well. His brother's experience as a Peace Corps administrator would make him valuable in that respect. He would hire Prince immediately, give him the job of assistant—

Robert lit a joint and handed it to Daniel, who sucked on it and rambled happily about the changes he would bring to his project while Robert drifted into fantasies of reunion with Marie.

When Robert went out to the doublecab an hour later he found Pa Bangura curled up on the back seat, snoring. He slipped behind the wheel, drove through the dark streets, following the brilliant flood of white light. The light revealed gloomy little mud houses set back from the road among trees that drooped with eerie whiteness. In the mirror he saw the bright glow of his own tail lights in thick billows of dust. Bats darted in and out of the light, foraging for insects.

Robert drove unhurriedly, savoring the night. He was pleased that it had been so easy, though it was clear that Daniel did not comprehend his loss of independence, nor the rigid accountability that Kevin would demand. But that understanding would come, and Daniel would accept those small oppressions as he had accepted the ministry's much greater oppressions. As he had accepted this night's humiliation.

He steered the doublecab through a traffic circle, turning right at the abandoned gas station, following the road for a mile, slowing gradually as it got rougher and rougher. And then he was at the end of the road. He stopped. The head lamps shone out into space, illuminating the tops of a dozen palm trees and the thatch roof of a hut. He turned and prodded Pa Bangura.

"Pa, wake up."

The old man yawned, stretched, and opened the door.

"Eight o'clock," Robert said.

"Yessah."

When Robert got back to the traffic circle he stopped. A swirl of following dust moved over the vehicle and into the headlight cones. He rummaged in the side pocket of his knapsack until he found the tin box, opened it, and found a roach in the loose jamba. He lit the roach, drove into the traffic circle, turned on the road to the Teacher's College.

He parked the doublecab in the yard, stepped over the snoring watchman and climbed the stairs and knocked on Kathleen's door.

A thin, feminine voice: "Who dey?"

"Robert."

There was a clatter of metal as the bolt slid back, then

the door swung open. "Robert! I heard you stayed—Jimmy Cox told me he saw you at the Marines' party."

"Why weren't you there?"

"I had malaria again." She stepped back and he entered. "Tell me what happened."

The air was heavy with the sandalwood scent of a smoldering mosquito coil. A candle fluttered on the table over a notebook and a pen. The corners of the room were dark. They sat at the table.

"Tell me about it."

He described the evening at Kevin's house.

"That's wonderful, Robert. You'll be working in Bo."

"Looks like it."

She rose and went to the cabinet. "Would you like some tea?"

"I brought you a case of Star Beer. I didn't know if you'd be alone, so I left it in the lorry—"

"Baba doesn't come any more. I found out he's got an African woman and a bunch of kids."

♈

Robert and Daniel made it to Freetown by noon the next day and found that Kevin had gone to lunch at the *Alliance Francais*. They found him at a table in the tiny thatch-covered yard and joined him. After lunch they went back to the Project office and upstairs to the meeting room where Kevin sat down behind a file folder that already rested at the head of the table. Daniel drew up a chair, opened his notebook, and tore out a sheet of paper, which he pushed across the table.

"My proposal," he said.

Kevin glanced at the paper. Daniel had written "8 requirements for my employment" across the top, and below that, eight numbered points. He had composed at least twenty versions of the document during the drive from Bo.

Kevin said that he had an offer that he hoped would address Mister Sulaiman's concerns. He told Daniel there would be no expense account, no lorry, no driver, no house,

116

no control of hiring or of rice allocation. As Robert's counterpart he would theoretically share authority with Robert, but he made it clear that Robert was in charge.

"I will increase your salary to 1900 leones. You will have one month of paid holiday, commencing after your first year. You will receive a per diem allowance of fifty leones, to be allocated when it is necessary that you spend nights away from Bo, for which you will obtain prior approval from Mister Kelley. You will have the privilege of buying one fifty-kilogram bag of rice from Zimi at the Project-subsidized price of 100 leones, and your family will of course have the full privilege of the Zimi Infirmary. And, as I said, you will have the use of a Honda and a monthly allocation of forty liters of petrol, which will be delivered to you in a twenty-liter rubber twice each month."

He pushed a piece of paper toward Daniel, clasped his hands together on the table and waited, his thin red hair plastered against his damp forehead, his face expressionless, his khaki shirt darkened by patches of sweat. Street sounds drifted in the open window.

Daniel looked at Kevin's paper for perhaps a minute, then picked up his "8 requirements for my employment" and began folding it. "How can my family live on one bag of rice?" he asked softly, his eyes on the paper he was folding.

"Salary and benefits are set by policy, Mister Sulaiman."

"My children cannot eat your policy."

"We are obliged to respect the policy of your government. All of our Sierra Leonean staff get less than that. We have no choice in this matter."

For a time there was no sound but the distant murmur of voices and the scrape and shuffle and clatter of activity in the street. Daniel continued folding the paper until it was a very small rectangle of white.

"How can we—we must have a lorry to do our work—"

"There will be no lorry, Mister Sulaiman."

"But how are we to carry fertilizer, tools, the fish tanks?"

"When you need to transport supplies, ZDP will provide transport."

Daniel smiled ruefully.

"You have the offer, Mister Sulaiman."

"And so I must tell you now if I accept your offer to let me become an employee in my own project?"

"No, Mister Sulaiman, you can take as much time as you like."

"It is rice that I need, not time."

Kevin made no response.

"If not the bone, nothing," Daniel said, still toying with the piece of paper.

Kevin opened the file folder. He withdrew two sheets of paper and slid them across the table to Daniel.

Daniel glanced at the contract, signed both copies and slid them back across the table to Kevin.

"Now, the matter of the frame survey—you have discussed it?"

"Yes," Robert said.

"Have you worked out a plan?"

"Not in detail."

"I want the two of you to sit together and work out a plan for it. Gunter told me he would like to participate. If you can use him, I think it's a good idea. He knows the area." He looked at Robert, then at Daniel. "Is there anything else to settle today? No? Then let us meet again tomorrow at four o'clock. At that time I will expect to see a survey plan."

Robert's eyebrows went up. "We agreed that I could have some time off—and I haven't even signed my contract."

"You're right—I'd forgotten about your contract. We must take care of that. Let me get your file."

"I've made plans to go to Mali," Robert said.

"There's no way you can make it to Mali on that leg."

"What about my expenses?" Daniel said.

"I will give you 150 leones right now," Kevin said, rising. "Come to my office and I'll give you the money."

"Wait a minute," Robert protested. "We need to settle this business about when I'm to start."

Kevin was already heading for the stairs. "What d'you mean?" he called over his shoulder. "You've already started. You're on the payroll and you got your Honda days ago."

"It's not possible," Robert said, but Kevin was already clumping down the stairs.

♈

The Leb came out on the porch with a beer in each hand. He gave one to the young woman sitting on the concrete rail. She smiled up at him and said something. He was a sturdy thickset fellow with wavy black hair, white pants and shirt, white shoes. His laugh echoed across the street. The woman looked like Peace Corps. Sun-blond hair. Long full skirt, faded, as if from many hand washings. Suitable for motorcycle travel, that skirt. And a blouse that showed the shape of her breasts very nicely. Right at home there on the porch of the City Hotel in the company of a West African Leb. Robert didn't recognize her—she hadn't been at the Marine's party. Three years ago he would have known immediately if she was Peace Corps, probably even known her name and village.

A lorry came bouncing down Charlotte Street, its jerky head lamps sweeping like searchlights over locked and iron-gated doors and windows, illuminating the fungus-blackened walls that surrounded the blacktop yard of the City Hotel, then sweeping over a cluster of blacks loitering about the line of tables at the corner. The lorry hesitated at the corner, turned left, thundered off down Lightfoot Boston Street, bouncing its lights over dusty broken buildings.

Robert took one more hit on the joint, pinched the fire off into the tin ashtray. He held the smoke in his lungs for a few seconds before breathing it past window bars out into the night. He had tried for three hours to get through to Marie. Three hours of sitting in the smoky waiting room at SLET, watching others get up and go down the hall to a telephone booth. He had come back to the hotel feeling depressed and lonely. Needing this good friend, this dependable companion.

Dependable sometimes. If you had good in you mary-jane made you better; but if you had bad in you maryjane

119

made you worse. Pot *had* betrayed him, but seldom. Not many bad trips, really, considering the thousands of trips. He could think of only one that was noteworthy enough to remember: a flight to Dakar to meet Marie. He'd smelled the jamba and gone to the back of the plane and found a couple of Lebs laughing with the Nigerian flight attendant, and he'd asked for a hit, and one of the Lebs gave him the roach and the stewardess pointed to the john, and he went inside and lit up and then joined the Lebs talking to the stewardess, and the pot had hardly got working when the plane fell out from under them, throwing pillows and dirt and cigarette butts and people and beer cans up against the ceiling and there was the clatter of things banging, the grunt and thud of people hitting things, and then screams, and he'd been one of the screamers and didn't even know it until he was on the floor with one of the Lebs wiggling on top of him and realized he was still yelling. And even when it was over and the plane was flying straight and level again with the calm British-sounding voice on the intercom assuring them that everything was okay, nothing to worry about, and he'd gotten into his seat and strapped himself in; even then, five minutes after the event, the pot had exaggerated the residual fear to just this side of outright panic and he'd spent a quivery half hour holding on against the panic, wishing he was on the ground, wishing he was straight.

He realized that the pot was turning on him now, like then; magnifying the bad that was stewing inside him, focusing on the fear that he had killed the good thing that was Marie's love. He shouldn't have smoked the joint, not while he was feeling so miserable about her. Why wouldn't she answer his fucking calls? He thought of the promise he had made to his brother; that he would call his father. It was something to do, and while he was there he could try Marie one more time. He turned away from the window and got his knapsack and helmet and blew the candle out and locked the door and limped down the dark staircase behind his flashlight.

♈

120

"So you're not coming, eh?" The voice vivid and jocular, like Robert remembered it.

"Kevin offered me another job."

"So your brother told me. Was it a good offer?"

"Nearly double what I was making."

"Doesn't sound that great to me."

"It's relative, Dad."

"I suppose. Listen, don't pay any attention to your brother. He doesn't speak for me."

Robert waited; when his father did not amplify, he asked, "What do you mean?"

Impatiently, like Robert expected: "I mean don't pay any attention to him. He doesn't speak for me."

"I'm not following you, Dad."

"Your brother is a bit fucked up right now. Feeling put-upon. Thinks he works too hard, thinks he's missing life. Mid-life crisis. The example you provide isn't helping."

"What can I say? That I will be happy to make myself miserable so my brother will have a more favorable example?"

"Don't wise-ass me. If you want to waste your life in Africa, it's your life. I'm just telling you what's going on. In case you might want to know."

"Okay. I know."

"And, wise-ass, if you'd come home for a visit last month like you said, you wouldn't have missed the best fly-fishing I ever saw—and you'll *never* see, as long as you're in Africa."

Flyfishing: for a few years the center of his life: the passion that would never diminish. And now he never thought about it. "Where?" he asked, because it was expected.

"The Selway. I never saw it so good. Flew in, like we did that time in seventy-eight."

"Seventy-seven."

"It was supposed to be a surprise. When you didn't show I just said fuck it, I'm going anyway, so I went alone."

Robert didn't bother pointing out that he had never promised he was coming home. Instead, he said, "We had snow on the last day—remember?"

"Fucking right I remember. I remember you throwing

121

that October caddis and taking a cut every third cast and wondering how you were doing it."

"Wasn't every third cast, Dad."

"Okay, every fourth cast. At the time I wasn't counting—at the time I was thinking we had a fifty-mile walk ahead of us, in snow, to get out of there. But it was bright sunny days this time. Cold at night, but bright warm days. Indian summer. Caught my first fish ten minutes after we landed. Didn't see another human for five days."

He realized the awful emptiness he had brought with him to the SLET office was gone, filled now with something good: the good that was the Selway trip with the snow coming down on that last morning, and the exhilarating knowledge that the snow and fifty miles of wilderness was between them and the crossroads town of Lowell, and the graceful looping of the line out through the slanting snow, and the big October caddis turning at the end of it and slapping down right in the seam in exactly the place he'd wanted it, knowing there had to be a cutthroat on the slack water side of the seam and sure enough a big dumb cut came up and casually sipped the orange-bellied caddis off the surface, showing only mouth, then shining dark back.

"Thought I was going to lose you to the rivers. When you were a teenager I thought you'd end up a flyfishing bum and you ended up a bum in Africa. Of all things. I can't believe I'm losing you to Africa. What the hell is holding you *there*?"

Silence for several seconds. He felt the good seeping out of him. "It's where I live."

"Wise-ass answer."

"No. It's where I live. It feels like I always lived here."

"Romantic bullshit. You went there to escape home, not to go home. Mid-life crisis. Only you had yours when you were thirty, unlike your brother, who's having his at forty. Jesus. What a pair to draw to. I never even *heard* of a mid-life crisis until I was too old for one."

"Doctor Kelley."

"What did you say, wise-ass?"

"I said Doctor Kelley, know-it-all wise-ass Doctor Kelley. You always knew it all."

"I don't need to listen to this crap from you. I got things to do."

"Fine. Go do your things."

"Goodbye, wise-ass."

Three tables were occupied: one by a fat American and his fat wife; one by Francesca and her husband, Carlo, and daughter, Delilah; the other by four boisterous Brits: sunburned men whose appraising eyes often slid over to Delilah. A white man and a black woman perched on stools at the bar. The man, slovenly shaggy, black bearded, round shouldered—and already drunk—sat leaning against the black woman and mumbling nonsense across the bar to Farrah, who ignored him.

Delilah was saying, "It stinks and the food is bad and there's nothing to do. Nothing. I *knew* it would be like this."

Carlo gazed at the black water of the bay, pretending that he did not understand.

"Except for you, of course—when men are around, you always have something to do." She began naming her other grievances, but it was clear she was just going through the motions.

The old man spoke to Francesca in Italian. "I think the food will be better here." He looked around approvingly. "It is apparent that this is a white man's establishment. Look, even the sand is smooth and clean. And the waiters have clean clothing. And I noticed that the tables and chairs are all wiped free of dust."

The young woman rolled her eyes. "We are marooned—maybe forever, who knows—and *he* thinks it is wonderful that the tables are not dusty."

Francesca ignored her daughter, who was still a child and therefore understood little of anything—except her own needs and appetites, of course; those she understood very well. And Carlo ignored his daughter also, mainly because he did not like her, had never liked her, and saw no reason to like her, but also because he just plain refused to relinquish the pleasant mood he had enjoyed since he woke from his nap a hour before—the only pleasure he'd experienced since the plane touched down at Lungi. Francesca buttered a piece of bread, placed it on her plate, cut it in two pieces, one of which she offered to him. He accepted, thanking her with a gentlemanly nod.

The waiter came with a plate of falafel. "Mistah Farrah de say, wid he compliment."

Francesca looked toward the bar, saw Farrah standing with crossed arms, looking at her.

Carlo shot a look at the bar, then at Francesca. His face clouded.

"How do you know *him*?" Delilah asked incredulously.

"*Chi `e lui?*" Carlo asked.

"*Il proprietario,*" she said.

"When were you here? You didn't say you came here."

That morning, to get away from her daughter and husband, she had taken her bag and gone for a walk. At the roundabout she had come to an open place that allowed her to view the entire bay, a pond of mirror-flat water, sandy-beached all around except at the rocky opening to the sea. She'd seen a low structure gleaming white under a canopy of coconut palms and mango trees a few hundred meters around the perimeter of the bay and had walked along the beach to reach it.

The restaurant had been deserted: stools up on the bar, sand raked smooth, cabinets behind the bar closed and locked. She'd found a folding chair leaning against the bar and took it to a shaded table and sat and opened her bag and got her diary and her book. She'd opened the diary and began writing.

"We're not open," he'd said, and she'd looked up at a big man in shorts and T-shirt standing in the shadowy passageway, a cigarette drooping from the center of his lips.

His T-shirt, which was stained with grease and food, rode up a little, exposing a patch of hairy belly. "What are you doing?" The cigarette bounced around when he spoke.

She'd told him she had seen the restaurant from across the bay and thought it was open.

"You can see it's closed."

She closed her diary and reached down for her bag.

"But you can stay if you want." He came out of the passage, walked across the sand to her table. "What are you writing? Are you a journalist?"

"No."

"Sometimes a journalist comes. Once a woman from Berlin. She lived with me for a month while she wrote her articles. And many came for the OAU meetings, and of course they came to see Momoh when the Old Pa picked him. They always come to Farrah's. They like it here."

She didn't say anything.

"So what are you are writing about?"

"Personal things. And things about Freetown—"

"Freetown is not interesting. How Salone *used* to be and how the jungle bunnies ruined it—that is interesting. That is what I tell the journalists to write."

"Jungle bunnies—?"

"Niggers. Jungle bunnies, niggers. Same thing."

"Ah—"

"Well—not exactly the same. The bad ones are niggers. They are the leaders. They eat the jungle bunnies, who are not bad, just lazy and stupid; they are the people. You can write that down."

"Is that what the whites say?"

"*I* say it. You can write in your book that *Farrah* says it. It's what I tell the journalists. But they never write it down."

"No, I mean—"

"I know what you mean. They never write about how the blacks kill and eat one another. But if I say the whites do the killing, they always write *that* down. It's a big lie, but it is today's lie, so they write it down. You are like the journalists. You won't write it down. But I could care fucking less. I am only making conversation."

"How do you know I won't?"

"You are white—and it is not the lie that whites are believing now."

"You don't believe it and you are white."

"I am Sierra Leonean. Born in Freetown, as was my father. But I can't talk any more, I have a job to do, which is to repair a gas oven that a stupid fucking jungle bunny spoiled."

He had gone back into the passage and a minute later a young black had come out with a warm Coke, which he'd put on the table in front of her. After that she'd written the things he said into her diary, and when she tired of writing, opened her book. From time to time she heard distant voices and things clinking and banging. Later she had gone to the open kitchen door and looked in. Only the young black was there, cleaning a big fish that was laid out on a table.

"That's why we came here tonight, isn't it," Delilah said. "Because you met that man here."

"We came here because I am weary of hearing you complain about the hotel."

"Oh, we came here for me. But it *is* quite convenient for you. Look, your new man is coming."

♈

A full moon had risen out of the mountains, lighting the terrain so well they could have driven without lights, simply followed the white ribbon of gravel. They crested the hill and headed down the seaward side past the Bintomani Hotel, toward Man-O-War Bay. Max talked all the way, complaining about a day spent trying to repair the damage caused by Neggie's Thanksgiving Day speech.

Robert wasn't listening. He was thinking about what he would say to Marie. He had driven out to Juba to kill time— he would not try to call again until after ten o'clock—and he had stopped to see Max, without really *wanting* to see him, intending to stay for only a few minutes. Max had talked him into going to Farrah's for a beer.

The driver turned the Cadillac into the graveled parking lot behind Farrah's, coasting to a stop beside a Land Rover. The parking lot was nearly empty. They walked through the passageway to the bar, which was lit by lanterns hanging from the thatch roof. Robert recognized the fat couple at the nearest table: a Methodist missionary and his wife. The missionary nodded at Robert, his mouth full and his jaw pumping. Robert returned his greeting and turned to the bar. Molai was opening a Star Beer and placing it in front of Hans. The black woman looked around Hans' shoulder at Robert. One cloudy eye looked off to the side.

"Hello Isatu, hello Hans," Robert said.

"Evening, Robert," she said. Hans grunted at his beer.

Robert climbed up on a stool, raised his left foot, removed the sandal, examined the bandage.

Molai snapped the caps off two bottles and put them on the bar.

"I want a cold beer," Max said. "This isn't cold."

"We no get cold beer, sah, we no get 'lectricity."

"No cold beers. Molai, we are witnessing it. The end of civilization."

"Yessah."

♈

The young waiter brought plates of food. Carlo, who sat with his chair turned away from the table, glanced disdainfully at the plate, then looked back at the black water. Francesca picked up her fork and looked down at the grilled barracuda and the chips and a few gray peas. Farrah lit another cigarette, blew smoke into the air over their heads.

Francesca tried the fish. "Delicious," she murmured.

"The fish is good, the rest is shit. Until the market has fresh vegetables everything but the fish comes out of tins."

Delilah made a face and shoved the plate away.

Farrah continued. "So, if you want to see a little of Freetown you can go with me to the bakery and the market. I go every morning."

"I know what you want, you're going to take my mother to some—" Delilah began, then stopped. Her voice became sweetly soft. "Mother, Robert is there at the bar. You remember Robert—the one you tried to pick up two days ago? Or was it yesterday?"

Francesca speared a piece of fish, stuck it in her mouth. Delilah pushed her chair back, but the legs had sunk into the sand. The chair fell over behind her. She stepped around it and walked past the Brits, who stopped talking and watched her pass their table.

"Robert, how nice to see you again," she called, so loudly that everyone looked at her. Everyone but her father, who faced the bay.

Robert saw the skirt and blouse swaying out of the darkness, looked beyond her, saw Farrah in the shadows turning in his chair, and across the table from him the woman from the beach baffa.

"I was hoping to meet you again," she said to Robert. "I enjoyed our conversation very much."

"My name is Max Bush."

She eyed Max for a second, then said, "I am Delilah Giuliani."

"Yes, you *are* delightful," Max said.

She looked pleased. "Delilah, not delightful."

"Delilah yes, but delightful—oh *yes!*"

"Max—calm down," Robert said.

"Sorry—I get carried away in the presence of beauty."

"May I join you? My mother and father are at the table with the owner and I do not want to sit with him. He is a disgusting man."

"I don't like him either," Max said, edging into the space between Robert and Delilah. "Molai, bring this lady a beer."

"Do you work with Robert?"

"No—I'm a diplomatist."

"Diploma*tist*? What the hell's *that*?" Robert said.

"A diplomat?" Delilah asked.

"Deputy Chief of Mission, American Embassy."

"Really!"

"Clerk," Robert said. "He gets a fancy title instead of money."

Max smiled modestly. "Robert is right. The only time I'm Ambassador is when the real Ambassador's gone. About half the time, I guess." He got a stool, which he planted in the sand. "You can sit here, beside me."

She saw her mother approaching, slipped back against the bar between Robert's shoulder and Hans' back. "No, I want to stand with my friend Robert." She slipped her arm over Robert's shoulder and moved her body against his.

Robert looked up at her, surprised. And then a hand shot past his nose, grabbed the girl's free arm. He caught a glimpse of Francesca's red face and bulging eyes and then there was grunting and cursing and Delilah was yelling right in his ear. The stool tilted and before he could recover, Robert was on his face in the sand, with the girl, now screaming, on top of him. And then *he* was screaming: "*My foot! Get the fuck off my fucking foot!*"

♈

Robert and Delilah heard Max curse. They were waist deep in the low surf, and he was trying to kiss her, and she was—not quite, but almost—letting him. They drew apart and watched Max crawl out of the water, fight his way to his feet, sway for a moment, then lurch—an absurd naked whiteness ghosting drunkenly over white sand—up the beach toward the Cadillac, which gleamed in the moonlight beneath a pair of coconut palms at the road edge. They heard him shout something at Alimamy, who got out of the car and opened the door. Max pushed Alimamy out of the way and leaned into the car and came out with an arm load of clothing, which he threw up into the air, then reached into the car again and with his arms raked clothes and shoes and knapsack out onto the sand. Then—still bare-assed—he climbed onto the backseat and slammed the door.

The driver looked down at the pile of clothing and shoes and then at Robert and Delilah, both of whom now suspected Max's intent and were wading out of the water. Alimamy heard his master bellow something unintelligible, whereupon he walked with slow dignity around the car and got in. By then Robert was limping up the beach as fast as he could move. The car lurched up onto the blacktop and accelerated away.

"Where is he going?" she asked anxiously.

With his arms full of clothes Robert straightened and

looked at her. He had not seen much of her when they undressed. They had done it rapidly—she with embarrassed haste—and he had only glimpsed the triangular whiteness of her back and the dancing globes of her buttocks as she ran into the water. Now, standing in moonlight so bright you had to squint, mysteries only hinted at were revealed: the small dark nipples that seemed to demand the touch of fingers, a breathtaking complexity of curve where belly and hip and thigh came together at that sweeping shadowy delta—the only unrevealed place—and the surprising muscularity of her swimmer's rounded belly above that void, and the pucker lines around the indent of her navel, and— and his unrepentant dick awoke to its unrepentant purpose and began to prepare itself. He dropped the clothing in a heap and approached her and her worried look changed immediately to anger and she pushed him away.

She was right. And his dick knew it. The three of them were three miles from the hotels and two miles from Max's house; on a deserted beach, which they both knew was enemy territory at night. He bent over the pile of clothing and began sorting through it while she stood with her arms crossed over her breasts and gazed uneasily across the road into the black tangle of the mangroves. They dressed and found that they had clothing left over; Max had thrown his own clothing out of the car with theirs.

She wanted to go north along the beach, to the hotels. He said no, he wanted his motorcycle, and began limping southward along the road edge. She followed, pleading.

He struggled along in clumsy sidewise steps. The pain and the warm squishiness soon forced him to stop and deal with his foot. He sat in the sand and with his knife he cut away the bandage, which was black with blood, then cut the back out of Max's shirt and tore it into strips, which he wrapped round his foot.

They followed the road away from the beach, out of the moonlight into the darkness beneath the mango and breadfruit trees lining the road. A dog barked in the distance, another took it up, and another, and then a dozen dogs were exchanging volleys that echoed across the valley. Beyond the trees on both sides of the road the walled expatriate compounds were dark and quiet. An hour and a half later they stood at the iron gate before Max's house. Tinka came yawning and stretching out of the tiny guard shack, as if it was the most natural thing in the world for Robert to limp bloody-footed up the driveway in the early morning with a young woman, looking for his motorcycle. He opened the gate and watched as Robert got the motorcycle started and drove it out onto the road. He accelerated and she grabbed his waist.

The motorcycle headlamp lit the street for blocks. Here and there the yellow of a candle flickered in a window or a flashlight beam jerked about in the distance. They passed the Chinese restaurant, with its wide, long porch, which in the early evening was always warmly lit by candles inside a multitude of paper lanterns, and then the houses along the road became more closely crowded together, and they were in Congo Town. Then they came to the curve where Wilkerson Road forked, the left road a gravelly track curving down the hill to the Cockle Bay Bridge and the Cape, where the girl's mother waited. Robert slowed and entered the curve, his headlamp sweeping over the ruin of a petrol station on one side of the gravel road. He steered across the road and into a parking lot. A hand-painted sign on the wall identified the building as the Kit Kat Klub. He pushed the kickstand down.

"Get off," he said over his shoulder. "We're gonna have a beer."

She tightened her arms around his waist. "I don't want a beer, I want to go back to my hotel. Please, Robert, please."

"It's that way," he said, pointing down the gravel road. "A couple of miles." He waited for her to get off. When she didn't move, he looked over his shoulder. "Get off."

She followed him inside. Plank tables and benches surrounded a concrete dance floor, and booths lined three walls. Most of the tables and booths were empty. On every patch of wall, posters showed light-skinned Africans with white features leaning on Volvos and Porches, laughing and smoking Marlboro, Players, and Galois, and drinking Guinness and Becks and St. Pauli. Kerosene fumes stung the eye. A black man sat on a stool in the darkness behind the bar, watching them.

Robert limped across the dance floor and leaned on the bar.

"Star Beer," Robert said.

"Stah done finish."

"You get Beck's?"

"No."

"Guinness?"

"No, beer done finish."

"I don't want anything," Delilah said. "Let's go."

"Sassman?" Robert said.

The black man nodded.

"Sassman and Coke."

The barman brought a small plastic bottle of the cheap local gin and a bottle of Coca Cola and a glass.

Robert put a packet of two-leone notes on the bar. The barman picked up the packet and began counting them.

Robert poured the clear liquor into the glass, then topped it off with Coke. He stirred it with his finger and raised the glass.

"How long are we going to stay," Delilah whispered nervously.

"Until he closes, I suppose."

"Oh-h-h—please, Robert, after you have your drink, take me to the hotel. You can come back after that."

"If you start crying I'll leave you here."

"I'm not crying, I just want to go to my hotel."

"First you want to go to *my* hotel, then you want to go to yours." Robert turned and spoke to the barman: "Na German man?" He pointed to the corner booth.

The barman nodded.

"Hans," Robert said to Delilah. "Those people in the corner booth. It's Hans and Isatu. Old friends from Bo. Hans used to work for Gunter, but poor Hans is a drunk, so Gunter fired him. Sad story."

"I was only *talking* about going to your hotel, I didn't really mean it. I want to go to *my* hotel. Please Robert—"

"I think we ought to say hello to Hans and Isatu."

"Robert, I don't want—"

133

"Of course you do, they're old friends." He was already limping across the concrete dance floor, which was littered with cigarette butts and gritty with sand. She hurried behind.

Isatu watched them approach. "Hello, Robert," she called. Hans, his back to Robert, remained hunched over his beer.

Robert nodded and slid into the booth beside her.

"Move, let her sit," Isatu said to Hans.

Hans managed to look annoyed as he pushed his beer over and moved behind it.

"You should not drink dat Sassman," Isatu said to Robert. "Make you craze."

"Bread is better," Hans rumbled, not looking up. "Liquid bread." He raised the bottle of beer to show Robert, then banged it down on the table.

Robert looked at Delilah. "Sit down."

"How long are we going to stay?" she quavered, sitting on Hans' side, as close to the edge as possible.

"What is your name?" Isatu asked.

Delilah told her.

Isatu nodded, smiling. "Bible name, notoso?"

Delilah smiled uneasily.

"You like Salone?"

"It's very—umm, I came with my mother and father—and—"

"And she wants to go back to her mother," Robert said. "But I am thinking that maybe I should take her before I take her—if you get my drift."

Isatu frowned at Robert. "You should not talk so."

"I can't help it, Sassman makes you crazy."

"You do not talk like Robert," Isatu said. "You should not drink dat Sassman."

Hans looked up from his beer, grinning lopsidedly. "Ve seen her. She vas at Farrah's tonight wis her new American." His eyes moved slyly toward Robert. "A gold miner. Very rich."

Robert poured Sassman into his glass, splashed a little Coke over it, stirred it with his finger, raised the glass and drank.

Hans grinned triumphantly down at his bottle, his black hair falling over his eyes.

Robert glanced at Isatu.

"He is talking about Victoria," Isatu said. "The sister of Josephine Garrison—the friend of your friend Mister Bush. She talked about you and him."

"Oh. Right. Didn't remember her name."

Hans snorted derisively. "She hass clap, and now I sink you haf clap, too." He slapped the table and laughed uproariously.

Isatu shook her head. "He is confused."

"She says you luf her, and dat she gif you clap and now she gif ze new American clap. I sink she likes Americans."

"It is not true, Robert, she was drunk and making a joke."

Hans grinned at his bottle while Robert toyed with his drink and Isatu glared at Hans, and Delilah stared at Robert. Abruptly Robert drained his glass and rose.

"C'mon," he said. "I'm taking you home to mamma." He limped across the dance floor toward the door, calling behind him, "See you around, Isatu."

Delilah scurried after him.

WHAM! WHAM! WHAM! WHAM! WHAM! WHAM! WHAM! WHAM!

Robert cranked his eyes open. Slanting yellow light flooded the room. Cheerful light and soft air reminiscent of trees and damp earth and baking bread, a cool pungency ever so faintly scented by the open sewers. Morning air, on the cusp of cool and warm, flowing clean off the mountain—and yet he didn't even notice the sweetness of it. Nor did the racket that woke him hold his attention for very long.

As he came half awake fragments of memory appeared, coalescing to image: that was him leaning over the gray mattress in the fluttery light of a candle; that was her rattling the bed springs as she fell back, her mouth slack, her conked hair sticking out in all directions. That was him, peeling her naked, dragging her up on the bed, stripping off his shorts and shirt and slipping under the netting, and screwing her while she snored. He groaned aloud. He wanted to remember *not* fucking her, not *fucking* her.

But there was something surreal about that swirl of image; it did not *seem* like memory. Could it be hallucination? The fabrication of a fevered brain? Or bits of dream? It *could* be dream—it seemed more like dream than reality. But there was no consolation in that, for experience often feeds dream; sometimes one relives reality in dream.

WHAM! WHAM! WHAM! WHAM! WHAM!

He looked at his arm to find the time and found instead that he'd lost his watch. He studied the sunlight slanting in the window, knew he still had time to sleep, wondered if the shade-tree mechanic might stop; and after another dozen metallic explosions decided that the banging was long-term, not short-term. He pushed the netting out of the way, got his crutches, hopped to the window.

It was a brown four-door Datsun. A rattletrap taxi with no trunk lid, showing wounds everywhere: rusty gouges and disfiguring dents painted over with religious slogans imploring God to forgive sinners, exulting in the flames God was preparing for sinners, blaming God for the world's ugliness. *Nar God*: God's will: it's on you, God. The front end of the Datsun was up on blocks. A pair of black legs stuck out from under it.

♈

He got a bean sandwich from Mrs. Gooding and ate it while he sat on the porch. When he finished he took the rag she offered and wiped the red palm oil off his hands and chin, and watched the old watchman roll his motorcycle out of the hall and down the two stairs to the street. He drove the half dozen blocks to the office, parked the Honda and crutched his way up the stairs to the glass door and pushed it open.

"Who's that?" Kevin's voice came from the back room. There was a rattle of cooking pans.

"It's me, Robert."

Some more rattling, then Kevin appeared in the doorway, wiping his wet hands on a cloth. "What are you doing here? It's only seven."

"Couldn't sleep."

Kevin watched Robert limp across the floor to the chair beside Mrs. Kruma's desk.

"You look terrible."

"I'm okay. You making coffee?"

"Yes—and I've got bread and cheese and jam."

Kevin disappeared into the back room. His voice came over the rattle of dishes: "Maybe we should put this off for a few days. Doesn't seem like a smart thing right now, what with your foot done in like it is."

137

"No, I'm all right."

More clatter, then Kevin appeared with a tray, which he placed on the desk near Robert. He got another chair, dragged it to the desk, and sat.

"Here, let me cut you some bread. And some of this excellent stilton. Or maybe you prefer this frog cheese—some like this soft stuff, but not me, I like it big and demanding. Stilton's just the thing over Rachel's raspberry jam and a slice of bread. What d'you think? Ought we call Gunter and Rex and Alexander and tell 'em it's off for a few days? Won't hurt a thing, you know. We can do it in a couple of weeks, might even be better to wait until the dry season's full upon us."

"It doesn't make any difference to my foot whether it's in Pujehun or Freetown. Pa Bangura's doing the driving."

In the end, Kevin insisted that Robert get Mike Martino's okay before leaving, so at nine o'clock they drove off to the American Embassy, found that it was clinic day at the Peace Corps office and that Martino had already gone there. Kevin left Robert, telling him he'd return in an hour.

"So, the fellow gets a dose of clap to liven things up. As if this isn't enough medical excitement." Martino was removing the blood-stiffened bandage. "But what the hell, a dose of clap's easy, we can deal with that when we deal with this. Two for the price of one." He dropped Robert's foot, got up from his stool, went across the room, and returned with a hand mirror. "I want you to see this." He sat on the stool and lifted Robert's leg and held the mirror so that Robert could see the cut. "Pretty, isn't it. The way the flesh is pushed out? Like it's trying to turn you inside-out. That's not proud flesh, my friend—no healing going on in there. That lovely smell—maybe you thought it was a B.O.? Well, it wasn't. The bad guys are winning. That's *rot* you smell. If you had gangrene that's what you'd smell like, only worse." He put the mirror aside. "I wonder—what does it take to get your attention? To make you understand? Would amputation make you understand?" He manipulated the wound with his fingers. "I can't suture this. It's like trying to sew hamburger. I'll say it one more time, in case I finally got your attention: you gotta keep this foot clean. Do you understand?" He glared at Robert until Robert muttered, "Yeah." Then he made Robert limp over to the sink where he lifted the wounded foot to the edge of the porcelain bowl and cut the old sutures out.

When the brush touched the raw flesh Robert went pale. He closed his eyes, leaned into the crutches; held on against the pain, now awake and caroming like a cannon ball through his chest and head. He released not a murmur, emitted not a whimper, nor a grunt; forced himself—as he went light-headed, then nauseous—to breathe in-one out-two, in-one out-two; concentrated on the breathing; refused to even hint how much he wanted the percodan high or the morphine oblivion that he knew Martino possessed. And then he realized Martino was finished, that he had stopped scrubbing and was patting the foot dry and wrapping it in a towel. He pointed and Robert dazedly crutched himself back and fell into the chair, thrusting his hands under his arms so that Martino would not see the shaking, biting his lower lip against the pain still rocketing up and down his leg.

Martino smeared the wound with antiseptic salve and rebandaged the foot. Then he went back to the counter, unlocked the top drawer, pulled out a brown bottle, filled a vial with tablets, then got another bottle and filled the second vial. He wrote something on a pair of labels, glued them to the vials and brought them to Robert. "Come back in a week and we'll try suturing it again." He looked closely at Robert's eyes. "Are you okay?"

"Yes."

"You look like shit. You're not driving that suicide machine, are you?"

Robert shook his head. His mouth, which had been dry, was getting watery now, and his stomach jerked and shuddered.

"You planning on driving it today?"

Robert shook his head again. Sweat dampened his forehead. He wondered if he could get outside before he puked.

"I'm gonna give you a shot of morphine and some penicillin and it's gonna—Robert, are you hearing me?"

Robert nodded.

"It's gonna wipe you out—if you drive that bike you'll kill yourself."

Robert belched, but it didn't help. The rumbling intensified.

"Did you hear me? Are you driving that—"

"I'm not driving," Robert croaked irritably. "Kevin's picking me up."

"Taking you home?"

Robert nodded.

"Good. I want you in bed."

Martino rose and went to the counter and prepared two injections. He gave the morphine first, then the penicillin. Robert made his way out of the office and through a waiting room full of just-out-of-training PCVs, come to get their condoms; who watched with big sober eyes as he hobbled over the tile floor and started down the spiral of stairs. He fought the nausea, hoping he would make it past the receptionist's desk to the door before he puked the bean sandwich and the stilton cheese.

Robert was leaning back against the cotton tree in front of the Peace Corps office, the crutches under his arms, when Pa Bangura pulled up. He climbed laboriously up on the back seat with Kevin, who studied his ashen face as the doublecab moved off.

"You look terrible. You sick?"

"I'm fine."

"What'd he do?"

"Changed the bandage, gave me a shot. No big deal."

"What'd he say about traveling? I don't like the way you look."

"Traveling's no problem."

"What'd he say?"

"That I have to stay off it, that's all."

"Does Martino know—"

"Jesus, Kevin, I'm not *marching* to Pujehun. I won't even drive. I'll be sitting on my ass. Which is exactly what I'd be doing here."

Kevin looked doubtful.

Robert stared straight ahead, determined that they would proceed with the survey. He *had* to get to Mali and

140

talk to Marie, and he couldn't go until they finished the survey.

♈

Morphine and exhaustion: an irresistible sleeping potion. Robert sat beside Mrs. Kruma's desk, wanting sleep and fighting it, nodding as she rattled on about her daughter's wedding, to which—he dimly perceived—she was inviting him as an honored guest, with broad hints that her daughter wanted a radio that would receive the BBC.

Through waves of drowsiness he pretended that he knew what was going on. He nodded knowingly—and didn't have any idea what Kevin was talking about—when Kevin told him he was sending Pa Bangura back to the compound at Juba Hill for a couple of extra rubbers of petrol; and sat rigidly upright (at least *he* thought he was rigidly upright) while Kevin read him the inventory of supplies they would take—petrol, spare tires, pump and patch kit, tools, first aid kit, a briefcase full of leone notes, food and water. Then Kevin was talking about a plan change proposed by Alexander. Daniel said irritably that it was nonsense, Alexander was simply making trouble. Kevin agreed, but said it was nonetheless important that Alexander be part of the survey—the survey area was too close to Bonthe to exclude him. If a victory was his price—well, it was a harmless victory and they could afford it. When Kevin looked at Robert for agreement, he broke into a grin. "You don't have the foggiest what we're talking about, do you? You look drunk."

Robert mumbled, "What d'you think I ought to look like?" and his eyes thudded shut, his head fell forward, and he caught himself as he began to slide off the chair.

Kevin rolled his eyes over at Daniel: "He's not going anywhere."

"Yes I am," Robert murmured at his lap. "I'm gonna see Marie." And then he was snoring.

♈

Gunter's voice was fuzzy and broken by static. "How's Robert?"

"He's better," Kevin answered. "Mike's got him so doped up he can't get out of bed."

The crackly voice came strong, then faded, the German accent recognizable even through the static: "When will he be ready?"

"I'm guessing a week. Is that going to be a problem?"

"It's no problem on this end."

"Gunter, thanks for putting up with our fits and starts and for helping Daniel get this thing organized. Know it's a damned nuisance."

"I did nothing. Daniel and Rex did it all."

"I have someone here who wants to say hello." Kevin held the microphone out toward the young woman.

She took the mike and pushed the talk button. "Hello Gunter, this is Marie."

"Marie! How did you get to Freetown?"

"Motorcycle. They told me Lungi was closed, so I came by motorcycle."

Gunter's incredulity came through the static: "From *Bamako*?"

♈

Kevin looked up at the waiter, handed him the menu. "The lady will have the shrimp salad and I'll have the ham sandwich. And bring us some bottled water."

The young man went to the open window gave the order to the cook, then got a bottle of water from the cooler and returned to the table.

"And so Bonthe ended as a big disappointment," Kevin was saying. "Robert was very angry about it, and of course he had a right to his anger—he put a lot of himself into the station. I offered him the new position as soon as he returned to Freetown. At first he was spoiling for a fight, but in the end he saw the possibilities of the project and we came together. Which brings us to the present moment—why you're here. To take him away from me, I'm guessing."

"Yes."

Kevin nodded, looked down at the glass of water. Condensation was beading up and running down the side. He picked the glass up, drank, refilled it.

"What's Robert saying?" he asked.

"About that? Oh, he's still too confused. Still trying to get it in his head I'm actually here. He wakes up thinking he's dreaming it."

"Hate to lose him. He's a good one. Bit of an eccentric, and too much of an outlaw, though I have to say there's more good than bad in that. The thing he's got going for him is he gets things *done*. That is the best talent a man can have, you know, getting things done. Africa wrings that talent out of most of us. But not Robert. Hate to lose him."

A pair of young white women came out of the dining room to the thatch-shaded dining patio. They had the same weathered, young look that Marie had—like they worked in the sun—and they were dressed much like Marie: loose blouses and long full skirts that were suitable for motorcycle travel, the fabric bleached out by the sun and brutalized by many hand-washings. They took a table nearby and the waiter came to them.

"You've never told me exactly what you do," Kevin said. "Except of course that you're in women's programs."

"Yes, I did. That first day, in the baffa."

"Umm."

"But I'll tell you again: rural market development and health infrastructure."

"I remember. For how long?"

"Two years, in Mopti."

"What is your training? Peace Corps? University?"

"Why are you asking me this?"

"Professional interest. A recruiter's curiosity. I have been moving toward consolidation of our women's programs under single leadership. Rachel's been urging me in that direction, and I must say the times do call for it."

"Kevin, you don't know a thing about me."

"That's why I am talking to you—to learn about you. And you are wrong, I *do* know important things about you."

"I am not—"

"I know you just ended a remarkable three-day motorcycle journey, alone, through Mali and Guinea and Sierra Leone. There's a lot of information about you in that fact."

She smiled. "Kevin, do I smell bullshit?"

Soberly: "I don't think so. There are no cattle in Salone. Tsetse flies and sleeping sickness, you know."

"This conversation is about Robert, not me. I'm not interested in some job you create to induce me stay and keep Robert happy."

"That would be unethical. I would not do it."

"I already have a job. A good one." A pause. "You're gonna try to fuck it up, aren't you."

"Pardon?"

"Robert and me."

"I would not do that, either."

♈

"My foot is not even involved."

"Mike wouldn't like this."

"That's okay, he's not invited."

"You shouldn't be doing this, you're not ready yet."

"Not ready? Gimme your hand, I'll show you some ready. I feel great. Look, I promise to keep my foot out of the way—and completely still. You can get on top. Take your skirt off."

"You didn't keep it still this morning. You were all over the bed."

"It was the first time in three months."

"With me."

His expression sobered, but his gaze did not leave her face.

"You talked about Aminata. Who is she—some titi at Bonthe?"

He nodded. She touched his cheek with the back of her fingers, the message of her touch at odds with her words.

"What's the deal?"

"My housekeeper."

"That's not what it sounded like."

"Take off your skirt—please."

"Mike's upstairs. He might come down."

144

"He knows you're here, he won't come down."

"This is his hospital, not your bedroom." Behind her were three hospital beds and locked cabinets filled with medicines and medical instruments.

He grasped one of her hands and placed it at his crotch. She pulled her hand away. "We need to talk about Aminata."

He took her hand, placed it once again on the sheet at his crotch. "We need to make love."

She pulled the sheet down to his feet. "Lift your ass," she said. He obliged and she pulled his underwear down to the bulky white dressing on his foot. "What if he comes down the stairs while I'm doing this?"

"Oh, wow—oh!"

She raised her head and began unbuttoning her blouse. "I think I want you in me."

"I *was* in you."

"In the other end of me."

"I'll do both. And then afterwards I'll throw in a blow job for you. How's that sound? Is it a deal? Now be a good girl and put it back in your mouth."

As he talked he watched her push her skirt and panties down to her ankles, unclasp and drop her bra.

She climbed up on the bed, positioned herself astraddle his hips, holding herself high on her knees so he could get his hand between her legs. Looking down lazy-eyed: "What if Mike comes downstairs?"

"I don't care if he does, he's not getting any."

She lifted her chin, closed her eyes, concentrated on his hands.

♈

She turned the bike east. The road followed the thinly-treed ridge line toward the south flank of Leicester Peak. He shouted something over her shoulder, but all she heard was "Hill Station—colonials—malaria—" He pointed at a pair of two-story buildings built on stilts, which shared the shade of a pair of towering breadfruit trees. For a half-mile the road on either side was bordered by high-walled compounds with two- and three-story houses guarded by iron gates and uniformed Africans. The road meandered in and out of the forest, rising and falling over rolling swells of rocky earth that rose higher and higher toward the mountain pass along the south flank of Leicester Peak, where the blacktop would begin a long switchback descent through rain forest to the plain near the ancient slave holding compound at the Bunce River delta and the trading village of Waterloo. There it would join the Freetown-Bo road.

The air was cooler than in Freetown, and drier: soothing air that stroked her arms and face, grabbed and billowed her skirt. They were as high now as most of the peaks of the peninsula range, in a verdant, lush terrain of brush and elephant grass and locust, mango, breadfruit, guava, pawpaw, and tamerind trees, in air that was rainy season clear. With no people about, none at all. All were down there in that termite mound of a place.

The road was rising up against the southern flank of Leicester Peak when Marie slowed the bike, turned off the main road onto a single lane of blacktop that ran between six-foot walls of elephant grass for a quarter-mile, then began its spiraling ascent of the mountain. She downshifted and turned the throttle ring. The bike leaped up the narrow, steep road. After a long time the road leveled abruptly and widened, the raw red earth and broken rock of the road cut retreating to grass and brush. They coasted past the broken gate of a collapsed fence, from which the wire had been stripped, and into the big blacktopped yard that occupied the top of the mountain. In the middle of the yard was a high tower. Beside the tower was the wreckage of a flat-roofed, concrete-block building. She stopped the bike at the base of the tower and waited until he removed himself and his crutches before dropping the kick stand.

Pulling her helmet up over her ears, she shook her hair loose and walked across the yard to the building and looked through a gaping window that was bordered by shards of broken glass into a room filled with sodden trash and the debris of a broken wall. She shaded her eyes and gazed up at the tower top.

"They've even taken the wires," she said, pointing up at

a line of insulators that rose along one side of the tower, from which the cut ends of wire protruded. She went around the building and found a ladder fixed to the rear wall, climbed it and walked across the gravelly roof to the other side and looked down the mountainside to the west and north, where Freetown spread itself about the base of Mount Auriol, the northern-most peak in the range of hills and mountains that angled southeastward away from them. She recognized the valley between Juba Hill and Signal Hill, Man-O-War Bay, the lighthouse at Cape Sierra Leone, the orange-brown walls of the prison, Parliament Hill, and the huge Cotton Tree in the middle of town. But the elevations suggested by the crowded contour lines of the map did not prepare her for the reality of the colors and the dramatic ups and downs of the place: white, tan, green, and rusty brownish-orange, the brown-orange predominating; the city a dirty rusty orange skirt over the green undulating hips of Mount Auriol. She heard the crunch of gravel and felt his presence.

Marie looked southward over green peaks and shadowed valleys that ran down into the sea. She pointed. "Look—the waves on the horizon. It must be 50 kilometers."

"Probably," he said. The sun was low, reflecting off the sea in a brilliant swath that was difficult to look at for very long. To the south along the line of peaks and hills dark clouds rolled and turned. "There'll be storms tonight."

She looked east, where cumulonimbus clouds climbed tier upon tier for tens of thousands of feet, towers of cloud trailing mare's tails down to the earth.

He opened his knapsack and removed the blanket and the bag of apples and cheese and bread and the bottles of beer. She spread the blanket along the edge of the roof and they sat, dangling their legs and looking south along the mountains while they ate.

"I want to know about her," Marie said.

Robert bit into the apple, chewed slowly. "We were lucky to find apples. I haven't seen an apple since you were here in May. The Lebs don't like to import them. Too many go bad. These are French." He looked out over the mountains and the sea. "My housekeeper." He bit into the apple again.

The silence lengthened.

She spoke again. "You already told me that."

"Pa Bia brought her to me. To be my housekeeper. After a few months—"

"How old?"

He shrugged.

"How old?"

"This is Africa."

"How old?"

"Probably fifteen."

"Now or then?"

"Then."

He bit into the apple, chewed slowly.

"Go on," she said, finally.

"After a few months she began staying—"

"You began fucking her—"

"I began fucking her."

"A little girl."

"This is Africa. She's not a little girl."

"And you have been fucking her all of the time you have been fucking me and telling me how much you love me. Do you tell *her* how much you love her? *Do* you love her?"

He drew a breath to begin a denial, but caught himself. He realized denial could be fatal: she'd probably push him off the fucking roof and leave him to rot in the brush and rocks. He sat and listened to what she had to say about loyalty and predatory white men acting like an African Big Man.

♈

The rain did come, pouring out of the darkness, a waterfall of marbles rattling on her helmet, stinging her arms and chest and legs, roaring on the pavement, beating the brown water on the road to froth, fogging her goggles. With one hand she dragged the goggles off her eyes. Lightning darted along the tops of hills, the explosions rolling over them like volleys of cannon that they felt in their stomachs, in their teeth, in their bones. A car came round a curve, throwing a bright light that turned the curtain of rain into a shimmering brilliance; she moved the bike a little to the right, thinking about the rocky hillside below them, tensed, held her breath. Then the car was by and they were passing through its roostertail of dirty water.

They were descending from the base of the clouds, which were lit by blinding stabs of light that turned the world into strobe-lit scenes of swaying blackness. And then the road leveled and the lights of a walled compound flashed by and she knew they were through the ravines and nearing the fork. They moved onto the wider, smoother stretch of road that ran along the crest past Wilberforce Barracks and the President's Mansion, the rain still pounding down, the lightning still tearing through the clouds close overhead, the barrage of thunder still hammering.

They were over the crest and through the roundabout and heading down and the air ahead of them was bright with the street lights that always illuminated the stretch of road in front of the President's Mansion. And then the air around them shone with the light of a sun, and she felt Robert stiffen and heard him shout, "Stop!" She kicked the Honda into second gear and it slowed, the engine whining. And then she heard angry shouts through the whine of the engine and the rattle of rain on her helmet, and she hit the brakes, and the bike skidded to a stop, throwing him halfway up her back. The bike fell silent, the machine held upright by her legs planted on the pavement on either side. Its tailpipe hissed with rain.

A string of blinding headlamps streaked by, and from all around the motorcycle there came a thudding of boots on pavement and angry shouts, and then they were surrounded by uniformed figures jabbering and waving guns and jumping about in the rain.

Robert got off the bike and stood beside her, trying to calm the soldiers.

"Mohdafohka! Mohdafohka!"

A sergeant broke through the ring of gesticulating soldiers: "Mohdafohka, de Pres-den de come! You no de stop, mohdafohka!"

"Padi, we done sorry, we no bin see the lights," Robert said, his voice placating.

The absurdity of that plea sent the sergeant into a rage. "Mohdafohka!"

There was a violent movement and Robert grunted in pain and fell back against her, and she went off-balance and fell with the bike, and then there was a flash and an explosion that slapped like a fist, and she was on the pavement with her ears ringing and her brain hurting. Robert scrambled over to her, yelling "Are you all right?" He grabbed her and pulled her from under the bike, then lost his balance again and tumbled over into the rushing water in the gutter, still yelling, "Are you all right?"

Marie looked up into the bright shimmering night, backlit by all those speeding suns, saw numberless glittering bullets streaking in out of the blackness to explode against the pavement around her and against her face and helmet and arms and her blouse and skirt; observed the gaggle of soldiers frozen in position above her; understood that they were as stunned as she, shocked out of their rage into silence by their own audacity in crossing from threat to violence—violence against whites.

There was a skidding of tires and a gleaming blackness loomed up behind the soldiers. A yellow light shown over a bulky, gray-haired African in a black bow tie and black dinner jacket; he moved out of that yellow light into the rain among the soldiers, who parted for him. He looked down at her.

"Are you all right?" he asked, offering his hand.

She dazedly took his hand, felt him pull her up.

The gray-haired African looked at the soldier who had fired his rifle. "Wetin na you name?" he snapped.

The soldier stiffened to attention. "Sah! Ah name na Sah-gent Alusine Lansana, sah!"

"You will hear from your superior about this, Sergeant Lansana. Now lef we."

"Yes *sah!*" he said, his right hand springing up in a stiff salute. He turned, stamping his feet with parade ground precision, and yelled something to the others, who had gathered into a ragged line. They shuffled off toward the guard station.

The African looked at Marie. "You are not hurt?"

She removed the helmet, shook her head.

He looked at Robert. "I've seen you before."

"Yes, your Excellency. We met at the American DCM's house. At a reception."

"I remember—you are Mister Bush's friend, the follow who runs the Bonthe station for Mister Beachley." He glanced at the motorcycle, laying on its side. "You must be more careful around the soldiers. They are very nervous these days. You could have been killed." He looked at Marie, his eyes moving down from her face to her chest, where his gaze lingered on the fabric of her blouse, which was plastered wetly over her breasts. He looked back up to her face. "You go tell God tanki," he said. He got back into the car, said something to the driver, and the car accelerated away.

"Talk about dumb luck," Robert muttered. "That was Minah."

A cluster of sodden Africans had gathered in the rain in the haloed light of the guard station. Sergeant Lansana stood among them, his hands on his hips.

"Help me lift the bike, we need to get out of here."

They bent over the motorcycle, righted it.

"Want me to drive?" Robert asked.

She pushed strands of wet hair out of her face, pulled the helmet down, then put her leg over the saddle and settled herself. She kicked the engine to life. "Get on," she said.

♈

He looked up at her—a paleness against the darkness—and offered the joint. She took it, drew on it, offered it back. He waved it off and she pinched the fire into the ashtray on the window sill. The storm had passed; the sky glittered with stars and the streets once again murmured with activity. Late as it was, traders had returned to the street corners with their tables, lit their candles and lanterns, spread their goods. The old Leb waiter shuffled across the porch of the City Hotel, lighting lanterns. She felt Robert's hand move over her buttocks. She looked down at him.

151

"I want you," he said.

She smiled. "I thought you just had me."

"I want *more* of you."

She touched his hand, stroked his forearm. "Not right now. In a little while."

"Then light the candle so I can look at you."

"You know what I look like."

"I haven't seen you for over an hour. I want to look at you."

"It wasn't an hour ago and I haven't changed."

"Maybe you have. Light the candle."

She went to the table and lit the candle and faced him, her arms out, her palms up.

"See?" she said, turning in a circle.

"You *have* changed. You're more beautiful."

"You are so full of bullshit," she said, leaning over the candle.

"Let it burn. I need to look at you some more."

She blew the candle out, came to the bed, pulled the mosquito netting down, then slipped under it and stretched out beside him. He turned on his side, put his hand on her belly, moved it up to enclose one of her breasts. She lay unmoving, her eyes closed, her hands clasped behind her head.

"Talk to Kevin about the job," he said. "Please, just talk to him. Then stay an extra couple of days and let's drive out to Zimi and look it over. You can make up your mind then."

"I have the job I want and I'm not giving it up."

Silence. He turned on to his back, looked up at the dark underside of the roof.

"What harm can it do?"

"Besides, you're not in any shape to travel."

"Why won't you even talk about it?"

She raised herself on her elbow and looked down at him.

"I haven't asked *you* to give up anything for *me*. Not even your little girl."

"She's not a little girl. Look, I was willing to leave Salone and come to Mali for you."

"I didn't ask you to come to Mali. It was your idea."

"I volunteered to come to Mali so we could be together."

"Yes. And you weren't giving up a damned thing. Except your little girl."

"Goddamn it, she isn't a little girl."

"And whoever the hell else you've been fucking."

♈

Farrah came to the table with a bottle of the Algerian red. He poured the four glasses full.

"It's a decent red," Farrah said. "Perhaps not the wine we got in the good days, but it'll do."

The truth—which they all knew—was that Billy Darwish had purchased it on a buying trip to Europe because it was cheap; and it was cheap because it had suffered heat damage in some French warehouse. But, acidic as it was, it was the best wine you could find in Freetown stores. Farrah had bought several cases for his wine room. Indeed, it was the only wine he had in his wine room.

"Vinegar wine and Chernobyl cheese," Kevin said, when Farrah had gone back to the bar. "You pay as much in Salone for this trash as you would for quality in Europe. A dumping ground for garbage. A country full of victims, isn't it?" He said this to Robert, but Robert, leaning on his elbows and holding a glass of the red wine in front of him, was looking somberly off into space. Kevin looked at Marie picking at her plate of fish and chips, arched an eyebrow at Rachel. Rachel understood exactly what was going on; she had seen the situation the moment Robert and Marie had come out of the Tropic and climbed to the back seat of the doublecab. Of course Kevin had also noted the tension between the young couple—had observed Marie's thin lips and the blotches of red on her cheeks, the tightness of Robert's jaw and the way he knotted his forehead and the fact that during the drive out to Farrah's neither Robert nor Marie said a word to one another.

Something caught Kevin's eye out in the darkness: a naked boy edged into the light put out by the candles on the tables nearest the beach. Marie, seated beside Kevin, saw the boy scuttle closer, keeping the table between himself and the bar.

"Bread," he whispered. He looked from Kevin to Marie, his expression tense and pleading.

Robert and Rachel turned in their chairs.

"My goodness," Rachel said. She looked back at Kevin, then at the basket of sliced bread.

Kevin shook his head. "Not a good idea, not while we're eating."

The boy looked anxiously toward the bar, then at Rachel. "Bread," he whispered again.

An Englishman at the next table spoke up: "I say, Farrah—they're here again."

From behind the bar Farrah looked out toward the beach.

The boy crouched lower, urgently whispered, "Bread!"

Marie picked up the basket of bread and went around the table, approaching the boy with the basket. He jumped forward, scooped the bread out of the basket, and scampered into the darkness.

"Wish you wouldn't do that," Farrah said as he approached. "Just encourages the little bastards."

Marie went back to her chair and said to Farrah: "We have no bread—please bring some."

"And some more of this fine Algerian red," Kevin added, holding up his glass.

Farrah muttered something and went back to the bar.

"Farrah does have a point, you know," Kevin said.

"You were right," Rachel said to Marie.

Kevin shrugged. "I doubt it. Those squatters up on the hill by the hotel took the clothes off the skinniest youngster in the camp and sent him over here. That's the reality."

"It doesn't matter, Marie's impulse was correct and so was her action," Rachel said.

"It encourages inappropriate behavior. You could give these poor people all you have—everything—and it would solve nothing. One day later they would be as hungry as they were before you gave them anything. And what have you accomplished, except impoverishing yourself? What d'you think, Robert?"

154

It was at this point that Robert's blood should have warmed and he should have joined the argument. Indeed, that was what Kevin expected, and it was the reason he said what he said. But Robert just looked at him with a preoccupied expression.

"You have expressed it as a moral dilemma," Rachel said, "but it is a moral dilemma only if you measure goodness in economic terms. It is a false argument, because good cannot be measured that way."

"But one *can* measure goodness in economic terms. Some would say it is the only way."

"It is sophistry."

"You are sounding just like Robert, my dear. In fact, there are philosophies based upon it."

Kevin grinned at Robert, inviting response, but Robert was gazing toward the bar with such intensity that Kevin turned to look. He saw a black woman with rather pretty European features and straight-conked hair approaching unsteadily. A tall middle-aged white man stood embarrassedly behind her. She stopped a couple of paces away from their table, gathered herself dramatically.

"That man—*raped* me," she said with a theatrical toss of her head.

There was laughter from the shaggy-headed German who sat at the bar with the wall-eyed black woman and from the table of Englishmen. Holding her head high she tried to glare at Robert, but that task was one too many for her overburdened motor functions: she managed to focus both eyes on Robert for only a second, then tilted abruptly backwards, landing with a thud flat on her back.

"Oh-h-h!" she groaned in surprise.

For several seconds Paul Simon's voice, coming from the tape player behind the bar, was the only sound, then laughter exploded once again from the table of Englishmen. The middle-aged white man who had come in with her looked shocked. He turned and walked quickly toward the passageway that led to the parking lot. Marie jumped to her feet and went to the black woman and kneeled beside her.

♈

155

They talked in the noonday sun for an hour: Marie in her boots and sunglasses and long skirt and jacket, her goggles up on her forehead, her gloves in one hand, her helmet dangling from the handlebar; Robert in T-shirt, halfbacks, and shorts, leaning into his crutches. Sweat ran down her face and darkened her blouse. Sweat trickled down the small of his back under his T-shirt, soaking the waist band of his shorts. Neither of them cared about the sweat; neither did they care about the hardness of the sun's heat; nor the fact that Kevin watched them through the curtains of the second floor meeting room.

"I don't know what's going to happen," Marie was saying. "I can't think straight when I'm with you—so I don't know."

"But what are you thinking?"

"I said I haven't made up my mind. I hate this Aminata business. And the other women you're fucking. Even if I didn't care *who* you fucked it would be a health issue. But I do care. I'm not going to be an African woman. Not even for you."

"You keep saying that."

"Yes, and you keep trivializing it."

Silence. Then, "I don't understand you. I'm not making you—"

Her face stiffened. "That's what I'm talking about, exactly that—that you can't seem to understand. Or won't understand."

At that moment she caught the movement of the curtain out of the corner of her eye, glanced up over Robert's shoulder, saw Kevin's face looking down at her. That he had been watching them since she and Robert had come out of the office did not bother her. She knew he had a bit of a crush on her, but there was no threat in that circumstance, for it was also clear that his affection was not predatory. Kevin did not need to have her to enjoy her. As a matter of fact his crush had more to do with admiration of her independence than sexual appetite. Possessing her would have denied that independence, would have changed the very quality he most admired in her. Some men saw threat in a woman's independence, but not Kevin. To him it was a woman's most

156

exciting attribute. It was what originally drew him to Rachel. It had taken many months of correspondence to reduce *her* independence to the point where she would follow him to Africa. Following him for twenty years thereafter, from one posting to another in Africa, had further eroded whatever independence remained in her, in the end making her a completely different person from the person he fell in love with. Now she *talked* independence; she certainly spoke her mind—which of course Kevin encouraged—but speaking one's mind was not independence. The bottom line on independence was—well, acting independently. As in every other sphere of life, it was action that counted, not words. Independence was going your own way. That was the bottom line on it. Kevin could not hear their words, but the intensity of the conversation in the street below the window showed in their expressions—which suggested pretty clearly that Marie was going to remain independent.

Kevin knew that this kind of intense talking had been going on for several days. But of course that wasn't the only thing they'd been doing—they'd spent a lot of time fucking as well. You could smell it on them. And flitting about the countryside on her motorcycle. A lot of that, too. Robert was a lucky devil. Or perhaps unlucky, if the look on his face at that moment meant anything.

She donned her helmet, finally, and slung her knapsack across her back. While she fastened the helmet strap under her chin and pulled her gloves on, Robert checked the straps holding the two petrol rubbers on the carrier. She came into his arms and they held one another for a long time; then she pulled away, got on the bike, accelerated to the corner, and turned into the traffic on Siaka Stevens Street.

Robert woke to the distant mutter of a generator and the voice of the BBC news presenter. Then he heard Gunter's soft voice, followed by Alexander's, which was loud and dominating. He listened for a minute, then lifted the netting and swung his legs out of bed. He got into shorts and T-shirt, and when he finished washing he made his way down the hall to the living room.

"Good morning, Mister Kelley," Alexander called from the dining room table, where he had surrounded himself with the ham and butter and jam, and was spreading brie over a slice of bread.

Gunter was pulling out a chair. "Good morning, Robert. Alhadji, bring coffee for Mister Kelley."

"Morning, Gunter. Morning, Mister Alexander."

"I congratulate you on your new situation, Mister Kelley," Alexander said. "A man of your abilities—I was not surprised to hear it."

"Thank you. How was your trip?"

"Frightful! It is a miracle that I was not drowned. Terrible waves!" Alexander watched Robert lean his crutches against the wall and lower himself into a chair. "Mister Wagner said you injured your foot. I am sorry to hear it."

"Nothing serious. A small inconvenience."

They made small talk while they ate. Alexander thanked Gunter for his generosity in sending a car all the way to Matruh, and for putting him up for the night, even though the stupid driver had gotten them lost and they had not found their way to Bo until well after midnight. He described once again the horror of the crossing, which was a foolish risk for a man to take for a thing as frivolous as this frame survey—but English money was paying for it so who was he to complain. Indeed, he was honored they had asked him to share his experience with them.

The sun was just above the horizon when they arrived at the project office where they spread their maps over the table in the meeting room, reviewed their plan, and waited for the rest of the survey team to assemble. When one of the interpreters didn't show up Gunter sent his driver for him. The driver came back and said the interpreter had malaria.

"Robert, we can get Prince," Daniel exclaimed. "He is fluent in Mende, he has worked among those villagers."

Gunter and Rex became very interested in the maps; neither of them wanted any part of this conversation. Gunter had rejected Prince's applications for positions as cooperatives organizer, program leader, even driver, and Rex knew him from the time when Prince managed the Bo Peace Corps office. Alexander noticed the change in atmosphere and looked curiously from Daniel to Robert to Gunter.

Robert shrugged. A job for the few days they would be in the bush was piece work, not a commitment. "Okay, let's go and talk to him."

When they got to Daniel's house they found Prince sitting on the porch thumbing through a tattered magazine. Daniel leaped out of the doublecab and hurried across the earthen yard. Robert climbed out behind him.

"Prince, get your clothes, quickly, Robert has a job for you. Hurry, we must leave soon."

Prince looked startled.

"Hurry!" Daniel said.

Prince rose to his feet, looked uncertainly from Daniel to Robert.

Robert stopped halfway across the yard, leaned into his crutches. "We need a Mende speaker to interpret. The job is for the time we are in the bush. Maybe five days. The pay is fifty leones a day. Are you interested?"

"Yes. Yes, of course," Prince said. "I'll get my clothes."

Eileen opened the front door and stepped to the porch, a baby on her hip.

"Prince will work for Zimi," Daniel said.

Eileen looked at Robert.

"For a few days," Robert said.

Prince came out of the house carrying a plastic shopping bag, which contained his wardrobe—a pair of nondescript trousers and a couple of frayed T-shirts.

♈

They sat in the high-walled common room in a circle of chairs, sharing the murky light of two smoking kerosene lanterns. Robert's presentation was to be the last of the evening, after which they would break and move across the room to the long table where Regina would serve groundnut soup and rice.

Alexander sat frowning and fidgeting, and looking at his watch every two or three minutes. On this evening as on the other evenings he had muscled his way onto the floor first, given his abbreviated presentation—in less than five minutes—and sat down and crossed his arms, frowning to discourage questions. But, as usual, his brevity influenced no one. Rex had followed him with a windy ramble of thirty-five minutes (Alexander acidly commenting when Rex finished that he had given the same amount of information in under five minutes), after which Gunter had followed with a half-hour talk, followed by questions that went on and on. Then Daniel had talked twenty minutes beyond *his* allotted time, droning interminably and irrelevantly about a clutch of unimportant huts peopled by ignorant, thieving farmers who were exactly like the ignorant, thieving farmers who had been lying to them for four days. As Robert began his talk Alexander sighed noisily, looked ostentatiously at his watch, and muttered about his stomach eating itself.

They expected this of Alexander. He complained as naturally as others breathed. Why rise so early—it was absurd to be on the road before dawn. And why did they stay in the bush so long every day? These hamlets were all alike, so why did they bother to visit so many? Indeed, why visit more than one? Or any, for that matter? They had but to ask him and he would tell them anything they needed to know about these thieving farmers. He complained most bitterly about the uselessness of these evening debriefings, where everyone took much too much time to say the same thing every night.

Robert ignored Alexander's sighs and fidgets and went on with his talk. That morning he, Daniel, Pa Bangura, and the interpreter Ladipor Conteh, had driven into the village of Vama and asked to see the headman. A small graying man in shorts and plastic half-backs had pushed his way through a throng of women and children, greeting Robert with bobbing head and obsequious gestures. Robert said that he and his colleagues came to talk to the villagers about their problems.

After the headman sent children off to fetch the farmers, he led the visitors and a procession of women and children along the road between the mud houses to a baffa in the middle of the village. Women brought chairs and a table. Robert and Daniel and Ladipor seated themselves behind the table. The conversation with the headman became a welcoming speech, and he was still speaking as the last of the elders arrived. By then scores of men and women milled around in the sun outside the baffa.

After more speeches, the Imam rose and chanted a prayer. Robert stood and made his own speech, which was very short by Salone standards, so short it was almost curt. He thanked the villagers, explaining that he did not come to offer them anything, but to learn about their problems.

Every man and woman wanted to speak; and they did, one after another; of too little land, too many people, and too many pests. At one time the village produced rice enough to eat, with some left over to sell for tools, medicine, and even luxuries such as kerosene and radio batteries. But now the farmers' land seldom yielded enough to get them through the hungry season. The pests—monkeys, cutting-grass, birds, baboons, bush deer—harvested as much as they did. Sometimes Liberians came with guns and nets, offering to kill the monkeys and birds, but they demanded money for this and the villagers seldom had money. Guns was the best way to kill the pests, the villagers said—would ZDP provide guns and bullets? No, Robert said, they did not come to give anything, they came to learn. He asked about the fallow cycle.

The farmers said the fallow period, which was traditionally twenty years or more, was now only six years. There were so many people now that the farmers had to clear and cultivate the land before it was ready. Robert asked them if they cultivated their swamps. They did not like planting in the swamps, because the work was hard and they were already overworked. And when they blocked the water flow the swamps became sandy, quickly losing fertility. It was best to leave the swamps open, planting only where they were naturally suitable. Robert asked if they had dammed the streams in the past?

Yes, yes—the IAD had come before the civil war and told the villagers they could grow more food if they would turn their swamps into rice paddies. Until that time the farmers had grown only upland rice. Only white men, in their plantations in the marshes along the River Sewa and the lakes along the coast, had tried cultivating swamp rice and they had failed and gone away. The IAD nonetheless pressed the villagers to develop their swamps, even offered sixty leones per acre to get them to do it. That was in the days when the leone was worth half an English pound, so it was a great deal of money. But the money turned out to be loans, not gifts, loans the IAD people handed over to the government to administer. The government sent collectors and then soldiers with guns. Under much pressure, the villagers made payments year after year, and were still paying, though they had long ago repaid the so-called loans. When the farmers complained to the UN, the IAD administrators told the government and the soldiers came again. Now the UN refused to operate in the area, but the government men still came with soldiers and guns, taking their rice and money.

Robert had moved to questions about the swamps to determine whether the villagers would accept the heavy work of developing their swamps into fish ponds, but they associated his questions with the IAD problem. To reassure them, he told the villagers he would try to help them. What about using the swamps for growing fish, he asked, to get them back on track. Had they heard of that? Would they be interested in developing some of their swamps into ponds for fish? They did not know, they said. It would depend on how much help the project offered, for they had no money and they already worked very hard in farming their land.

One farmer complained that the Zimi project should not have raised the price for oil palm seedlings—the village could not afford to pay one leone for each seedling. Ladipor began translating this complaint, then stopped. He looked confused for a moment, finishing in a lame evasion. Robert saw that he was concealing something. He summoned what little Mende he could speak, asking the farmer what price he paid for the seedlings. Ladipor looked uncomfortable. The farmer repeated that the villagers paid one leone for each seedling. Robert knew that Zimi had provided the seedlings through a government extension agent—Ladipor Conteh's colleague. It was apparent that the agent, a Temne woman, had raised the price and pocketed the difference. A routine scam. Annoyed that he could not keep the discussion focused on the fish ponds, Robert said he would look into the matter, and that the village would get back the money they overpaid. By then the farmers saw that the white man was not going to give them anything, and they wandered off in ones and twos, and the baffa began to empty.

Regina came into the room and said their supper was ready. Robert thanked her, saying they would come in a few minutes. He turned back to the others. "That IAD business—I am concerned about how that experience will affect our plan. I'm wondering if we can get them to work in the swamps for—"

"Lies," Alexander interjected. "When you loan these farmers money it is a gift. When you loan them tools it is a gift. Everything is a gift to them, even the things they steal. The farmers borrowed money, and they knew it when they borrowed it. They are lying about the money and they are lying about the soldiers."

Robert glanced at Gunter, who looked exhausted, then at Rex, who stared off into space. It was clear they were all finished for the night. "Okay," he said, "It's late—let's adjourn for the evening."

They moved to the table and ate. The only sounds were the clink of spoons on china, the slurp of water, the spitting of bones upon the table. When they finished Robert sent Regina into his bedroom for one of the cases of Star Beer he'd bought in Bo. She passed the beers around and talk started up again, but it was not talk about the survey. They were tired of it; they had lived the survey for four days, from the time they rose from their beds in darkness until they fell into bed eighteen hours later.

As the case emptied the talk picked up, became lively, became the conversation of friends. Robert watched and listened. They had worked hard and gotten good results. He felt a surge of affection and respect for Daniel, Prince, Rex, Ladipor, even Alexander. Though he and Gunter were only sojourners in their world, Robert understood that world, even experienced its realities from time to time. But mostly he and Gunter viewed it like a Big Man viewed it—from a place of power, a place that was as safe as theirs was dangerous: from the security that comes from living in a white skin.

Their sturdiness was remarkable when you considered the degree of their insecurity. He wondered if he had the stuff to survive what they survived. Physical sturdiness he possessed, a modicum of courage too, he reckoned, though he knew he had never been truly tested. Not like they were tested every day.

He looked at Prince, who had once been his superior. Once Prince had been recognized as one of the Big Men in Bo. As big as Alexander was in *his* world. Now Prince held a position just above that of Pa Bangura. He ate upstairs with his superiors and he shared a room with Ladipor Conteh, the other interpreter, but he did not speak at the debriefings—except to answer questions relevant to his job. He sat quietly, as befitted a man of his position at the table of his boss, the Big Man Robert. Robert thought about those visits years ago to Prince's concrete block house on the outskirts of Bo, where he and Daniel and Prince sat on the porch, drank palm wine, talked about women and the future of Africa.

Now, as he watched Prince drink his beer, he made himself think like he thought then, made himself see Prince as he had seen him then. In those years Prince was no radical. Far from it. He was seen as a man on the make. He had good clothes, a camera, a watch, a refrigerator, a radio that received BBC, a stereo, a generator. He had leones, when leones were worth something. And professional status, a driver, and a Peace Corps Land Rover that he loved so much that he often risked loss of dignity by driving it himself. The inflation did Prince in, like it did so many other black professionals; but Prince's confidence put a special spin on his ruination. As the value of leones fell from a dollar to a dime he found a way to get dollars. Peace Corps dollars. At first not many—enough to maintain his style of living. He would probably have gotten away with his embezzlement if he hadn't become careless with a local money changer. Selling dollars wouldn't have been noticed in Freetown, but in Bo—well, the Peace Corps office manager was widely known and when he sold Peace Corps petrol or showed dollars about the town there was only one conclusion. When a zealous young volunteer went to the PCD's office in Freetown and demanded that the PCD put a stop to the flagrant blackmarketeering of the Peace Corps office manager in Bo, Prince was finished. Prince's problem was he'd been working for the Americans. Had he been in Alexander's position the misfeasance would not have even been noteworthy.

The Temne woman, the extension agent who had cheated the villagers—what of her? What should he do about *her* corruption? Or could you even say that she was corrupt? In the white man's frame of reference her action was a violation of trust, and therefore corrupt. But in *her* frame of reference—well, how was she wrong in putting a little on top for herself and her family? Her first duty was her family. Was she not exactly like the men who sat with

165

him now? These men hustled leones where and how they could. If they didn't, their families did not eat. Rex—who had studied for five years at Reading to earn his PhD—bought baskets of dried fish in villages along the coast, which he transported upline in project lorries—in violation of project regulations—to sell to the market women of project villages, earning by this labor a few dollars each month. To induce him to attend to project business Gunter bought his time by giving him loans which they both knew were gifts. And Daniel—well, Daniel begged bundles of netting from Robert, which he sold so he could buy rice. Daniel knew Robert knew, and Daniel was unembarrassed by it. He engaged in petty trade when he could, buying and selling cloth, tins of dried milk, or anything else that would bring a small profit. And Alexander: the fox in charge of the henhouse. He would clean out the Bonthe henhouse at his leisure—chicken by chicken—and when the job was finished and the station abandoned, rejoin his colleagues in the offices of Fisheries Division in Freetown, his stature greater, his girth larger, his family stronger. The villagers at York Island and Gbap and Bonthe would go back to living the way they had lived before Robert came.

When the case emptied Robert sent Regina for another. He himself drank little, preferring a hit of jamba, which he took when he went out to the toilet on the balcony. By the time the second case was half empty the talk died down. Ladipor went off to bed, and Daniel, Prince, Rex, and Alexander sat back, their legs splayed out, their eyes drooping, belching and sighing from the fullness of their bellies. Alexander drained his bottle, took another out of the box, muttered that he wanted sleep, and went to his room. One after another, the rest said goodnight and went to their rooms.

Robert felt good. The mix of talents had produced a success. Gunter and Rex had added professional experience, and even Alexander's complaining had benefited the survey. He had challenged them, in a perversely positive way, to test every conclusion, to distrust every assumption. Now only the last and least important part remained, the survey of the river region and the lake villages along the coast—the area that intermittently supplied dried fish to the upland region.

Robert rose from the table and slipped the crutches under his arms. Gunter sat at the end of the table smoking a cigarette.

"Today was a good day," Robert said.

"We have it, I think."

"That IAD business—what do you make of it?"

"Thieves tiefing thieves."

"It's that simple?"

"I think so. The farmers borrowed the money and didn't pay it back and the government sent soldiers for it. The soldiers made the villagers pay, and when the soldiers got their hands on the money they liked the feel of it. They kept some and came the next year to get some more. And came again. Now it is their right to come for money."

"Did I make a mistake, promising to do something?"

"Maybe Kevin can do something at the ministerial level. I don't think so, but maybe." He put his cigarette out in the ash tray. "Robert, Prince asked me to speak for him."

Robert said nothing. He'd been expecting something from Prince, some kind of plea, either directly or through one of the others.

"He said he is going to talk to you, but he wanted me to speak to you first, to tell you what I think of his work. I told him I would."

"And?"

"It's obvious. He's done a good job."

"Are you going to offer him a position?"

Gunter smiled and shook his head. "He has a reputation in Bo—the Peace Corps fiasco, the radicalism, the rabble-rousing. It wouldn't work."

"He's a two-time loser, Gunter. Caught with his hands in the cookie jar not once, but twice. One time you can understand. And forgive. But twice? When the PCD made a job for him in the office in Freetown, he did it again. Sold twenty liters of petrol and got caught. Makes you wonder about his judgment. Then there's the nepotism thing."

"If you can control him—" Gunter let the words trail off.

"I know. If you can control him you've got a good man."

"He was valuable out there," Gunter said. "He managed the farmers very well. Kept them on the subject, saw through the bullshit when they lied. He was more than an interpreter. Even Alexander was impressed."

"Maybe *he* should offer him a job."

Gunter smiled.

"Daniel's been pressuring me," Robert said. "He can't get to Kevin on this. He thinks I can."

Gunter did not respond. The silence lengthened.

"And I suppose I can, now. If I push Kevin hard enough I can probably line something up. But I'm not sure Prince could take working for Kevin. Kevin can be an asshole. Then there's me. I'm not sure I want to put my credibility on the line for Prince."

"I think you should take him with you tomorrow. Observe him. Give him the opportunity to talk to you about this."

"Okay. You take Ladipor, I'll take Prince. That should make Daniel happy. They'll have me all day between them."

When he finished washing Robert went to his room and climbed under the netting into his bed. The damp of his hair chilled him. He pulled the sheet up and listened to the building creak, like a ship at sea, its joints shifting as the wood contracted. The dryness of Harmattan. Always surprising, coming as it did after months of dripping humidity and the itchy rashes that came from constant sweating. Marie had been surprised by Harmattan last Christmas—landing at Lungi on a day so white you could not see a half-kilometer—expecting coastal humidity, finding instead her own Mopti winter dryness, with desert dust as thick as fog, a finer-than-talcum snow that hung white in the air, sifting slowly out in a powdery red coat over everything, staining the pages of books, clothing, curtains, bed clothes. On that warm December day he'd borrowed a motorcycle from Kevin and picked her up at Lungi and backed her, with a knapsack of food and a twenty-liter rubber of petrol, up through the brushy hills around Ma Siaka and Port Loko and through the beginnings of the savannah around Kamakwie to the national park, where they'd lived in the guest tent for a week while they canoed the river and swam and hiked and watched the tree tops 150 feet above the river quake and quiver with the leaping of the big white-faced monkeys, and looked for the snouts and eyes of hippos raised suspiciously above the water; giving the beasts a wide berth, knowing they could swim twice as fast as you could paddle a canoe; listened to the park director (a morose American who was counting the days left on a three-year contract) as he went on and on about the hopelessness of his task and about his Sierra Leonean assistant, who resented the supervision of a white man, and who worked more diligently with hippo poachers than with his boss. And sweating profusely from making love two or three times a day in the intense up-country heat; their sweat drying so fast it left a rime of salt; and the swims in the river afterward, to wash away the gritty residue of sweat, not caring about the shistosomiasis or the tsetse flies or the black flies that carried river blindness.

Laying in darkness listening to the building groan, riding the gentle high from Pa Koker's fine Kabala jamba, remembering that hot Christmas in the white air of Harmattan with Marie perched behind him, holding him tightly between her legs: the recollection filled him with a deep yearning, got him thinking how much he loved her and wanted her, wanted her legs around him as tightly as when he backed her on that Honda, wanted her warm breasts sweating against him.

♈

The boat rested in the mud, without oars or life jackets or even thwarts on which to sit: a twenty-foot shell, everything except the engine removed and sold. When Alexander learned there were no life jackets he shook his head adamantly: he would not go. There followed a long discussion, which ended only when the station chief went to his storeroom and rummaged around in a heap of debris, finding a life jacket so bedraggled that it had been discarded as unsellable. He brought it out and said he'd sell it for 100 leones. Alexander took the life jacket out of the young man's hands and told him to go ask Minister Kargbo for the money.

They got the boat in the water, but could not start the old Yamaha engine. Robert removed the spark plug, cleaned it, put it back, checked the wiring, fuel pump, cleaned the fuel line. The boat operator tried it again. This time it coughed and spewed gouts of blue smoke. Robert adjusted the throttle linkage and the choke, and soon it was roaring smoothly. They pushed the boat out into the water and Robert and the boat operator ran it up and down the river for a few minutes, then came back to the landing and took the others aboard and pushed off again.

Robert sat on the bow, facing forward, his feet dangling over the water. Rex and Daniel stood on the floor boards, leaning on the starboard side, while Gunter leaned on the other gunwale, smoking and watching the grassy banks of the river glide by. Ladipor and Prince leaned on the gunwale beside Gunter, talking. Alexander stood in the middle of the boat, as far as he could get from any gunwale, tensing when the boat lurched or tilted.

A breeze came and went, rippling the water. The air was dry, the sky white and featureless, the sun a pale ball hanging above the eastern horizon. They rounded a bend and passed a pair of Kroo canoes paddled by women. The fields along the river were no more than a foot higher than the river, and were flat and green with marsh grass and patches of rice. They motored past a long, low island covered by a tangle of dead brush and a few palm trees. A pair of herons stood in muddy shallows watching them.

Behind them were the low brush-covered hills and trees of Gbundapi, around and before them the flat marshes. They passed an anomalous low hill, smoothly rounded and brightly green. This had to be the golfing hill, the place where the priest at Sama came on Saturdays and hit golf balls, which he paid village children to fetch.

The terrain changed. They saw more palms against the haze, more sand, and less of the black mud of the marshes. There were garden plots, more cultivated fields, more huts that could be called villages, though they lacked the human continuity of villages. They were merely clusters of shacks thrown together by upland farmers who came in the dry season and tilled the fertile marsh soil. From time to time they passed castnet fishermen working out of small canoes, and they encountered many herons, some gray and featureless, some a pure and ghostly white against the shadowy line of the grassy shore.

They passed Sama, the missionary village of metal-roofed buildings on a knoll high enough to be above the high water of rainy season. A stand of palms rose around the buildings. A white man came out and waved. Children ran to the water's edge, danced about and waved, their shouts skipping like pebbles over the water.

The boat moved past Sama, sliding along terrain so low they could look over the fields and from time to time see people walking in single file along paths, their profiles gray against the gray of haze. A hawk swooped down to the field beside the river, disappeared for a moment, then leaped back into the air with a small creature wiggling in its talons.

The wind picked up, for the first time carrying the clean iodine scent of the sea. They rounded a long bend and a vista of sky and water slowly spread before them.

"That is the ocean," Alexander exclaimed. "We cannot go there. Where is the map, Mister Kelley?"

"It's Lake Mabesi."

"I want to see the map."

Robert climbed down from the bow, opened his knapsack, pulled the map out, and unfolded it. Alexander edged closer to Robert, away from the center of the boat, sucking his breath in alarm as it tilted a little.

"We are here," Robert said, his finger on the map. "The sand bar is across the lake—two miles away. Beyond that is the ocean."

Alexander worriedly studied the map, looked across the bow at the gray sky coming down to meet the gray water. He shook his head. "No, you are wrong. Look. There is no sand bar. It is the ocean."

"It's there, beyond the haze," Robert said.

Daniel and Rex had come to Robert's other side and were looking down at the map, smiling. "Robert is right,"

Rex said to Alexander. "The sand bar is there, across the lake. I have been there many times."

Alexander looked intently into Rex's face.

"It is impossible to reach the sea by boat from this lake," Rex said, "unless you go down the river that goes out of the lake—you have to go all the way to Sherbro Strait, near Bonthe, to get out into the ocean."

"But look," Alexander said, pointing. "There is nothing but water."

"It is there, across the lake. You will see it soon. I promise you it is there."

The boat left the river mouth, moving out into the low chop the wind had built on the lake. Now the water sliding alongside the boat was a translucent green. Alexander looked worriedly over the side: he knew that green water was deeper than brown water.

They were half across the lake with the river mouth showing behind them as only a dark line across the gray of water and sky when the sandbar on the other side began to materialize, gained shape, showed itself finally as a long berm of sandy soil and a few wind-blown palms that rose out of stubby grass and brush. They turned and motored a couple of miles along the beach to a place of palms and cotton trees. The shoreline became more irregular, and then they came upon an inlet, with grass growing out of the shallows. The boat operator turned into the cove and drove the boat into the grass and aground; got out, pulled the bow up on the sand.

A dozen naked children came running out of the brush and trees, yelling and laughing and jumping about. Robert climbed over the bow, got the crutches under his arms, and moved away from the boat with the children darting about him, touching him, leaping back, laughing hysterically. Daniel and Prince pushed the boat out until it floated free. The boat operator yanked on the starter rope, the engine coughed and caught, and the boat moved off. Robert followed Prince and Daniel up the trail through grass and brush into the trees. The children cavorted behind Robert, daring one another to run up to the white man and touch him.

Beneath the trees were a dozen mud huts. A fish-drying banda stood over a fire pit in the middle. A pair of old men and some women met them where the trail entered the village. Prince greeted them and asked for the headman. One of the old men said the headman was fishing. He invited them to come and sit in the baffa, which was nothing more than a thatch roof held aloft by bush poles, with uncomfortable benches of bamboo. Many fish traps hung from the rafters.

Robert asked questions. How many fishermen lived in the village and how many canoes did the village possess? What role did the women have in the village? Did they fish? Or did they buy and smoke the fish caught by the men? How did they fish in the lake? With nets, or only with traps? Did they catch enough fish to sell outside the village? Did they grow rice? Cassava? Potato leaf? Okra? Was the farming women's work or men's, or did they share it? How long did a canoe last—one year? And how did they replace their canoes? Did they have to travel upline and buy the logs and make them there? And what of the trawlers from Ivory Coast? Did they have an impact on local fish stocks?

The answers to these and other questions confirmed that the villagers were subsistence fishermen: they caught enough to eat and that was all they wanted. Success was opportunistic, not purposeful. They were not motivated to fish for profit. When it became clear that Robert and Daniel and Prince were finished asking questions one of the women left the group and returned with a basket of fish, which she offered to Robert. He bought the fish as a gift for the drivers and guards and for Regina.

With time to kill, they went on through the village, looking at the condition of the huts and the tools laying about, and then went out of the cluster of trees, walking toward the sea. The soil became loose sand and the trees disappeared, replaced by patches of grass, low brush, and clumps of tiny succulents. The sand bar at this point was a quarter-mile wide, comprising one storm berm after another, separated by low places in which grass and brush grew. The highest berm was the seaward berm, which sloped steeply down into the low surf. Countless thousands of small crabs skit-

tered in and out of the surf, darting up and down the steep
beach, which stretched northwest to southeast, as straight as
if it had been designed by engineers, disappearing in a distant glow of surf haze below the Harmattan whiteness.
Robert noticed then that Prince was standing beside him
and that Daniel, hands in pockets, was strolling along the
berm crest a hundred feet away. Robert waited for Prince to
speak.

"We were friends for a long time," Prince said. "You
and Daniel and me—we were like brothers."

Robert nodded.

"You have been very generous to forgive me and to give
me this job. Now I am ashamed of the things I said."

"It's nothing."

"No, you can never take back what you say. The best
thing is that you will be forgiven."

"It's forgiven and forgotten."

"It was out of anger. And shame. I did not mean it. Not
the things I said about you."

"It's forgotten."

"Thank you, Robert."

Silence.

"Robert—I asked Gunter to speak for me. Has he—"
The words trailed off.

"He did. He told me you have been a valuable team
member. It is what I expected."

"I asked him about some work and he said it was not
possible. Because of my—because of my misbehaviors in
Bo."

"So he told me."

"But he said he would be glad to have me as part of his
team. If not for that."

"Yes."

"He said I was very valuable. That I made important
contributions."

"So he told me."

"But he cannot give me a job in Bo."

"Yes, he told me."

"In Freetown my—reputation—it would not be a problem."

"Prince, Zimi has only a small presence in Freetown. A

secretary, Kevin about half the time, Chesty, a couple of drivers, a mechanic. That's all."

"But I am very valuable. Gunter said so. I can do anything. Surely you know that. I can interpret, I can manage programs, I can drive. Maybe Mister Beachley will give me a job in Zimi. Robert, please speak for me. Tell Mister Beachley that I am a new man, that I will take any job. Any job. Daniel cannot keep feeding me. He cannot even feed his family. Please, Robert, do this for me. I promise you I will not betray you again. I promise you. Duya, Robert, I beg."

Robert was looking out toward the invisible horizon. "Okay, I'll speak to Kevin. I make no promises, but I will speak to him."

♈

The sky, which had become faintly blue during the brightest part of the day turned white as the sun fell. By the time they were motoring up the river through the marsh the sun was low in the sky and turning from silver to orange. Robert could look out over the marsh grass and see the black silhouettes of women with babies strapped to their backs, the shoulders and heads of children, the torsos of men, the high peaks of thatch-roofed houses, some far off, some near, some in clumps of three or four, some alone. And the trees—no palms here: cotton trees, banana trees, and others that Robert did not know.

They drove into Pujehun after dark, too late, too tired, and too hungry for their debriefing session. Regina had prepared a supper of grin-grin plasas and rice. Robert asked her to bring out a case of beer, but they were too tired to drink much. Alexander finished eating first, got up and went off with soap and towel to the balcony showers. Prince followed, then Rex. Robert and Gunter stayed at the table long enough to study the map and agree that on the last survey day Robert, Daniel, and Prince would interview in another village on the shores of Lake Mabesi, while Gunter, Rex, Alexander, and Ladipor would go north to Kormendi and interview there.

175

During the night Robert came half awake from the noise of the building creaking and popping, then drifted back to sleep. A few minutes later he woke again, this time from the chill. He pulled his clothing up on the bed, spread it over the sheet, curled himself into a ball, listened to the popping, thinking drowsily that it was like that dark morning in the Cascades, the first time his father had taken him on the high hunt, out of Salmon La Sac: twenty-some years ago, opening day, the night still pooled in the valleys, the sun's light sweeping cold and blue across the sky above the mountain, the air around them on that logging road sharp-edged with cold, the steam rising out of Thermos cups of coffee. His father and the two other men shrugging the cold and slurping coffee and murmuring over the topo spread on the hood of the pickup; Robert standing with them, trying to be one of them, holding the thirty-ought-six familiarly, like they did. Then the first pop. He'd looked around wanting to ask what *that* was, and then he knew what it was, because this was opening day; and seconds later another; then another; then more. Like now. He drifted back to sleep.

Gunter was the first to drag himself out of bed. He lit a lantern and went to the door, followed by Daniel and then Robert on his crutches. Alexander, Rex, Prince, and Ladipor hung back, watching. The corporal said there had been some trouble and his sergeant had ordered him to put guards on the Pujehun Project compound, as a precaution against looting. He had posted soldiers at the gate.

Robert asked him what kind of trouble.

"Well, I no saby, sah, I t'ink say some bad Mende people make hala-hala." There had been damage to houses in the outskirts of Pujehun, he said, but the soldiers had come and scattered the troublemakers, arresting some and taking them away. It was quiet now.

Was there shooting? The corporal said he didn't know; maybe some bad people had been shooting guns, but if they had he was sure they had been arrested. Robert asked if the survey teams would be permitted to drive out into the bush and continue their work. The corporal said they could go where they wanted. They questioned him for a while longer, but it was evident he knew as little as they did.

They went back inside and sat about the table talking and slapping at mosquitoes. Alexander grumbled that he was going back to bed. The others drifted off to their rooms, dressed, and returned to the table. Robert sent for Regina and asked her to prepare coffee.

"I think it is the Mende making trouble again," Prince said. "Like they did in the civil war."

"The President will not let them do it again," Daniel replied. "The soldiers will stop the rioting very firmly."

"It was not a civil war," Ladipor said resentfully—he was a Mende, and all this talk about Mende trouble-making annoyed him. "The villagers were talking against the price of rice and the soldiers killed some of them. It made the people angry. It is the same now, it is the First Vice-President's people doing it, not the Mende. The Mende people never made trouble, the Mende support the President's New Order."

"*Some* Mende support the President," Rex admitted, to mollify Ladipor. "Remember last year there was that big hala-hala when Dr. Timbo's men caught one of the First Vice-President's men burying juju things in the Timbo compound before the election. A lot of people were killed. That was not a Mende problem?"

"First Vice-President Minah can do nothing here. Paramount Chief Kamara is the most important man in Pujehun, and he is firm in his support of the President's New Order," Daniel said.

"That is what he *says*," Ladipor muttered.

The talk continued in this random, gossipy vein while Regina made the coffee and served it with bread and jam.

"I suppose we ought to decide something," Robert said. "Do we finish the survey and return to Bo like we planned or do we stay close to the resthouse?" He looked round the table.

They looked at one another in silence. No one spoke.

Finally, Robert spoke again. "Daniel—what d'you say?"

Daniel shrugged. "I do not think there is any danger when we get out of Pujehun. The villagers do not care about these problems. The troublemakers are in Pujehun."

Robert looked at Ladipor.

"The people in Pujehun are angry about the price of rice," Ladipor said. "The trouble is here, not in the bush."

The others nodded.

"Prince?" said Robert.

"Ladipor is right. The people in the villages know noth-

178

ing of these quarrels. I think we are safer in the bush, away from these quarrels."

"Gunter?"

"Perhaps we should prepare ourselves to go and when it is full light check on the situation. If it's quiet, we can finish it."

Rex said, "Yes, that is what we should do. We can talk to the police and the soldiers and if everything is quiet, we can go. We will have to go soon anyway, even if it is only to return to Bo."

Robert looked around the table. "It seems we agree."

At dawn Gunter left with one of the soldiers. He returned a half-hour later and told the assembled teams that the sergeant knew little. There had been a disturbance—he thought there had been shooting from the rioters, but he wasn't sure, it could have been soldiers. When asked if the survey teams could go about their business, the sergeant said yes, they could go where they wanted.

They sat at the table for a few minutes more and decided they would finish and return to Bo as they had planned. They carried their bags and the unused supplies down the stairs, paid Regina for the meals they'd eaten, and gave her and the watchmen the expected tips. Robert's doublecab left first, Gunter's van going off in the opposite direction.

The doublecab headed toward the silver ball of the sun, throwing up a cloud of dust. Normally they would have seen farmers in fields or walking along the road with head-loads of wood, or with cutlasses and hoes, but on this white-skyed, foggy morning the men and women stood in clusters in bare yards and at crossroads near traders huts, talking. Soon they were in the bush on a dirt road.

They were not far out of Pujehun when they came out of a foggy bottom and saw a roadblock—a tree branch laid across the road—with soldiers hurrying into position behind it. The soldiers wore a patchwork of uniform parts and carried an assortment of rifles—turn-of-the-century Springfields, vintage M1s, AK47s. They looked childishly young, and frightened. On either side of the road, beyond the barricade, a clutch of farmers had been talking to the young soldiers; they drew back expectantly.

Pa Bangura stopped. The soldiers fingered their weapons. A corporal approached cautiously. He returned Pa Bangura's greeting with a suspicious nod, peered inside the doublecab at each of the passengers, walked to the rear where he leaned in, poked at the bags and boxes, then went around the back of the vehicle and approached Robert's side.

Robert had already gotten his work permit and his identification out of his knapsack. He handed it to the corporal, who scrutinized the picture, looked at Robert, looked again at the picture.

"Usai you de go?" he asked suspiciously.

"Lake Mabesi."

"Wetin du?"

"For talk for dem farmer—for help am."

The corporal looked at Pa Bangura, said something in Temne. Pa Bangura passed his identification across to the corporal, who took it, scrutinized it, passed it back. He looked in the back window, said something to Prince and Daniel.

Daniel passed his identification to the corporal. Prince followed suit.

"Krio," the corporal said contemptuously, tossing the identification booklets back to Daniel. He said something to Pa Bangura, who started the doublecab and drove it off the road. He turned the engine off , saying, "He de say we get for wait, sah. For 'im leftenant."

Robert looked over his shoulder at Daniel. "What'd he say to you?"

Daniel shrugged. "He said the Krios oppress the people. I told him we are loyal Sierra Leoneans, that you are an important man, that you know many important people."

"Does he want money? Is that the reason he's stopping us?"

Daniel hesitated. "I think if you give him money he will let us go."

Robert opened the door and stepped down and Daniel put his head out the back window. "Robert. Be careful how you approach him. He is nervous—and he's quite suspicious of you."

Robert approached the corporal, who had returned to his men at the road block. "Padi, duya, make we talk."

The corporal eyed him.

Robert explained that his friend Third Assistant Minister Kargbo had asked him to help some of the farmers of Pujehun and that he and his colleagues had come to find out what the farmers needed. Of course he understood that the corporal and his men must perform their own duty as well, which was one of vigilance. Could they not find a way for both to perform their duties?

The corporal stared at him. Several soldiers came around them.

Robert suggested that perhaps he could give the corporal a piece of paper explaining his purpose, which he could give to his officer. As evidence of his good faith he would gladly leave something of value—perhaps some money. The soldiers stirred and slid their eyes at one another and a murmur went round. But the corporal said nothing, merely stared at Robert. Robert began to think he had made a mistake.

"Five hundred leone," the corporal said abruptly.

Robert was startled by the demand; he had been thinking fifty leones. But he recovered quickly. "You can give we pass for other soldiers?" he asked.

"I no get papah."

"I go give you paper."

"I no able for write," the corporal said, his expression once again clouding with suspicion.

Robert knew it had gone as far as he could take it. He opened his knapsack and extracted some bundles of two-leone notes. He was glad that he had enough in his knapsack—he did not much like the idea of having to open a briefcase full of leones in front of the corporal.

As they drove away Prince muttered that he did not like the way the soldier talked to them.

"It is because we are near Pujehun," Daniel said. "It will be better in the bush."

♈

Komuku village was small—a scatter of mud and wattle huts occupied by a few fishermen and their wives and scores of dusty, mostly naked children. Nothing recommended it to the visitor except its location, at a crossroads on a dusty slope between the muddy flats of Lake Mabesi and a grove of trees along a low ridge.

It was market day. One of the market women pointed to the cloud of dust along the shore and murmurs of alarm spread among the other women. They scooped their dried fish and cassava roots and potato leaf and the peppers and the little mounds of rice into baskets, which they lifted to their heads, and hurried off to their huts or up the trail toward the trees. The old Mazda flatbed that in better times came once a week with passengers and farm produce for the crossroads market had not come for a year, so the vehicle making the dust had to be the government lorry, full of soldiers, coming to check market prices. No one paid any attention to the price controls except bands of soldiers who saw opportunity in the law: the soldiers forced market women to sell them produce at ruinously low controlled prices, then took the produce to towns like Bo, Pujehun, Sefadu, and Makeni where they sold it at prevailing, and illegal, market prices, pocketing good profits.

When the doublecab came into view the villagers saw that there was a white man inside and that there were no soldiers. They came chattering and laughing out of the houses and down the hill from the trees.

$$\gamma$$

The sun was low and turning yellow when they finished at Komuku. They had planned to visit one last village farther up the lake before starting back to Bo, but they had been delayed by two road blocks. The road blocks had made them uneasy, but Daniel quite rightly observed that it was nothing new, that soldiers had always extorted money from the people in this way. Robert and Daniel and Prince talked of these and other things as Pa Bangura navigated the doublecab into deepening gloom eastward along the lake shore. Daniel looked for and found much that validated his original project. The upland villagers needed protein in their diet, and that had to come from fish. It was clear that they were too poor to buy dried fish from the coast, even if there was transport to bring it upline, and even if the coastal fishermen produced enough to sell—which they didn't. It was clear that the only practical way to meet the need would be by growing their own fish, in ponds.

As Robert looked out into the fading day and listened to Prince and Daniel it felt like those distant evenings when he and Prince and Daniel sat on the steps of Prince's house in Bo and drank palm wine and beer, and argued development theory and the legitimacy of Siaka Stevens' one-party constitution, and the place of western democracy in Africa, and of Africa in the modern world. And women, always women. In that time Prince and Daniel had been his teachers—two ambitious young professionals full of energy and confidence and hope, doing their time in the trenches in exchange for the Big Man's favor while they learned how to *be* a Big Man; each confident that one day he would be the Big Man dispensing favor; generously sharing their knowledge and experience with their friend, the white sojourner; happy to train the bright young dilettante from America. Now the sojourner was the native, the dilettante was the expert, the student was the teacher, the acolyte was the Big Man—the Big Man whom Prince the thief had petitioned for mercy. Robert listened to Prince in the framework of these subtleties, understanding the humiliation of his old friend. He wondered if he could convince Kevin.

The doublecab lurched and bounced over the deep potholes and gullies, making five kilometers per hour as the sun, a shimmering red disk, slipped slowly into the slot of night. When the last wavering sliver winked out darkness spread over the world.

♈

Pa Bangura got them lost several times, though he did not admit it even once. Despite the old man's objections Robert often ordered him go one direction when Pa Bangura knew they ought to be going in another; or made him stop at some dark collection of huts to confer with a bevy of sleepy locals who knew how to get to the next village but were hazy about which road went to Pujehun or Bo. After midnight they finally came upon a true road, a potholed strip of dusty earth, which they recognized and knew was only a few miles from the ferry crossing at Taniniahun village. There they would cross the river and find the road to Bo.

Generously refraining from telling Robert that "I done tol' you, sah," Pa Bangura put the doublecab into third gear and pressed the accelerator. The vehicle danced and rattled as he pushed the speed to thirty-five kilometers per hour. After hours of creeping along bush trails that were more foot path than road, at little more than walking speed, that moderate velocity seemed to Robert like racing. The sensation of speed became even more marked when the vehicle entered the brilliantly under-lit tunnel of trees just outside Taniniahun.

Robert was thinking about whether he wanted to try a crossing in the dark. The ferry was little more than a rusted-out barge covered by rough-sawn planks, and it was a tricky business even when the river was running low. When they got to the village they would talk to the ferrymen. They came around the curve just outside the village and saw a palm tree laying across the road. Several soldiers scurried across the clearing behind the tree, rifles in one hand, shirts and trousers flying, their eyes squinting into the brilliant head lamps. The lorry skidded to a stop, dragging a cloud of dust behind it, the dust rolling forward over the vehicle and over the fallen tree and the soldiers behind it.

"Shit," Robert muttered. He spoke over his shoulder to Daniel and Prince, both of whom had been sleeping. "Another road block. Pass me my knapsack, I'm gonna need some—"

PA-PA-POW—a sparkling web of light sprang across the windshield, concussion slammed his ears, engulfed his body; brought a thousand pricks of bee-sting pain to his face and arms. "No de shoot we, no de shoot we!" Prince yelled, and from the darkness there came a huge bellow, followed by silence; then Pa Bangura said with surprising steadiness, "Sah, he de say we get for lef de lorry." Robert, unmindful of the blood beading up like sweat on his face and upper arms, opened the door, stepped to the ground, and without command thrust his arms toward the stars.

♈

The light was brilliant, blinding: twin halogen head lamps on high beam, burning his eyes from twenty feet. His whole head hurt: his eyes from the light, his face from the cuts and scratches, his lips and ear from the bruises administered by the sergeant's fist. The screaming had stopped—Prince was now an inert and shockingly deflated lump of bloody stuff on the dusty earth among the opened bags and the scattered clothing and the empty beer bottles. Daniel sat on the ground beside Robert, his eyes swollen shut, the front of his shirt dark with blood. They had dragged Pa Bangura off beyond the lights.

The village—a scatter of huts in the trees near the ferry landing—was deserted, the villagers having fled in panic when the sergeant attacked Prince. He had bewildered even his soldiers with the suddenness of his violence. Robert had stepped toward the sergeant, saying, "Padi, I beg, no de hit am, no de hit am, I beg," and with the light in his eyes he had not seen the fist, just the dark bulk of the man turning, and then that shocking thunderous WHAP had sent him sprawling and left the side of his head tingling and his ears ringing as he looked up at the under-lit canopy of trees—amazed that this was happening to *him*: he was a white man; a *white* man. Prince crying and pleading in Temne; Daniel sobbing, in terror of drawing the sergeant's violence. Robert not wanting to move, but forcing himself to a sitting position, also fearing the sergeant's attention—making himself at least try to rise because it was his duty to protect—and guiltily glad that his head spun, that the world tilted, that he could not rise, that he had to put his hands behind him feeling for the earth, as he pleaded for Prince: "Padi, duya, I beg—" but not finding the earth, and letting himself go. Thankfully, guiltily, he'd remained motionless while the grunts and the thuds continued, the cries diminished, and then stopped; then for a few seconds there was only the panting of an animal, and a murmur as someone clambered up on the bed of the doublecab and heaved the bags to the ground. Robert had gathered himself, rolled over, and pushed himself to a sitting position, and watched the sergeant tearing at the bags like a greedy out-of-control child going at Christmas presents, scattering clothing and toiletries and books. There was the sound of doors opening and slamming, and cries of surprise and excitement: they'd opened the briefcase. Then they'd emptied Robert's knapsack on the ground and scrambled for the bundles of two-leone notes, kicking his notebooks off to the side. And they'd discovered that the old tire patch kit, which he'd carried for five years, contained jamba and papers and matches, and they'd rolled the jamba into joints, which they lit and smoked while they emptied his Bo bag, scattering the checks and his work permit and his identification card and his Salone driver's license; and then someone got into the two cases of Star Beer, and suddenly every hand contained a beer; at which point the sergeant saw that he was losing control of the young soldiers, that they were working themselves up to something that he did not like, and he waded into *them*, knocking one down, cowing the others. Contemptuously, he shoved them away from the briefcase, closed it. He'd opened one of Robert's note books—the one containing his field notes, with the many sketches of village layouts showing water and roads and markets and meeting places—and studied the drawings; turning to Prince again, apparently greatly provoked by the drawings, and kicking him, again and again, kicking him so fucking hard, like he was kicking a door down, so hard the air grunted involuntarily out of Prince's unresponsive body and the sweat flew from the sergeant's face as Daniel crouched beside Robert, groaning and shivering and finally pissing his pants; Prince too far gone to even cry out from his many hurts, the sergeant finally turning away in rage and coming to Robert, panting, sweat dripping; dragging Robert to his feet and knocking him down, then kicking him again and again, finally stopping when he was breathless and unable to kick any more. Then he started in on Daniel. But Daniel was

186

lucky, the sergeant was too tired to do much more than bloody his nose and close his eyes. After that the soldiers drank the beer and smoked the jamba and talked excitedly among themselves beyond the light.

Robert heard Pa Bangura's voice, the words coming in Temne. And then there were more thuds and grunts, and Pa Bangura's voice raised in a bellow. A moment later two soldiers shoved him into the light and made him sit in the dirt with Daniel and Robert. The two soldiers disappeared behind the lights and there was a hiss of bottles opening, the clink of glass, smacking lips, nervous voices.

"Why are they doing this?" Robert whispered.

"He de say you na English mercenary man. He de look you book, an' say look am, na spy book."

"Why did he attack Prince like that?"

"He de saby Prince, he de say Prince talk-talk beaucoup 'bout over-t'row gommint. He de say Prince na traitor, he de say Prince get *Green Book*—" He worked his mouth, spat some blood off to the side. He told Robert that the sergeant had seen Prince talking against President Siaka Stevens and about President Momoh's New Order. But why this violence? Robert asked. Because there had been trouble in Freetown and Bo. The soldiers thought that some Lebanese, some mercenaries, and the Freetown Krios had taken over the government and killed a lot of soldiers in Freetown. The soldiers believed other mercenaries waited out there in the darkness with guns to kill them. They wanted to leave but the sergeant wouldn't let them. As he talked, Pa Bangura stared at the lump laying in the dirt in front of the doublecab. He paused, then whispered, "De soldiers done kill Prince?"

Daniel, who had been sitting with his head hanging, looked up. "No! He's not dead!"

The sergeant appeared, walked past them toward the river. He came back a few minutes later and said something to the soldiers, who bustled about gathering their food, ammunition, and personal things into plastic shopping bags, then lifted Prince and threw him into the bed of the double-cab. Pa Bangura, with the sergeant in the passenger seat beside him, drove the vehicle through the village and down to the ferry landing, while Robert limped along beside Daniel and the soldiers brought up the rear.

The road ended at the landing, a concrete pad in a lazy back eddy created by a breakwater of stones, beyond which the river ran flat and swift. A rectangular hull floated low in the water against the concrete pad. Angle-iron stanchions rose from the deck at the bow and at the stern, the top of each stanchion closing in a loop over a cable that ran from a pylon behind the concrete pad across the river to an identical pylon on the other shore. Pa Bangura stopped the doublecab on the pad. Its headlamps shot out over the ferry and the brown river into the trees on the other side.

The sergeant got out and went on the ferry. He turned and signaled for Pa Bangura to drive forward. The hull listed alarmingly as Pa Bangura edged the front wheels onto it. He stopped. The sergeant studied the deck of the ferry from one angle, then moved and studied it from another. As if he knew what he was doing, he showed the flashlight along the waterline, then dropped to his knees and looked through the planks into the bilge. It was half full of water. He chewed his lip thoughtfully, then shrugged. He motioned to Pa Bangura to drive the doublecab aboard.

Three men arranged themselves at the cable and the sergeant shouted something. The men grasped the cable and pulled. The ferry, very low in the water, drifted sluggishly away from the concrete pad—one boat length, then two, and then it was out of the eddy and in the current, and it groaned downstream, pulling the cable like a bow string, shuddering forward as water piled up on the upstream side. The hull tilted slowly until water edged up on the deck and flowed down into the bilge, increasing the list and the flow of water into the bilge, until it was a cascade. The sergeant was shouting and the soldiers did not understand, and then one soldier lost his footing and slid screaming into the water, dragging another with him. With a groan the rear cable stanchion tore loose at the deck, and the stern of the ferry swung downstream. As it swung with the current the doublecab lurched sideways and rolled ponderously over into the river, Daniel clinging to the side. Robert dropped to the deck and held on as the hull bounced up and down. The doublecab, its lights still on, righted itself and floated off downstream, the lights sinking below the surface and glowing eerily for a few seconds.

The ferry dangled on the taut cable, groaning, and then the current wrenched the remaining stanchion out and the ferry drifted into the darkness, water pouring in through the broken bow. A ghostly gray hump appeared in the darkness close alongside, and they were past it before Robert realized it was the doublecab, gone aground, the river washing around it. "Daniel!" he screamed into the darkness. No answer, nothing but the cries of the young soldiers, some in the water, some still with him on the ferry, then the water was over the deck and Robert was swimming.

"Mrs. Yombo!"

An ancient black woman came to the kitchen door. Filaments of smoke trailed from her pipe.

"More rice for Mister Robert," the priest said.

She came to the long table, took Robert's bowl, and went back to the kitchen.

The priest filled Robert's glass with water, his own glass with wine, lit a cigarette, watched Robert lift his foot off the floor and place it on a chair.

"You must drink more water," the priest said. "The sulfadiazine."

Robert drank the glass down. Mrs. Yombo came with a bowl of rice and fish. The priest watched Robert spoon the rice into his mouth. He filled the glass from the pitcher and signaled for Robert to drink again.

"They won't bother whites," he said. "They didn't last time."

"This is Minah's territory," Robert said. "If this thing is between Momoh and Minah, there will be fighting."

"Momoh is too strong for Minah. It will be over quickly. Before it gets bloody. It won't be like last time."

"It's already bloody." Robert pushed the bowl away. "I'd like to look at your radio."

"You can fix it?"

"I don't know. What's wrong with it?"

The priest shrugged. "It stopped working."

Robert limped across the room to the desk, which was positioned under a wide, iron-barred window that looked out on bare earth sloping down to the landing beach. The dugout remained where he had pulled it ashore. The priest had welcomed him and given him coffee, then sat him down on the bench in the kitchen and cut away the muddy bandage and cleaned the wound. After Robert had showered he gave him the sulfadiazine tablets for the infection, some codeine, bandaged his foot and sat him down to food and questions. Robert had seen the radio as soon as he'd come into the room and had asked to use it and the priest had told him that it was broken. Now he stood looking down at the set.

"What do you need?" the priest asked.

"Screw driver, steel wool, alcohol, cotton swabs."

Robert lifted the radio off its table and placed it on the desk where he had light from the window. He leaned over it, examined the wires leading down to the battery connectors. The priest went into the kitchen and came back with a small tool box. Robert took a screw driver and began removing the cover.

"I don't suppose you have a meter?"

"A what?"

"A multimeter."

The priest shook his head.

"What about the manual?"

The priest shrugged. "I have never seen one." He watched Robert poke around inside. "What are you doing?"

"Looking for corrosion—it's the most obvious problem. I need the steel wool and the alcohol."

The priest went through the kitchen door. Robert pulled a chair up to the desk, sat, removed a circuit board from the radio, examined it, saw nothing unusual. A little corrosion, but no broken solder, no burned places. He put the board on the desk and settled back in the chair to wait for the priest. He raised his hand and touched the side of his face. His ear was still swollen, but the ringing had stopped. He ran his fingers over the stubble of beard. The scabs covering the scores of tiny cuts felt as coarse as his beard.

His gaze wandered to the window. An old woman had landed a dugout next to the one he had stolen and was pulling it up on the muddy shore. She lifted a basket to her head and started up the beach. A young man in dirty shorts and a shirt with a skull and *The Grateful Dead* printed across its back came into view and greeted the woman. Then Mrs. Yombo appeared in her orange and black lapa and white brassiere.

Robert allowed his eyelids to close and his face relaxed and his head drooped; he began sliding; deliciously, irresistibly. He heard voices and his head jerked up. He saw the iron bars, the two dugouts, the woman with the basket on her head, and Mrs. Yombo and the young man, still talking. And then the priest came from the kitchen with a bottle of alcohol, some steel wool, and a wad of cotton.

When Robert finished cleaning the connections the priest went outside and started the generator. Robert turned the radio on. Nothing. He worked his way through the set, checking one connection after another. Finally, he pushed back, looked up at the priest. "There's nothing obvious—without a meter or the manual or a spare board—" He shrugged.

"We'll know soon enough, anyway. All we have to do is wait and we will hear."

♈

Afternoon heat woke him. His body was slick with sweat. He rolled out of bed and limped across the hall to the bathroom, washed, changed into the khaki shirt and shorts the priest had laid out for him, then went to the living room—a long whitewashed, stucco-walled space. Gauzy white curtains were drawn back from the windows. The room was sparely furnished: a long rough-hewn table with a half-dozen chairs, side tables with lanterns and candles, and on every wall shelves of books. The floor was a checkerboard of black and beige tiles. A golf bag with a half-dozen clubs leaned against the kitchen door. Bits of moist grass clung to the club heads. The priest was at his desk, writing, the back of his khaki shirt dark and damp. Smoke from his cigarette rose from the ashtray and drifted out the window. He heard Robert and turned.

"You slept long," he said, rising and going to the table. He pulled a chair out. "Come and sit."

"Any word of the others?"

"Alusine and I went upriver, to the mound. Some farmers saw us and came and told us soldiers had come and found bodies in the river. Two soldiers and an old man with a blue shirt and trousers."

"Pa Bangura."

"Your driver?"

"Yes—what about the others?"

"Nothing."

"I'm gonna take the canoe upriver."

"We looked for them. Very thoroughly. We went as far as your lorry and we found no trace."

Robert looked out the window at the dugout, still on the landing beach where he had pulled it up early that morning.

"The soldiers—" Robert said, his eyes still on the dugout.

"I didn't see any."

"If I went up as far as the doublecab—"

"It's no use. We searched thoroughly."

Robert looked at the priest. "Down river then? Anybody looked there?"

"No. It *is* possible they got out of the river."

Robert thought of Prince lying semiconscious in the bed of the doublecab, and his last sight of Daniel, clinging to the side of the vehicle as it slid off the barge into the river.

"How is your foot?"

"Sore as hell."

"I want to look at it."

The priest got his scissors and cut the bandage off. He wrinkled his nose, held the bandage up to Robert. Robert shook his head; he already knew the smell.

"It seems worse. We'll increase the sulfadiazine. Stand and loosen your trousers and let me look at your lymph nodes."

Robert stood and pushed his shorts down to his knees.

The priest ran his fingers down the crease of skin between Robert's torso and thigh. He stopped when he felt bumps.

"Sore?"

Robert nodded.

The priest motioned for him to pull his shorts up, got to his feet and went into the kitchen, then reappeared a minute later. "Mrs. Yombo is preparing a potassium permanganate soak. And Alusine is making you a crutch."

Robert told the priest then that he had decided to make his way by canoe to Bonthe. He would look for Daniel and Prince on his way down river. The priest looked surprised.

"My friend, you cannot make that journey in a canoe—not with that foot. You do not know—"

"I've traveled the lake and I've worked for years with the villagers in the Kitammi, below Gbap."

"But the swamp."

"There's only a few miles of it—after that there's Gbap. When I get there the fishermen will take me to Bonthe. I can contact Freetown from there."

The priest shook his head. "You have no papers. If you run into soldiers—"

"There are no soldiers down there."

"Your foot—"

"I'm going and you ought to go with me."

The priest's eyebrows arched. "Me? Go into that swamp?"

"The civil war started right here. This is where it will start again."

"The soldiers will not harm me."

"If there is fighting they'll kill whoever seems to oppose them. They're all terrified of white mercenaries."

"We still don't even know what's happened."

"We know enough. I think you ought to go with me."

"No. I need to be here."

♈

Robert rested the paddle across the dugout in front of him and opened one of the plastic bottles of water the priest had put in the canoe. To his right he saw trees in the haze, to his left the white sky merging seamlessly with the silvery lake. His arms and shoulders ached and his shirt and shorts showed lines of dried sweat. His lower back had begun cramping again and his legs were numb. He took one more drink from the bottle and leaned back against the stern and closed his eyes and tried to relax the soreness and the cramps away.

He had pushed himself very hard to get as far as possible down the lake before the onshore wind came up, knowing that it would come right in his face and the work would be twice as hard. But the morning had remained calm, the lake flat, the silence interrupted only by the splash of his paddle. As he'd slid along over miles of river and then lake, and the long morning became afternoon, he had looked for Daniel and Prince, with little hope of finding them; and wondered about how things were in Freetown, wondered if there was fighting, wondered if Gunter and Rex and Alexander had been taken.

He felt his strength trickle back, thought about the tire patch kit, and wished he had some of the fine Kabala jamba. He pulled himself back to a sitting position and drank more water, then reached forward and got a piece of bread and a tin of sardines out of his knapsack. He opened the sardines and made a sandwich, and with the oil dripping on his legs, ate it, swigging water to get it down.

He guessed he was near the head of the river, but he did not know how it came out of the lake—whether through many small channels in the mangroves, or less ambiguously in a single wide channel that he could easily identify. There was no map of the area, but he did not need one; he had only to keep the shoreline on his right and he would come to the head of the river.

He finished his sandwich, swallowed some more sulfa-diazine, and drank more of the water. He resumed paddling, at a leisurely pace, in no hurry now that he had traveled much of the distance he had hoped to make on this day. When he found the river the going would be easier.

He moved steadily along the meandering shoreline, entering every little embayment that opened up in front of him, following each to its termination at a wall of mangroves, expecting to find in each the head of the river. Not finding it, he would paddle on around the end of the bay and out into the lake again. Coming out of one such embayment he saw a shadow out in the lake and stopped paddling. It was a patch of gray against the white. As the patch moved slowly along it took on the shape of a man in a canoe. He paddled toward it. After a few minutes he saw that it had stopped. By then he was close enough to make out the profile of a fisherman bending forward. Robert shouted a greeting. The head came up, turned in his direction, and in turning revealed a woman's profile. He waved the paddle. The woman watched him approach. In front of her in the canoe were several cylindrical fish traps and a basket of small fish. When she saw that he was a white man, she began paddling toward him.

He greeted her in Krio, telling her he was traveling to Gbap. He asked her where he could find the head of the river.

She responded in Sherbro, speaking too rapidly for him to understand. He interrupted, asking her to speak slowly. Pointing across the lake, she told him the river flowed out of the lake close to the beach near her village, which was called Bengani. She had heard from fisherwomen in a village one day's travel up the lake that white men had come to help the people. She asked if he was one of them.

He told her that he was one of the white men, that he had gotten separated from his friends and was traveling by canoe to Bonthe. He asked her if she would take him to the river.

She said it was too late, she would bring him to her village, and the next morning she would show him the way.

γ

The thatch roofs of the houses of Bengani were old and gray and smelled of rot. Mud had dissolved out of the walls of most, revealing sections of wattle skeleton. Under a cotton tree not far from the lake shore the villagers had built a baffa. Beyond that was the bushpole framework of a smoke-blackened banda. Over it all hung the smoky, acrid smell of dried fish, which even a strong onshore breeze did not dispel.

An old woman, a pair of old men, and many children came to the landing beach when they saw that one of the canoes carried a white man. One of the old men waded into the mud and pulled the bow of Robert's canoe up on the grass. Robert steadied himself with his crutch, stepped gingerly out of the dugout. The children crowded round him, laughing and screaming.

♈

The evening breeze kept the mosquitoes down. The flies were more troublesome: when the wind dropped even a little they came up from the ground in thousands. Robert put on the socks, long pants, and long sleeve shirt that the priest had packed into the knapsack.

He sat with several young fishermen and the two old men who had met his canoe in the afternoon. The smell of fish—dried and fresh—permeated everything, mingling with the smoke and the pungent sour sweat odor of the men who sat close around him in the baffa. Dusty potbellied children lingered outside the baffa, staring at Robert as they had all afternoon, intently and endlessly, not quite able to fathom his whiteness. On the earthen floor of the baffa an empty two-gallon antifreeze container rested on its side. It had recently contained palm wine. They had drunk it all. A cooking fire smoldered nearby, flaring up from time to time as an eddy of air pushed through the stones surrounding it.

The fishermen had heard from their cousins up the lake that white men had come and asked many questions about the problems of fishermen and farmers. They were very happy to see him, for they also had many problems. With only the barest preamble of courtesy they set about telling Robert their needs. They wanted guns to kill the animals that swam in the lake and tore the women's traps apart. They wanted the white men to force the big shrimp trawlers from Ivory Coast to go far offshore where they belonged, and stop destroying the long lines. They wanted better fishing gear and more of it. They wanted the white men to come

197

and help them get fresh water to drink, for they had to drink the brackish lake water, even though it made them sick. They wanted medicine for malaria and cholera and worms and polio and the other diseases that killed their children. They complained about the high cost of palm oil, which they could seldom buy nowadays, though everyone knew that without palm oil even the best upland rice and the biggest fish were poor food. And, of course there was the transport problem. Always, everlastingly, transport: the problem of all problems.

Robert tried to explain that he and his colleagues had come to learn about the problems so that they could help the villagers help themselves, but his command of Sherbro was inadequate. The young fishermen could not believe they heard him right because his words made no sense. After he spoke they looked at one another in puzzlement, then talked all at once. After a while Robert gave up explaining; he simply let them believe what they wanted to believe.

In late afternoon the girl who had led him to the village returned with her fish traps and her catch. As the fishermen talked about all the things they wanted he had watched her move about the smoking banda arranging her fish on the drying frame. Her eyes came up from her work often to see if he still looked at her. A little later he observed her at the cooking fire as she worked with the other women. Still later he watched her as she moved about the baffa, serving food and pouring the brackish water for the men. The upright springiness of her breasts and the small, hard muscularity of her belly and the bones showing beneath the skin of her back reminded him of Aminata.

Before the light was gone the women brought rice on a piece of flat metal that was shaped like a tray, over which they'd poured grin-grin plasas, which, though it had only a flavoring of palm oil, contained big pieces of fish. Robert ate like the others, with the fingers of one hand while he waved flies off the food with the other. To make up for the poverty of palm oil the women had made the plasas peppery hot. This made him thirsty, but he did not drink their water, and he did not drink his own, for he knew if he brought it out simple courtesy would require that he pass it around.

Then it would be gone and he would have nothing but swamp water for the next day. They resolved the problem for him by topping some coconuts and then by bringing out the big yellow antifreeze jug full of palm wine.

Later Mister Sama, the headman, took him to one of the huts, which a young family had given up so that Robert could have it to himself. He got a candle from his knapsack and in its light he and Mister Sama tied his mosquito net to bushpole rafters so that the netting formed a tent above the dirt floor. Mister Sama ostentatiously admired the netting, hinting that he would love to have a thing like this—he would like it more than a gun, he said. Robert ignored the hints. When they finished Robert spread his sleeping mat and sheet under the netting and waited for Mister Sama to leave. But the headman lingered. Finally he spoke of the girl, saying she was strong and good to look at. Robert told him he was tired, and had to sleep now.

♈

He rolled over and saw, a foot from his face, a spider as big as his hand, clinging to the mosquito net. He reached over the girl and fumbled about in the knapsack for the priest's flashlight. Turning it on the spider, he saw that the creature was on the outside of the net. He slapped it with the flashlight. It bounced across the dirt floor toward the door-less doorway, recovered and darted off into a dark corner.

He sat up. The girl was curled on her side next to him with the sheet pulled round her. Scores of tiny braids trailed across her face. She stirred, murmuring something low and musical. He had been so full of codeine and exhaustion the night before he'd not discovered Mister Sama had sent her to him until sometime in the early morning when discomfort had brought him momentarily awake.

He rolled out from under the net, wincing from the pain that darted up his left leg, pushed himself to his feet and pulled his shorts up, then got his crutch and slipped his feet into his halfbacks and hobbled out of the hut. Wisps of fog hung in the air over the lake, little streamers of shadowy gray against the gray of first light.

His arms and shoulders were sore, his hands stiff, but these small discomforts did not diminish him; quite the contrary; he felt strong, rested. Perhaps the sulfadiazine *was* working. He went back inside, got a handful of the yellow tablets from his knapsack, which he swallowed with water, and then got some toilet paper and limped in the half light past several huts, working his way along a trail through grass along the shoreline, until he came to a brushy place where the sweet, rotten smell of old shit hung in the air. Mister Sama had told him where he would find this place. He found a clear spot, stepped out of his shorts, squatted.

When he came back he took the cooking pan from the knapsack and got some water from the lake and returned to the hut. The girl was sitting cross-legged in the tent of mosquito netting, with the sheet pulled round her shoulders, yawning. Through the netting she watched him wash, her dark eyes roaming frankly over his chest and crotch and legs, studying him like the children had studied him, with open-mouthed intensity, as if seeking to understand the disfiguring whiteness of him—particularly that pallid band of sickly translucence around his torso from his belly down to his thighs.

When he was through washing he went to his knees and slipped under the netting. The scent of soap lingered in his nostrils. Against that freshness she smelled strongly of dried sweat. She looked up at him through strings of plaited hair, her eyes big, her lips full. But for breasts and the patch of black hair between her legs, she could have been taken for a child. He knelt before her, to get his knapsack, and she, thinking he was readying himself for her, stretched herself out and opened her legs to him. She looked intently up at his face, her white teeth peeking out from behind big outward thrusting lips, her face the fat-tight face of a child.

He got the knapsack, stood, got into his shorts, began taking down the mosquito netting.

♈

He followed her canoe through tendrils of fog that hung vertically above the silvery lake. She stopped paddling and he glided up to the side of her canoe, reached across the water and grasped the side of it and brought the two dugouts together. The canoes rocked gently, turning slowly.

She pointed. Two hundred yards away walls of mangroves receded into the haze. He looked back at her. She knelt in the canoe, her weight back on her heels, her lapa round her waist, her upper torso bare. Piled in front of her in the canoe were a half-dozen fish traps—light, graceful, fragile cylinders of reed and grass.

He opened one of the side pockets of his knapsack, which the priest had stuffed full of two-leone notes, and pulled some of the money out, passing the bills over the water to her. Her eyes lit up and she smiled and bobbed her head and murmured her thanks. He said good-bye and pushed off, paddling toward the gray void that opened between the mangrove walls. After a few minutes he glanced over his shoulder. All he saw was the silvery lake merging into dimensionless white sky.

It was as Mister Sama and the others had said. The water moved, but very slowly, almost too slowly to notice. They had said the river was really part of the lake, except that it moved through many narrow, meandering channels that came together every few miles in a body of almost still water, which would be perhaps a mile long and a quarter mile wide, then the water would flow back into narrow channels. They had warned him to be careful about the side channels, to stay always in the biggest stream, so that he did not lose his way. If he came to a place where he was not certain of which channel to take he was to put a leaf in each of the channels and take the channel in which the water moved. He must proceed carefully and patiently. If he did not make it through to the Sewa on the first day, he should find a place where the channel meandered close to the storm berm that separated the ocean from the mangrove swamp. There were sandy places where the mangroves were thin, and he should beach his canoe at one of these, go up on the storm berm, and sleep on the ocean side to get away from the mosquitoes.

It seemed clear enough when they talked about it, but it was confusing in reality. Most of the time he was uncertain if he was in the river or in some side channel. The swamp was a place of black mud, still water, and motionless heavy air; of luminous greenish light and no sun; of rank shoots and runners that wove themselves together in a warp so impenetrable that even the light was dimmed by its roof of thick greenery, through which he saw not even a glimmer of the white sky.

He lost his way in the hottest part of the afternoon. His movement over the water had awakened the mosquitoes and his sweat kept washing the repellent off his legs and arms and face; his whole body tingled and itched maddeningly from the hundreds of bites. In his growing impatience he paddled the canoe more swiftly. When he came to a place where the channel split into two waterways, he chose too quickly and a half hour later found himself in a dead end of mud and tangled runners, a mile from the main channel. He could not even turn the canoe around. He had to turn *himself* around in the canoe—a difficult, painful maneuver—before he could paddle it back to the main channel. He came to one of the meanders the villagers had told him about, recognizing it only because he saw light through the mangrove wall. He paddled the canoe up to the place where he saw the light and grasped one of the runners and pulled the canoe up against the mud shelf. He reached up and grasped a runner, raised himself to his feet, looked into the tangle, and saw a patch of dead grass beyond the black mud.

He lowered himself back into the dugout and got the tape from the first aid kit, slipped his bandaged foot into the sandal and, setting his jaw against the pain, ran a band of tape under his heel and around his ankle over the bandage. He taped the other sandal on his right foot and grasped the runner above his head and raised himself to his feet once again, slipped his arms through the straps of the knapsack and settled it on his back, then stepped out of the canoe, reaching behind him as he did so and pulling it on to the mud.

It took much effort to work the bow of the dugout into a break in the mangrove wall. He was sweating heavily when he got his crutch and began working his way into the web of shoots and runners, which kept grabbing him, slowing him.

The mangroves petered out over a hundred yards, the last fifty yards of which he negotiated without sinking more than ankle deep in the black mud. By then pain enveloped his entire leg. The sandy, brushy face of the berm rose to a height of twenty feet. He limped slowly up the slope through patches of brittle gray grass. At the top he found low dunes, grass, and scattered palm trees, and he heard the rumble of surf. He looked back over the swamp, which extended in an unbroken green carpet that became greenish gray, then dark gray, then a light shade of gray against the white sky. There was no feature that he could memorize and come back to. It was all the same and it looked like it went on forever. He gouged at the sandy soil with his crutch until he had disturbed it enough to see it from a distance, then hobbled off toward the ocean. He came to a shallow depression that ran along the length of the berm and parallel to the beach on the other side. He limped down into the depression and crossed it, climbed up the other side and passed through dead grass and another stand of palms, stopping from time to time to dig at the ground with his crutch until he had made a mark he could easily find. He crossed two more depressions before he came to the ocean.

By then he was moving against the pain more than the terrain. Moving toward the sea to wash his feet clean of the fetid black mud and himself clean of the sweat. And wash himself clean of the pain with the codeine, but that only when he had reached the ocean and washed the sweat and mud away; only then would he allow himself to swallow the codeine, for the pain would not stop even with the codeine if he was moving about. He focused on the things he had to do: getting through the pain to the sea; washing in the salt water; resting. And of course the codeine; and on eating—though the pain had driven hunger out, he knew he had to eat—and on making a place to sleep; and then, when he had something in his belly, swallowing more of the priest's sulfadiazine.

He dropped the knapsack at the top of a steep face of coarse yellow sand, his presence sending hundreds of crabs skittering down into the surf. He sat in the sand, got his knife out of the knapsack, and with shaking hands cut the

tape away from his halfbacks and slipped them off. After
cutting away the blackened bandage he pushed himself to
his feet and limped down the beach face to the water's edge,
stripped off his clothes, and stepped into water as warm as
a bath. The sandy bottom was steep; in three or four steps
he was up to his chest in the warm water. He pushed off,
dove, rose and swam out into the ocean. He turned.
Amazingly, the beach was moving, perceptibly moving.
The water was transporting him toward the northwest, in the
direction he had traveled all day: a strong longshore current
moving him as fast as he could swim. He laughed, delight-
ing in the absurdity of the ocean moving so much faster than
its daughter, the river; thinking he could forget about the
river and the swamp and that fucking ass-numbing back-
cramping dugout, he could turn on his back and rest and
stare at the white sky while the ocean carried him to Sherbro
Strait. Then he sobered, realized that he was no longer
twenty feet off the beach, he was *fifty yards* from the beach.
He panicked, threw himself toward the band of yellow sand,
kicking and stroking, flailing at the water with an energy
that he did not know was still in him. It took all of that
energy, every ounce of it, to get the sand beneath him again.
He stood, waist deep, his chest heaving, his legs quivering,
his arms hanging like logs, the water tugging at him like a
mountain stream. Shivering with the chill of water evapo-
rating into the dry air, and from exhaustion, he pulled himself up on the beach, scattering crabs. As he limped back
toward his clothing, some 200 yards away, he came upon
sea-whitened nubs sticking out of the sand, the only feature
breaking the smooth yellow coarseness of the steep beach
face for as far as he could see. He stopped. One of the white
nubs rose high enough out of the sand for him to see that it
was a bone, a curve of white that could have been a rib. He
knelt to look more closely, saw among the nubs of bone a
fragment of cloth. He pushed himself to his feet, backed
away from the remains of some fisherman, a cousin perhaps
of the young woman with whom he had lain the night
before. He looked down at the nubs of bone for a long time,
then turned and limped along the water's edge toward the
pile of his clothing, which the crabs swarmed over and
picked at, looking for the rotten stuff of which the clothing

smelled. Beyond the clothing, going off into the distance, the surf haze hung above the steep face of the beach, mingling with the Harmattan haze, and beneath the haze, as far as he could see, thousands of crabs scurried in and out of the surf. He limped along, ankle deep in water, scattering the crabs before him, welcoming the chill that came as the water evaporated from his skin. He rinsed his sweat-wet clothes while the surf broke and rolled around him, then climbed the face of the beach. He opened his bedroll and spread his blanket and sat on it, then opened the knapsack and got one of the water bottles.

He brushed sand off his swollen foot and with a shaking hand poured water over the wound. He let the air dry it, then got the antiseptic salve and smeared it over the exposed flesh. Only then did he let himself swallow some of the codeine. He bandaged his foot and stretched out on the blanket and closed his eyes, remembered then that he had eaten nothing but the coconut jelly the girl had offered him that morning. He sat up and opened the knapsack and got the dried fish that she had wrapped in a banana leaf. He bit off pieces of the fish and looked up at the silver disk of sun, which was falling through the white sky toward the sea. It would turn to yellow soon and then it would redden and disappear.

The fish was the best that the villagers had to give: big pieces of kuta, brown from the smoke on the outside and white and firm inside. Not at all like the herring and the bonga shad that was the upland staple—small, desiccated, leathery, smoke-blackened, and not much bigger than a hand; caught in thousands in the ringnets of Ghana boats and dried by thousands over smoky fire—guts, skin, head, and all—with a taste of smoke and rancid fish fat even when fresh off the banda. No, the fish in his hand was solid and tasted good even without palm oil. He raised the piece of fish to his mouth—and saw that the white, shiny flesh *moved*. Astonished, he looked more closely. Oh God! Maggots! Scores of glistening white things swimming in the white flesh of the fish. His stomach knotted, quivered, jerked. He pitched the fish down the face of the beach, scattering crabs, put his face to the sand and vomited.

He sensed that he was not alone. Were they both there? No, not both: it was inconceivable that Aminata would quietly abide the presence of her enemy. Except in dream; in his dream they had coexisted as happily as the wives of Pa Bangura, though now he could not remember in what circumstance. He stared up into darkness, recalling fragments of the dream. The rustling distracted him. What was going on? Which one of them was there in the darkness? Or was it both of them, and why were they hiding? He said Aminata's name, then Marie's. The rustling stopped.

"Marie." He said her name again; and again; and yet again; louder each time, the sound of her name reminding him of their last day together, at River Number Two: a day of truce after that infamous evening at Farrah's, which had started as a farewell party full of happiness and had ended in exhausting, night-long battle.

Marie kneeling in the sand over the black woman, then looking up and ordering Kevin to bring the doublecab around. Robert leaning into his crutches, saying nothing. Kevin and Farrah helping Marie drag the black woman to the Land Rover. The somber drive, first to Victoria's ruined shit-stinking house where they poured her drunk onto the gray mattress, then to the Tropic. Kevin's and Rachel's restrained good-byes, leaving the two of them alone to end their week of skirmishing with the *real* fighting. The lovemaking a rambunctious culmination of battle—interludes of armistice coming out of exhaustion, not resolution. He said her name again: "Marie!" No answer.

206

But no answer *was* the answer. That was what she'd said, that there was no answer to this problem. He was an African man. And she would not let herself love an African man. "That's not going to happen to me, I'm not going to be wife number one, or wife number anything." Raising his head in surprise, he had looked down into her face, which had been ghostly in first light. "What the hell does *that* mean?"

"It means you love too many women."

"I love *you*."

"Well then, you *fuck* too many women. How many do I not know about?"

"None."

Silence. Lowering his head, he'd kissed her neck and she'd stroked his back.

"I'm not going to let myself love you," she'd said.

"You just said you loved me."

Running her hands down over his buttocks: "When you're inside me I can't help it."

"I'm gonna stay inside you." He'd moved his hips a little, to get another I-love-you out of her, but he was spent, utterly and completely spent, and the movement caused him to slip limply out. He told her again that he loved her, but this time it had sounded more like a capitulation than a protestation of love, and she had laughed at the unintended appropriateness of timing and tone; drew him down, kissed him, moved her hands over his back: "I know—and I love you." Then, more gently: "But after a while I won't. I'm not going to let it happen."

"You can't just turn it off."

"I can do anything I want."

"Okay, you can, but you shouldn't want to. If you love me you should want to be with me."

"Be with you? As one of your wives? What kind would I be? Maybe an African version of Rachel? To compete with the little-titi version of Aminata? Or the whore version of that creature at Farrah's?"

"Goddamn it! Where are you getting this *African* shit? I'm not an African. And what the hell's Rachel got to do with this?"

207

Angrily now: "Two or three wives like that little titi from Bonthe—that's what you deserve—not me." She'd pushed him off of her and the battle had started again.

That presence, that unsettling, rustling presence: still there—like someone attending him. Someone watching him when he couldn't watch back. It made him nervous. Marie? Why was she hiding from him? Why didn't she say something? Why didn't she turn on the lights? From all around him that rustling. "What are you doing?" he asked irritably. He blinked up at blackness, moved his hand, felt a cool hard thing. The telephone. He was not as confused as he was beginning to think. "Never mind," he said amiably. "I found it." He moved his fingers over it. What the hell kind of telephone is *this*? Hard things, sticking out, wiggling. Wiggling things on a telephone? A wave of revulsion brought him fully awake. What the fucking hell is going on? He hauled himself incautiously to a sitting position. And paid for it: he'd forgotten Pain; had wakened Pain, who roared his anger up through Robert's leg and belly and chest and head. Robert yelled, fell back, struggled up against the roaring: "Oh fuck!—what the fuck is—oh, sonofabitch—oh shit oh shit—" He fumbled for the flashlight, found it, switched it on, discovered them everywhere, dancing on the sand as far as the beam of his flashlight reached, on his blanket, poking at his bandaged foot, dancing between his legs, scratching the sand where he had vomited: come to clean up his vomit, and him too—if he was as dead as he smelled. Hundreds of them, now in a panic, skittering pell-mell down the face of the beach and into the surf.

When he could control his hands he opened the bottle of codeine and swallowed some pills. He got the crutch that Alusine had made for him, and still as naked as when he'd emerged from the sea hours before, slung his knapsack over his back and swung himself across the sand, like those hundreds and hundreds of polio-crippled Freetown beggars. Away from the beach he spread his blanket, put on his long sleeved shirt, and struggled into the long pants. He stretched himself out and looked up into the darkness. No stars. No moon. Nothing. Just him and the rumble and the swash of surf, muted now. And an onshore wind that had the palms talking to him with their chattery, cheerful, papery murmur and kept the mosquitoes hunkered down in their sheltering mangroves. It was a stiff breeze, but it was warm, soft, even tender. And transient: it would die out soon and spring up again in the morning, from the east, bringing the mosquitoes from the swamp. He thought about putting the net up, went so far as to think through the geometry of lines he would string between a couple of the palms, decided he couldn't manage it. Instead, he put some repellent on his face and pulled the sheet up under his chin.

He stared, trying to see the shape of the nothingness above him, trying to find perspective in something *near* going out to something *far*, the *close* converging on the *distant*, but the blackness was impregnable: a vast impenetrable secret with no near, no far, no past, no future. He switched the flashlight on to convince himself he was not blind. A reassuring beam of white shot out into space; he directed it around until it found the top of a coconut palm, held it there for a moment, switched it off.

Above him darkness, beneath him yellow sand. On one side the sea, on the other side the mangrove swamp. Dread squeezed his chest when he thought about the dense thickets of the swamp, going on endlessly; farther than he had imagined—for miles, for days, for weeks. Forever. And the ocean: also dark, also going on farther than he could imagine, all the way to the place he came from. But the place he came from was no longer his place. He *was* an African now. This place *was* his place. He smiled, grateful for the size and the blackness and the wildness of the ocean that separated his place from the place he came from, grateful even for the soldier crabs that guarded its boundaries and ate its enemies.

The codeine gradually calmed Pain, persuaded Pain to settle down. He drifted in and out of sleep.

It was full light when his thirst and his bladder woke him: the priest's water, wanting in and wanting out. Reminding him of the sulfadiazine. He tossed the sheet off, sat up carefully, stretched against the soreness he felt throughout his body; moving slowly so that he did not awaken Pain. Using the crutch he got himself to his feet,

209

limped off a few paces and urinated. He looked around. Palm trees and patches of gray grass and coarse yellow sand and white sky. He went back to the blanket and lowered himself to a sitting position and dragged the knapsack to him and opened it and withdrew the khaki shorts and shirt. He got into the clothes, which were stiff from the salt of his sweat and the sea, and drank some water with a handful of the sulfadiazine tablets, then dug into his knapsack and got a tin of sardines and his last piece of bread. He made himself eat all of the sardines, even dipping the bread in the oil as he usually did, washing down each bite with gulps of water. When he finished he packed his knapsack and hobbled across the sand toward the mangroves, following the gouges back to the dugout.

By the time he had fought his way through the mud and the tangle of mangrove runners to the dugout Pain was awake. Awake and pissed. He pleaded with Pain to accept what had to be, explained that all of this was necessary. But Pain wasn't listening. Pain was pissed and Pain let him know about it. Sweat streamed off his face and arms, soaking his clothes, and the black slime climbed his legs. When he finally got himself situated in the dugout—breathless and quivering and still pleading with rampaging Pain—he swallowed more of the codeine and splashed the swamp water over his legs until the muck was gone, then cut the blackened bandage off, and with shaking hands gingerly spread the antiseptic salve over his wound. His toes poked weirdly out of the red, drum-tight roundness of his foot. Meandering cracks showed in the skin, seeping a brownish liquid. The swelling was up past his ankle now, and the skin of his puffed-up toes bubbled over with gas blisters. Burdened as he was with lassitude and a clotted-up thickness of thought, he was nonetheless rational, and being rational, he knew what he was looking at, understood what it meant, forced himself to look at it and think about it. But the reality was too harsh to comprehend: he escaped into his heady disorientation; the priest's sulfadiazine would hold it off until he got to Bonthe, where he would call Mike on the radio and Mike would send a helicopter for him, and when he got to Mike's basement clinic he would be okay. Mike would fix him like he had fixed him before. He opened the plastic bottle and got some more sulfadiazine.

He had no sense of time passing nor of movement along the narrow, turning waterway. The clumsiness of his canoe handling on the first day was no longer evident. He maneuvered the dugout effortlessly and naturally. For a while he was quite disciplined about it, stopping at every confluence of channels to drop a leaf. But this tiresome business took more concentration than he could muster. His mind wandered and he began to rely on intuition.

As long as he kept his blood loaded with the codeine and his foot undisturbed the lassitude brought on by the fever was tolerable; indeed, it was almost pleasant. The heady laziness was rather like being high, though he certainly didn't have the sense of pleasurable expectancy that came from being jamba high. Notwithstanding that, he rather liked the indiscipline of his thoughts. As soon as one idea settled in, another one appeared and shoved it aside. At one moment he was arguing with Kevin, loudly and quite vehemently, with gestures of the paddle to emphasize his point, and something Kevin said introduced Julie Bush, and his fever-damaged Thought Priority Control System, his TPCS—which he visualized as a lump of brain matter as big and wrinkly as a walnut—let Julie shove Kevin completely off the edge of his consciousness, in mid-sentence, and come to him and lean solicitously down and take his hand, and then his TPCS unplugged *her* and Marie was there on her knees again in front of that chair in the hotel giving him that amazing blowjob—the *first* one, which so surprised him; blew him away, actually, when she'd pulled his shorts down and pushed him back in the chair. The plastic had felt just like the icy sofa in Max's office, which was always so cold you had to wear a coat; and then he was listening to Max bitching as usual about Neggie, and he was pissed at Max—Max had interrupted something extremely pleasurable, but he couldn't remember what it was—and then it came to him that he'd left Marie in mid-blowjob, and he cursed his TPCS for admitting all these distractions. He tried to think only about Marie, but his TPCS lost control again, synapses snapping and popping, circuits flopping open and closed, kaleidoscopically flashing unpredictable

211

images that had nothing to do with her. By an extreme exertion of will he managed to get her face in front of him, but in a second she was gone again and he was looking at Aminata's skinny, bony shoulders and those little cups of tit on either side of her chest (his interest in which endlessly amused her), and just as suddenly a vague, faceless David was telling him solemnly that it was time.

He woke, his face and arms itching like hell from mosquito bites. He struggled slowly to an upright position, found the canoe hung up across a channel, laboriously freed it, continued on. His distance from himself seemed to have increased, but that didn't feel so bad; indeed, except for an occasional ill-tempered growl from Pain he felt almost okay. The sulfadiazine, he thought hazily. It *was* working. More, he thought. Take more. He put the paddle in the dugout and rummaged in his knapsack, found the bottle of tablets.

He did not see the change in the character of the river— the channels growing wider and the flow of water increasing, the waterways coalescing. A river was forming and he did not see it. Sometime late in the afternoon he came around a curve in a channel and found himself paddling slowly into a long body of silvery water. Ahead of him the water seemed to split into two bodies, both widening into the distance, both guarded by walls of mangroves. When he realized that the body on the right had to be the Sewa River, he stopped paddling and stared, only half believing, not really trusting his TPCS to sort out what was illusion and what was real. When he became convinced it was real he turned to the priest and said, "See, you fucker, I told you."

♈

Gbap showed up on only the most detailed maps of Sierra Leone. A residual dot, representing a residue of colonialism. At one time it possessed the only pier between Bonthe and Liberia, to which a small river steamer came and tied up once a week, bringing mail, beer, wine, and other comforts for the white owners who supervised scores of blacks toiling in the rice plantation.

In every way the body of water had the characteristics

of a lake, in no way the characteristics of a river. And yet, because it was so much longer than it was wide, and because rivers entered and left it, and because, like the rivers that fed and drained it (its course meandered north-westward, always within a mile or two of the ocean) it was called a river. The Kitammi.

Robert nudged his dugout ashore at Gbap, in darkness, guided the last couple of miles by the glimmer of cooking fires, and was discovered, after he climbed stiffly out of the dugout, by a child who had come down to the lake to defecate, and upon seeing him ran howling back to the huts and the cooking fires with yellow shit dribbling down his legs. The child knew Robert—had sat in Robert's lap a dozen times. But the child did not see Robert inside the lion-maned, shaggy-faced bush devil walking toward him over the blackness of the lake.

A fisherman came warily down the muddy slope to investigate. He immediately recognized Robert inside the shadowy devil, and greeted him with delight, yelled for his wife and for the others to come, grabbed Robert's hand, and pumping it, jabbered questions. Soon a dozen adults and a bee hive of children buzzed about him, laughing and chattering familiarly. Was Robert back in the Bonthe Station? Why did he come in a dugout? Where was Hassan and the sea car? And his foot—had he injured himself? Was he all right?

He slept that night among friends—the fisherwomen and fishermen, rice farmers and market women. They had taken over the land abandoned two generations before by the colonial rice farmers, who had carried their bags aboard the steamer one morning and never looked back, leaving houses and sheds to fall down in ruins and fences to sink into the marsh and iron-wheeled steam-powered tractors to rust and become drift fences for blowing sand and shelter for bamboo that rooted in the sand and collected more sand, and over a long time would make an anomalous, mysterious little mound around and over each tractor, rather like the siliceous material that accumulates over millions of years around a chunk of shit to form a thunder egg. But this thunder egg was still unfinished. Now it was rusty steel showing through the lushness of bamboo.

213

Behind a pair of these nascent hillocks was a banda. Nearby a double line of carious stumps ran out into the water: the ruin of the white man's pier. Women reached over the banda's waist-high drying platform through wisps of smoke to gather stiff, leathery little carcasses of fish, some three inches long, some as big as a hand. They packed the still-warm smoke-mummies one by one into spherical baskets that would be heavy headloads even for the sturdiest woman. The baskets would join others that had been accumulating near the ruined pier, some brought by the women of Gbap, some by women from villages with similar names but no dot on the map.

While the women cleared the banda and packed the baskets, the men sat talking worriedly with Robert. They were disturbed because they had smelled and seen the wounded foot. It had cracked open across the top, the skin beginning to peel back like the skin of a roasted chicken, and a foul-smelling brown and gray liquid came from the wound. They pleaded with him to let them carry him to a famous herbalist who lived a few miles up the Sewa River. Robert had dreamily said no, the foot would be all right, he was taking sulfadiazine for it. That was better than the medicine of native doctors. He even opened the knapsack and showed them the bottle of yellow tablets. They had looked doubtfully at the tablets, then started in on him again. This had been going on all morning, while the women listened from a distance, concerned, but busy packing the hundreds of dozens of tiny dried fish.

They heard the pampam coming through the haze before they saw it, the faint tut-tut-tut-tut-tut coming strong and then waning as a fitful mid-afternoon breeze came and went. It was a quarter-mile away when they saw it materialize, a long, dark, high-prowed vessel that was too narrow and too top-heavy to be seaworthy. The diesel engine stopped when the fifty-foot craft was still two boat-lengths off shore, the boat's momentum nosing it into the mud near the stumps of the pier. Several men dropped over the side into the waist-deep water. The women, some with babies slung on their backs, made their way forward between benches lining the gunwales and at the place where the gunwales rose sharply to meet the prow climbed over the side and down a ladder into the shallows and waded ashore, holding their lappas up out of the mud. The captain's two apprentice boys clambered up onto the deck above and passed down baskets, plastic tubs, string-tied boxes, cloth-wrapped bundles, and ties of firewood. In the stern the captain—young Ibrahim Turay—had the cover off the engine housing, and though the engine was too hot to touch, was tinkering with a hose that carried water into the cooling jacket. The problem had plagued him for two years. The engine would overheat and quit, and only after it had cooled could it be restarted. The engine had quit the afternoon before, in the worst possible place: the middle of Sherbro Strait on an ebbing tide. The tide had carried the pampam past the river mouth and out the Strait into the sea. The vessel had drifted with the current five miles up the seaward side of Bonthe Island before the captain got the engine started. By then the craft, which was loaded too high and too heavily to be in *any* sea, rolled so extremely that the passengers sobbed and groaned and held one another or hung their heads over the side, puking; knowing they were as good as dead, that it was only a matter of minutes before the sea capsized the pampam and swallowed them as it had swallowed the passengers of that pampam that had run up on the rock just a few miles away, on the north side of the island. Darkness was closing in when they came pitching and rolling through the ferocious rip of longshore current and tidal ebb at the mouth of the Strait and entered the quiet water of the river mouth. They tied up to mangroves in the darkness, giddily happy to be ashore and alive, congratulating one another on the miracle of their survival and excitedly telling and retelling the story of the unlucky pampam killed by the angry rock, discovering in the retelling the underlying logic of those fifty deaths and their own survival: the rock, they said, had once occupied an honorable place on an island beach, and it had been angered when children of a nearby village began using it as a place to shit and had gone to sea to wash itself; there it had seen the pampam and had gotten its revenge by moving cunningly into the path of the pampam, killing everyone—except of course the white man from Bonthe whose juju magic enabled him to simply walk ashore on top of the water.

That white man dazedly watched the unloading and the reloading of this pampam, *Shebar II*, and when it was done got his crutch and with the help of some fishermen made his way back to the hut of the headman, where he had slept. He thanked the headman's wife and gave her a gift of money. He realized he would not need the long pants and the long-sleeved shirt any more, so he gave the shirt to one fisherman, the pants to another. They thanked him profusely. Looking into the knapsack, he thought he might as well give the rest of it away. He gave the net to the headman, the sheet to his wife, the pan, the tins of sardines, and the plastic bottle to whomever was closest. He turned from the murmurings of thanks and some young fishermen helped him down the slope past the banda where the women still worked hurriedly to fill the last basket with the dried fish. One of the fisherman waded to the side of the pampam and handed the knapsack—empty now except for the medical kit and the sulfadiazine—to one of the captain's bobos, who tossed it up on the deck above the benches that lined the gunwale. The captain stepped up behind the boy and blind-sided him with a resounding slap across the side of his head. The boy yelped in much greater voice than pain, which earned him a kick from the captain and the sniggers of the other boy, who scrambled up on the deck, retrieved the knapsack, and passed it down to the captain, who carried it back to the seat of honor next to his own in the stern.

The headman said something and two sturdy fishermen sprang forward and made a seat behind Robert with their crossed arms. Robert sat, put his arms over their shoulders, and they carried him into the water. Their skin was dusty and strong-smelling and tight and smooth and black and hot, and ridged and rounded by hard muscles that moved smoothly beneath the tight skin. The captain helped lift Robert over the gunwale, then helped him make his way back between the benches to the captain's seat in the stern. Robert preferred to be in the bow, as far as possible from the rattle and the heat and the smell of the diesel engine, but he knew the young boat captain, and it would be insulting to decline to sit with him.

When the last of the baskets had been stowed on the deck above the rows of benches the passengers climbed aboard. Villagers waded out and shoved the bow of the pampam off the mud and the captain started the engine. He turned the craft toward the northern end of the long meandering lake, and the thirty market women and fishermen and children settled themselves to pass the time eating dried fish and mangos and bananas and oranges, and laughing, and telling stories, and sleeping, as the mixed shoreline of sand dunes, impenetrable mangrove, and marshy grass slid by.

♈

The air was a hot and livid pink from the fire that lingered in the western sky. As the pampam approached the landing beach its engine stopped; it slowed and its prow eased into the soft mud, coming to a stop fifty feet from the crumbling retaining wall.

The trip was uneventful. The engine had quit a couple of times, but not in situations that brought complication: once in the long lake, when young Ibrahim Turay had simply taken the engine cover off, sat back for an hour with his cap pulled down on his nose, and slept while the air cooled the engine; the second time at the river mouth, where the flow of the river and the flow of the flooding tide carried the drifting craft toward York Island. But that was the direction of their travel anyway, so no one minded.

The passengers were clambering over the side of the pampam into the muddy shallows when someone in the crowd shouted, "Mistah Robaht!"

Robert raised his head and turned toward the sound, but the darkness had thickened and he could not see who had shouted his name.

"Mistah Robaht!"

He looked again. Hassan? What would he be doing here? There was a murmur from the dozen villagers who had gathered to greet the passengers, but it was too dark to see who was there. The only light now came from the smear of deep red that lingered in the sky over the mangroves beyond the village, and from a couple of kerosene lanterns on traders' tables. He was perplexed—he seemed to know this place, had a feeling that he knew it well, but that intimate knowledge of this place was somehow not available to him: his fucked-up TPCS again. His gaze roamed down the beach, searching for something that would bring the knowledge back. When his gaze came to the familiar blocky grayness looming like a ghost against the black of trees his mouth dropped open. The image short-circuited his failing TPCS, connected the disconnected synapses, liberated a flood of recollection. The station—his village—*home*. He turned his wondering gaze back to the beach. That ripple of dark movement: he *knew* these people. Their calls had died down to a worried murmur as passengers moved with their headloads through the mud and then among them, telling them about their sick white man.

He looked back up the beach at the white station building with its balcony overhanging the porch and the heavy wooden doors that opened into the store. A faint glow of yellow came from beyond the French doors on the second floor. Aminata was home. She would help him. He would rest and take the sulfadiazine and Pain would leave his leg forever and soon he would be running the path again, as he had every morning for years.

Something on his shoulder. He looked up into Ibrahim Turay's face, in lantern light. Young. Worried. Smelling overpoweringly of stale sweat and tobacco and fish and diesel oil; teeth, sharpened in adolescence to ferocious spikes behind fat lips; cheeks and forehead tight with youth and well marked with ridges of decorative scars that made a lovely fearsome pattern that he envied very much. He wanted scars like that.

"Sah," the captain said, "we go carry you go upsai."

Robert gave himself to the many hands lifting him up and over the side, trusting these hands to carry him safely ashore and up the gravel walk and up the familiar wide concrete staircase and across the fruit salad tile of the airy high-ceilinged flat and put him into his bed, where Aminata waited.

♈

218

Pain had subsided into a growling, suspicious quiet. Robert let his gaze roam over the netting top, noted the tiny droppings of the bats that came at night and competed with the geckoes for insects. Aminata had rolled the sides of the netting and neatly tied them so that the net would come down with a simple pull of the string. He had taught her that.

The oily scent of kerosene, from the cooking stove. The soft air of a bright yellow morning. Rustling. Murmurs. Words of Krio, words of Sherbro. Clicking: the palms talking to the wind beyond the open window. Alexander looking down at him, face close and wet, eyes squinting—as if Pain had burrowed down into him as well.

"Can you understand me?"

Robert nodded slowly, rolling his eyes over to Aminata's face, which was all knotted up and wet. And another face, that of a frightened old man he did not know. Gray hair, wrinkled and dusty skin, dirty white shirt under a clownish remnant of black dinner jacket. All he needed was a top hat and he'd be ready to hit the town. Hat! Of course—he had never seen the old herbalist without his battered bowler. He nodded at the face of old Mister Benga, who acknowledged his nod with a solemn blink of eyes.

"—says we must." Alexander's face all screwed up like he was going to cry.

What's the matter with him now? Him and his tantrums. What a royal pain in the ass. And yet—and yet, you had to admit he got it done. You had to admit he got results. And he was no hypocrite about what he expected. He told you who he was and what he wanted—which was other people's things. Taking things from people who already don't have a thing except their skins—but what the fuck, that's the way life is, isn't it? That's *all* life is. A lot of people who don't have a thing giving what they have to a few who have everything already. That's what Robert had been doing all those years in Njala and then Bonthe: getting it. While piously believing he was giving. A white man needs to do that. Believe he is giving while he is taking. The African man doesn't. That was the difference between him and his brother, Alexander. What *is* his brother saying?

"Minister Kargbo has taken the radio—there's no way we can call—"

Robert lost the thread. Where the hell was Alexander taking this? And why so many words?

"Do you understand?"

He shook his head, still looking up into Alexander's strangely anguished face.

"There is no radio. We cannot call."

This seemed important, so he tried hard to understand, managed to capture the idea of *no radio*, held it tenaciously while his TPCS labored to reconnect enough of the frayed synapses for him to understand how that fact related to his present situation. "Okay," he croaked, "the sea car, Hassan can take me—"

"Minister Kargbo keeps the sea car in Freetown. And the engine of the pampam is spoiled. We have tried to make it, Hassan and Mister Turay are still working—"

Too many words!

"We cannot wait. Do you understand?"

The old herbalist's big eyes blinking down at him.

"Mister Benga says we cannot wait."

Hearing his name, the old man nodded soberly.

Robert's TPCS was doing a great job: he was beginning to understand, and the shock of what he understood left him breathless. "No," he croaked, his heart pounding, "no, no—the sea car—call Kargbo, make him—"

Mister Benga understood "no" and "sea car" and "Kargbo." He looked at Alexander.

Alexander withdrew. Mister Benga followed. Good. Jesus Christ—Robert's heart pounding so hugely that the sound of it blocked out the murmurs and shuffles and the clicking of the palms—Jesus Christ on a crutch, what the hell are they *thinking*! And then Robert's TPCS lost it again, let it all come unraveled, and he didn't have any idea what had excited him, knew only that a bubble of terror was swelling in his chest, crowding his heart. He looked anxiously for Aminata, saw her wet face across the room staring at him like he was a leper.

♈

220

The night sky glowed with stars. It was a rainy season sky, a sky swarming with life, the life evident in its busyness. The stately drift of satellites; occasional streaks of meteoric suicides so breathlessly quick they were gone before his brain knew his eye had captured them; the sky alive and swinging majestically one way, then another, reminding him of the way the blanket of lights had swept up Signal Hill that night so long ago, when he had dined with Kevin and Rachel.

Though he had awakened only minutes before, he knew where he was. The diesel and dried fish smells, the cargo deck above, the iodine scent of seawater, the rattly tut-tut-tut-tut, the languorous roll: these observations informed him that the long port side bench of *Shebar II* was under him, and the ocean was under *Shebar II*. And that bulky blackness on the starboard bench, silhouetted against the glow of the Milky Way—that was Alexander's profile. He wondered what could possibly bring Alexander out *here*?

"Mister Alexander," Robert whispered through paper dry lips. "I de want watah. Duya, I beg, make I get watah."

The silhouette jerked and there was a sound of sucking air. "Mister Kelley! My God! You are awake. Yes. Water." He jumped up, shouted: "Mister Benga, bring water! Quickly!"

A clatter from the stern; and voices: Alexander's, then Mister Benga's. Robert raised his right shoulder, got his elbow under him; tried to raise himself, but couldn't manage it. He fell back on something soft, felt a surly stab of pain from his foot, steeled himself for the rest of it, for Pain's onslaught. And there was pain, all right, sharp and penetrating pain. But not *Pain*. He waited tensely. Pain did not appear.

Alexander, all bulked out by his orange life vest, hanging a lantern. Bowler-hatted Mister Benga. Ibrahim Turay, his spiked teeth showing in a grin. Hassan, all eyes. Alexander kneeled, lifted Robert's head, held a cup to his lips. Robert sipped the fragrant liquid, followed its soothing coolness all the way to his stomach. The liquid grabbed at his mouth astringently, pleasantly. A familiar texture—what was it? He remembered: the juice of crushed pawpaw leaves in water. Aminata had given him that remedy more than once. For fever, even—ineffectively—for malaria. He drained the cup. And then another. And tried to drink more, but his stomach was full.

Alexander lowered Robert's head to the mattress.

"How mos time?" Robert croaked.

"It will soon be morning," Alexander said. "You have slept through two days."

Robert tried to comprehend sleeping for two days. He couldn't. "Usai we dey? Yawri Bay?"

"Mister Turay says we are through the bay. I think we have passed the Banana Islands." Alexander fell silent for several seconds, then spoke again, hesitantly. "Do you know—what has happened?"

Robert looked past Alexander's face and the lantern's glare to the night sky, which was not so beautiful now. The lantern ruined its richness, hid the best part of it, which was the glow of it's life. He wanted Alexander to kill the lantern.

"Do you know?" Alexander asked again.

Robert was looking for the life in the night sky.

"You were dying."

Robert looked sharply at Alexander, then Mister Benga, his heart suddenly pounding, his head light. "No—"

"You were dying—"

♈

Robert seemed not to notice that it was day; seemed uncaring that two miles to starboard the sun was spilling its light gloriously through a tumult of cloud down green mountain sides; seemed unaware that the warm morning breeze from off those mountains had in an hour's time strengthened to a near gale; seemed oblivious of *Shebar II's* struggle against an increasingly choppy whitecapped sea, which put the boat into a continuous pattern of extreme corkscrew rolls—snappy, whippy rolls that forced Ibrahim Turay to wedge himself into his seat beside the engine housing where he puffed his pipe and ate dried fish, and which had Alexander clinging in a death grip to one of the baggage deck supports and hanging his head over the side, puking, while Mister Benga and Hassan sat side by side on the deck at midships, their feet against the starboard bench, their backs against the port bench, stoically awaiting their fates.

An hour before, when the wind picked up, Mister Benga had helped Hassan jury rig a bulwark on the open side of the seat to contain Robert. They had wedged him in with blankets and life jackets—except Alexander's, which he refused to give up—and covered him with a plastic sheet to keep him dry. *Shebar II* had fought her way northwestward as far as Whale Bay before the wind began its late morning moderation. By the time they had motored another ten miles the whitecaps were gone and the sea was an oily smooth swell that was so long and low that you could not see it unless you looked toward the shore, a mile to starboard, and saw that the shoaling bottom crowded it up into a surf that spilled over white sand.

"Ree-vah Numbah Two," Ibrahim Turay said. He had come forward to check on Robert and Alexander had asked him where they were.

Robert stiffened. He turned his head but couldn't see over the bulwark. He tried to raise himself.

Alexander appeared and looked down at Robert, his face anxious. "What do you want, Mister Kelley? Water? Mister Benga, bring water!"

"I want to see."

Alexander took his hands and pulled him to a sitting position.

Robert looked down at his lap and his legs, which were under the sheet. His right leg ended at the tent of his foot. The sheet flattened out below his left knee. He stared at the place where his left leg should be. He moved the stump, flinched when it answered with a surge of pain. "My foot—I feel it," he murmured wonderingly. "I can even move my toes—I've been doing it all morning—moving my toes."

"We had to do it," Alexander said earnestly. "Please believe me, we had to do it—you were dying. It was very bad." He had said these words many times since Robert woke in the middle of the night but Robert never showed that he heard.

"Yes, I know."

223

Robert looked across the water. He knew this stretch of beach. He and Marie had spent many days together on that beach. She always got him to bring her here when she visited Salone; had even gotten to know some of the women who lived in the half-dozen huts back in the trees; had begun to regard them as friends and clients, these wives and mothers of families that managed to scratch a life out of fishing and cultivating patches of sweet potatoes and cassava and guarding the cars and motorcycles of weekending Freetown expats. But neither Marie nor Robert had seen River Number Two from the sea. Now he looked across a mile of flat green water to a low line of surf breaking on white beach. Tall ragged-topped palms lined the beach and inland of the palms the green sides of mountains slanted gradually upward, then more sharply up into rocky talus slopes and cliffs. From a mile offshore the river itself was invisible, though he could discern its location by the presence of the river valley and the patch of mangroves that flanked the estuary. There, where the whiteness of beach yielded to encroaching palms, were the sorry little beach baffas the villagers had erected to shelter the delicate skins of Freetown expats. A long time ago he and Marie had sheltered from a storm in one of them, and they had heard the rain rattling the palm thatch roof, heard it trickling through in rivulets that spilled down, almost warm, on his bare back and into her face as he moved in her, heard the little boys come to the entrance and stand there in the rain and giggle and beg for money.

He watched the mangroves and the valley and the baffas slide slowly behind, until they disappeared, replaced by a black rocky shoreline that was marked by white patches of sandy inlets.

Robert drank more of the astringent water and fell, exhausted, back on the mattress. He let his mind wander; dreamily remembered the miles from River Number Two to Freetown; calculated that *Shebar II's* seven knots would bring them to the King Jimmi landing in four hours—in the middle of the day, when the market would be hot and noisy and teeming with market women and customers and boats coming and going. He thought about the things he would do when they got to the landing. First he would send Hassan up the hill to the Zimi office to get Kevin, and then to the embassy for Mike, and before Mike took charge of him and carried him off to his basement hospital—where he would do God knows what to him, maybe cut some more off his leg—he would tell Kevin what he knew about Daniel and Prince and Pa Bangura, and he'd find out if Gunter and Rex and Ladipor had gotten out okay, and if there was fighting in Pujehun. And of course Marie: he would ask Kevin to send her a cable telling her about his leg. But no—not a cable: a cable would open more questions than it answered. Receiving a cable like that, not hearing the details from him—no, he would not send a cable, he'd call.

He made that call in his head as he looked up at the underside of the cargo deck, heard himself tell her that they had cut off his leg, heard her response—in several versions. The one that he liked best had her saying she was coming to Freetown immediately. She would come to Freetown and it would be just like before, only this time she would not say no to Kevin, this time there would be no anger, no quarreling; this time she was coming to stay. He played that version of their conversation several times as he watched clouds coalescing along the mountain tops. But his erratic TPCS did not let him think about it for very long. Soon Daniel and Prince and Pa Bangura were in his thoughts again.

"Mister Alexander. What happened in Pujehun? Was it Minah's people?"

"I know nothing. When Mister Wagner left me at Matruh, on the last day, it was quiet. We had no problems."

"What were they fighting about?"

"I don't know. I think it started in Freetown. Mister Turay was in Freetown when some soldiers and some Lebanese tried to seize the government. He said loyal soldiers killed some of them and captured the rest."

"But what about Daniel and Prince and Pa Bangura and Gunter and—"

Alexander shook his head. "I don't know."

♈

225

Mike's khaki legs appeared on the stone jetty among the many black legs. He squatted and looked in under the cargo deck. "They're bringing the litter down the stairs. We'll have you out of here in a minute."

Robert did not respond. He was staring at the underside of the cargo deck.

"You still with us?" Mike asked.

Robert looked over at him and watched him climb down into the boat.

"That morphine do it for you?" Mike asked.

Robert nodded sleepily.

"So as soon as he heard about Prince and Daniel and the driver he went upline," Max said. He had been telling Robert where Kevin was. "To take care of Daniel's family and to get the bodies. He and Gunter and an escort of soldiers went to Pujehun yesterday."

"It's confirmed then—" Robert murmured.

"Yes. Some farmers found Bangura and Prince on a sand bar. Daniel was shot. Don't know the circumstances, but it appears he was approaching some soldiers at a road block."

"Shit."

"Yeah, bum deal."

"Was it Minah?"

"Yes. And the usual Lebs. They even had an Englishmen in with them, which really fueled the mercenary rumors. Turns out he was just an accountant who worked for one of the Lebs. It wasn't much of a coup. Even by African standards it was a cluster fuck. We heard rumors of it for days before it happened. I think Momoh knew all about it from the start, and waited until Minah had committed himself so he could nail him for treason. It was over in two hours. Except in Pujehun. Momoh's people have scores to settle there, so the killing there went on for three or four days. Grimes is there now, looking for his PCVs. You feel like telling us what happened to you?"

"No, he doesn't," Mike said. "Later." He had pulled the sheet off Robert's legs and was bending over the stump. "These red streaks—septicemia. But not bad. Could have been a lot worse."

"It was the priest's sulfadiazine," Robert said sleepily.

"What?"

"The priest at Sama—"

"Father Meagan. You saw him?"

"He gave me sulfadiazine."

"Useless in this situation. We'll get you going on antibiotics." He inspected the bandage. "Mister Benga told me about the amputation. A most interesting procedure. And a most interesting old man. Incredible knowledge of plants and herbs."

"Fuck, they shot him," Robert murmured. His mind had drifted back to what Max told him about Daniel. "It was because he was with me. They thought I was a mercenary."

"His instruments and technique are right out of the eighteenth century," Mike was saying. "He's a time capsule. Reminded me of something I read in medical school, an article by a Royal Navy surgeon about amputating legs and arms at Trafalgar. Tubs and tubs of them. The old man knew what he was doing—explained where he made the incision, how he tied off the artery, how he sawed the bone back so he'd have enough meat to make a stump." He looked into Robert's face, pulled one of his eyelids up and studied his eye, then put his hand on Robert's forehead. "He even showed me how he tied off the artery. You leave about three inches of the string coming out the stump. I'll show you later. Most interesting—the string closes the artery until it heals, and while it heals the body's rejecting it. By the time the wound has healed all you have to do is tug on the string and out it comes, with a little piece of rotted artery. Pretty slick, eh?" He grinned down at Robert.

Robert was looking up at Mike, but he was thinking about Daniel and Prince and Pa Bangura, and about that last morning at the resthouse in Pujehun.

"He said you were conscious," Mike said. "They had you tied down. Do you remember any of it?"

"It was my decision," Robert murmured. "But I didn't make it, I let the group decide. I shouldn't have let anybody go out, we should have stayed in the resthouse until we *knew* what was happening out there."

They heard the porters yelling for people to get out of

the way, saw black legs shuffle, saw lappas swaying one way or another, saw children scuttling between legs, trying to get a better look down into *Shebar II*. And then the porters put the litter on the jetty and two of them climbed down into the boat. Mike and Max helped them hand Robert over the side to the other porters. They strapped him to the litter and the crowd parted as they carried him the length of the jetty to the stone stairs and then up the long flight in the hot sun to Lightfoot Boston Street where Mike's long van waited.

"Mike, I want to call Marie," Robert murmured as they approached the van.

"Max can call her."

Two of the porters climbed into the back of the van and lifted the front of the litter and drew it into the van.

"No, *I* have to."

"You're in no shape—"

"Please—Mike, I need to talk to her."

Mike hesitated, then shrugged.

They drove down Lightfoot Boston, past the abandoned Bata store and the crumbling City Hotel and the Tropic and stopped in front of SLET. The porters carried him into the waiting room, which was as hot as a sauna. The young clerk took the money from Max and went in the back with the yellow slip of paper. They waited with several Africans and a couple of Lebs, who sat on benches along the wall sweating and staring at Robert until the clerk called out a booth number and Robert's name. The porters carried him down the hall to a booth and stood patiently holding the litter off the floor so that Robert could reach the handset. The connection was bright and clear. When he heard her voice his heart quickened and he felt momentarily light-headed.

"Sweetheart! Oh, it's so good to hear your voice. How was your trip? Any problems?" His voice unnatural, nervous.

For several seconds there was no sound. Then, coolly, distantly: "It was okay. How're things there? We heard about the coup attempt."

"It was over in a couple of hours." His TPCS had organized the things he would say to her, had lined them up neatly in his head, but now he couldn't remember which came first. His leg? No, not yet—it didn't fit yet. And then it came to him. "You remember Daniel and Prince—they were killed in the coup. With Pa Bangura. All three of them."

"My God! What happened?"

"It was at a road block. The soldiers panicked—"

"Jesus—Daniel's got kids—"

"Kevin's up in Bo, now. Taking care of things." His voice sounding distant, thick, unnatural, the nervousness coming through. Another pause, then: "Marie, what we talked about—"

"Let's not start—"

"Don't say anything. What we talked about, you coming to Salone and working for the project—"

"I'm staying in Mopti."

"I know, I know. But you said you loved—"

"Robert, it's finished."

"I don't understand—you said—" Robert fell silent. He knew he wasn't making sense. His head was clogged with the heat, his mouth thick with thirst. The morphine sleepiness seemed to be caving in on him. His TPCS was losing control again and things were getting discontinuous, like seeing someone dancing in a sequence of strobe flashes separated by longer and longer intervals of darkness. He was beginning to think he was missing some very important parts.

"You sound strange, Robert. Are you okay? Is your leg infected again?"

He formed the words in his head: "No, they cut it off." But he wasn't ready to tell her about his leg, he wanted to talk about something else first. But he couldn't remember what. "I'm okay," he said. Laying on the litter, staring at the ceiling, he noted for the first time in all the scores of times he had come to SLET, how dust and greasy residue from tobacco smoke had, over four decades, given the ceiling a dark, furry coat of brown. "I just wanted—" The words trailed off. He couldn't remember what he wanted.

"Robert, this is just making it harder. Don't call me any more. This is too hard."

His TPCS had let things get completely fucked up. Thoughts were bouncing all over the place. "Well—"

"I need for you to be out of my life."

"I love you." That was the only thought he could get hold of, so he said it again: "I love you."

A sigh, then, "I have to go. Goodbye, Robert."

"They cut it off," Robert said abruptly. He'd remembered one of the things he was going to tell her. "Alexander and Mister Benga and Aminata. They cut it off at Bonthe." He listened for her response, but the line was silent. He stared at the furry brown ceiling with the handset still at his ear, while he waited for his TPCS to regain control of his head. And it did, valiantly, one piece at a time: he figured out that he was at SLET, that Mike had brought him there, that Marie had just hung up on him, that Mike waited down the hall to take him to his basement clinic where he would probably cut his own piece off of him. All that information he managed to organize and store in his head. The hard part was hoisting in what Marie had said. His TPCS just couldn't get around that one; just wouldn't accept it. No way. A minute passed; two minutes. He gave the handset to one of the porters, who returned it to its cradle. The porters carried him into the waiting room where Max and Mike stood talking.

His voice, even in his own ear, sounded distant and soft. "Okay, Mike."

"You all right?"

"Yeah."

"How's Marie?" Max asked. "She make it back okay?"

"Yeah."

Mike held the door open and the porters carried Robert out to the van. They loaded him and got in the back with him.

"I gotta get back to the embassy, Robert," Max said, "but I'll come see you this evening. I'll bring a bottle of whiskey and some women."

"You do that," Mike said. "He ought to be ready for a party by then."

"Max, is Lungi open yet?" Robert's voice ever so soft and distant, like he was walking down the street, away from himself.

"What?"

"Lungi—"

"You're not going any place," Mike said. "Not for a long time." He slammed the door.

"Max, find out about Lungi," Robert murmured at the closed door. "And book me to Bamako. Marie's waiting."